SILVER BULLET

A LOU THORNE THRILLER

KORY M. SHRUM

ISBN: 978-1-949577-58-7
Copyright © 2022 by Kory M. Shrum
Cover design by Christian Bentulan
Editing by Toby Selwyn

TIMBERLANE
PRESS

SILVER BULLET

AN EXCLUSIVE OFFER FOR YOU

Connecting with my readers is the best part of my job as a writer. One way that I like to connect is by sending 2–3 newsletters a month with a subscribers-only giveaway, free stories from your favorite series, and personal updates (read: pictures of my dog).

When you first sign up for the mailing list, I send you at least three free stories right away. If free stories and exclusive giveaways sound like something you're interested in, please look for the special offer in the back of this book.

Happy reading,

Kory M. Shrum

For Kimberly,
and the home we've made together

1

Konstantine crossed the Piazza della Santissima Annunziata with Stefano at his side. The air was cool and the light dim from the cloudy day. A moped rumbled past as they turned the corner and the church came into view.

His church. Konstantine had chosen it for its modest stone exterior. Nothing about it would invite wandering tourists. The façade was simple and smooth, unremarkable with one exception. He loved the beautiful stained-glass window depicting the Virgin Mary with her hands open in welcome.

Every morning he admired it before he entered the church.

This moment of serenity and reverence was cut short as cries broke through his musings. The children were yelling, becoming nothing more than a pile of kicking limbs on the steps outside the entrance.

The group of children who usually played here before school had, for some reason, turned into a pack of wild dogs.

Stefano swore beside him. "The little beasts."

"Grab whoever you can," Konstantine told him.

Konstantine himself stepped into the fray and grabbed Nario, the oldest and tallest of the boys. With his remaining free hand, he grabbed Matteo and hauled both boys to their feet. "What is going on here? Smettila! Smettetela tutti!"

The children stopped, scattering like startled pigeons.

Konstantine shook Nario's arm. "Speak up! Why are you acting this way in the street for everyone to see? Outside our church no less. Do you want someone to file a complaint? Do you want to bring attention to us?"

Konstantine cut his eyes to the other boys who stood in the circle, chests heaving. A couple of the littlest ones had begun to cry quietly, their trembling lips betraying them.

Konstantine looked to Matteo. "What happened here?"

Matteo looked down.

Konstantine did his best to hide that Matteo was his favorite, the one who held a special place in his heart, but he worried that at times like this, it must show.

"I admire your solidarity," Konstantine said, and meant it. "But that means you will all receive your punishment together."

"That's not fair!" Nario cried out, wrenching his arm from Konstantine's grip. "It's her fault!"

Nario was pointing an accusing finger at the newest addition to Konstantine's little band of street rats. A ten-year-old boy named Gabriele. Gabriele had approached Konstantine three months before, not long after he and Lou had wrapped up their terrible business with Riku Yamamoto. He had offered to run errands for Konstantine in exchange for a bit of money.

He claimed to be an orphan and had heard that Konstantine took in children like him, gave them jobs, food, and money.

All of this was true.

Just like Padre Leo before him, Konstantine refused to let the children of his city go uncared for. If he could help them, he did.

"What did you just say?" Konstantine said, searching Nario's face. "*Her?*"

It was too late. Gabriele had already launched himself across Konstantine and knocked Nario to the ground.

Konstantine heard the air leave Nario in a *whoosh* as the wind was knocked from his chest.

Konstantine swore and fought to lift Gabriele off the other boy before he could beat him to a pulp, but the child thrashed in his arms.

That's when Konstantine felt the bindings across her chest.

Her.

"Stop it," Konstantine said, trying to place her on her feet. "Stop it now or neither of you will walk again."

The girl tore herself from Konstantine's grip, standing apart from the group now. She looked ready to run, but Matteo whispered something under his breath and the girl stilled.

Nario lay on the flat of his back, his nose bloodied and eye bleeding. Konstantine offered him a hand and pulled him to his feet.

Konstantine looked at the children, his disappointment immense.

He took a deep, steadying breath. *What to do with them?*

His predecessor, Padre Leo, had been cruel at times like this. If the children behaved badly, he would hurt them. He'd had a post in the center of his courtyard that he would strap a boy to and whip him until the skin broke and his back bled.

Konstantine had been spared such treatment all except for once, when, defying Padre's orders, he'd challenged a rival who could have shot Konstantine dead—and almost had.

But Konstantine was not Padre Leo.

He could stab, torture, or cut a man. He could even carve out an eye or end a life, but he could not raise a hand against a child.

"Did any of you know that Gabriele was a girl?" he asked.

There was no point in pretending he did not know her secret now.

He looked around the little group, and no one met his eyes. Not even Nario, who touched his bloody nose and hissed.

"Matteo?" Konstantine asked directly, knowing that boy, at least, would not lie to him. "Did you know she was a girl?"

Matteo finally gave the smallest of nods.

Well then, Konstantine thought. *Deception amongst my own ranks.*

He motioned to Stefano. "Take Nario and clean him up. The rest of you, straighten your clothes and go to school. And you." He pointed at Gabriele. "You come with me."

Again, she looked ready to run.

Calmly, he said, "Do you think there is a place you could go in this city that I would not find you? *Vieni con me.* I only want to speak to you."

Matteo gave her hand a gentle squeeze, saying something under his breath again.

Gabriele rebuffed him by shrugging off his touch. Instead of running, she lifted her chin a little higher and fell into step behind Konstantine.

As she followed him through the church and to the court-yard at its center where Konstantine's office waited, he looked back several times to make sure she was still there. He half expected her to break and run.

But she didn't. She stepped inside his office and took the chair he offered before sitting down behind his own desk.

"Is your name really Gabriele?" he asked her. He wasn't sure where else to begin.

"Gabriella," she said.

"Take off your cap."

She did. Now he wondered how he hadn't seen it before. Her hair was short, but it was obviously cut by her own hand.

"Did you do that to make yourself look more like a boy?" he asked, gesturing at her head.

"*Sì*," she said, again with that tone of defiance. As if she were daring him to make fun of her.

"You didn't do a very good job," he said.

"I know," she replied simply. "I couldn't see the back."

"Show me," he said, and she turned enough to show him the back of her hair. Her black locks were a massacre of jagged lines.

"Why did you lie?" Konstantine asked. When she didn't answer, he asked again. "Gabriella, why did you lie to me and say you were a boy?"

"I'm thirteen," she said, as if this answered his question.

He shrugged. "And?"

"I hear the only work you give women is—It's—"

It was clear that she meant prostitution.

"I do not turn children into whores," he said, unable to hide his anger. "No matter what you've heard. I employ many women who do not do anything like that."

How could he explain to this child that his own mother had been forced to turn to prostitution once, and for that reason alone, he would never subject another to it?

Wasn't that how Konstantine had gotten involved with Padre Leo and the Ravengers to begin with? The economy had turned and his mother had lost her job selling postcards and trinkets to the tourists. She'd not been able to afford the rent on their small apartment anymore, and so she'd sold the only thing she thought she had left to sell.

Konstantine still remembered the way her shoulders had shaken as she'd lain in their bed crying afterward. How hard she'd worked to hide her tears for his sake.

He'd gone to Padre Leo the very next day and asked him for a job. He'd told the old priest that he'd do anything if it meant keeping his mother safe.

"I don't want to do that," Gabriella said again. Her dark blue eyes were large and insistent. "I never want to do that."

"I wouldn't have asked you to," he said. "But there is still the matter of you lying to me. I don't like liars."

She said nothing to this, but she didn't have to. The way she squirmed in her seat, keeping her eyes down on her lap, told him plenty.

"Can I keep working for you?" she asked.

"That depends," he said. "We will have to redo your interview, since now I cannot trust the answers you gave me before. Answer my questions *honestly*, and then I will tell you if you still have a job."

She dared to look at him.

"Your real name? All of it."

"Gabriella Luna Barone."

"And you're thirteen?" he asked. "You told me you were ten."

"I'm short for my age."

This wasn't true. Konstantine had thought she was tall for a ten-year-old. Taller than Matteo, who was twelve. But it made sense now that she wanted to buy herself some time and pass as a child for as long as possible.

"Do you have family in Florence?" he asked.

"No. There's no one."

Konstantine suspected she was lying by the way her eyes darted away.

"That is what you said last time," he replied. "It's why I agreed to let you sleep in the dormitory with the other boys."

The dormitory was the room at the back of the church that Konstantine kept for the boys who did not have families. They had beds and closets for their clothes. Personal shelves for their belongings, bookcases full of books. And he had two of his older women—Bella and Gianna—looking after them at night. Making sure the boys dressed and went to bed at a decent hour and woke in time to eat and go to school.

"I don't know how I feel about you sleeping in the dormitory as the only girl in a room full of boys," he said.

"Do you have a room for girls?" she asked.

He admitted that he did not. She was the first female child to ask him for help. Most of the women that came to him were older. And he owned apartments across the city for those who needed help finding an affordable place to live.

Her eyes were on her lap again. "If I sleep somewhere else, can I still keep the job?"

He could not see a child as his enemy. But that didn't mean she wasn't operating under someone else's orders. That her little hands couldn't deliver destruction all the same.

Until he could be sure of her intentions, it was best not to keep her in the church or around the other children.

"*Do* you have somewhere else to sleep?" he asked.

Ever so slowly, she began to nod. "I have somewhere to sleep."

"Is it inside? Is it clean, dry? Warm?"

"Sì," she said.

She was lying about something. He was sure of it. Only he couldn't be sure of what, or why she felt that she needed to deceive him.

Because your enemies mean to use her to destroy you. Your kindness toward women and children has been noticed and they will exploit and punish you for it.

He tried to push these thoughts down, but his unease remained. "You can keep your job only if you keep going to school and you don't sleep in the dormitory."

She relaxed a little at that.

"I will double your wage," he said, testing her reaction. "It's only fair since I will no longer be providing your room and board."

"Grazie," she said. But she was not happy.

Would she miss the dorms so much? Or was she instructed to get as close to him as she could?

You are paranoid. Until you know better, treat her like the child she is.

"You are welcome," he said.

"Do I have to go to school now?" she asked, sliding out of her seat.

"Soon," he said, rising from his own chair. "But first, we need to do something about your hair."

The killer stood in the rain. Cold droplets pelted his shoulders and the brim of his hat. He was well hidden in the shadow of the spruce tree with its thick branches.

Most of the houses on this street were quiet, their windows dark, with only a porch light beaming in the night. The house he watched, however, was lit up. Light poured from almost every window, falling across the neat lawn and the driveway where the white minivan rested, its engine still ticking as it released its heat into the chilly air.

He knew it had been well used on the long drive today. Following the daughter's social media, he'd tracked the quartet from Yosemite to Yellowstone. Social media could be *so* useful.

Yet when he'd selected the family weeks ago, it hadn't been the daughter who'd caught his eye. It had been the father.

The father, more than the mother and two children, had called to the beast within him.

As he thought of the mother, she appeared, passing the

upstairs window while carrying the littlest one on her hip. A suitcase was in her other hand.

The daughter stood in the doorway and paused in flossing her braces long enough to ask her mother a question.

He found the father in the lower-left window. The dining room. He wore a t-shirt and pajama pants now, scratching the back of his head as he looked out the window at the wet and gleaming street.

The father lifted a drink to his lips, and hissed through his teeth after sipping it.

The killer's heart beat faster, but he didn't step back, didn't retreat deeper into the shadows. He knew the movement would betray him. If he remained perfectly still, as still as the tree beside him, the father's eyes would slide over his body and down the street, seeing nothing.

And he was right.

With a yawn, the father turned away from the window. As the father turned away, hunger welled up within the killer again.

That low growl was coming from him, from the barely contained beast.

He bit down hard on the leather between his teeth. The muzzle fastened over his mouth immobilized his jaw. Its straps dug into his cheeks. The buckle at the back of his head creaked from the strain.

I want them, I want them, I want them, the beast begged as his stomach twisted with anticipation.

Soon, he told it.

Very soon.

LOUIE THORNE'S HAND STILLED, MID-MOTION. SHE'D BEEN about to fork another mouthful of scrambled eggs from her plate when a tug through her navel snagged her attention.

But before she fully registered what her compass was telling her, the energy dissipated and the urge to act disappeared.

Whatever the threat was, it was not fully formed.

She turned her head as if listening to something in the distance, but her compass remained quiet. The soft light of early-spring morning shone through the large windows of her apartment. The light filled her with a cheerful feeling, a sharp contrast to what she'd touched a moment before.

Something sinister. Menacing.

Lou turned her attention back to her fully-plated meal. She was finishing up her sixth week of eating like this regularly, beginning with an actual breakfast each morning. Today, after her workout at the gym with Dani and Piper, she'd decided on salmon and avocado on toast with a side of scrambled eggs.

She even ate an orange.

Her aunt Lucy—rest her soul—would have been so proud. After all her fruitless years of trying to force her stubborn niece into eating three meals a day, here she finally was.

Lou could admit, if only to herself, that she did feel pretty good. Who knew eating and properly caring for one's body rather than just treating it like a punching bag could *actually* lead to her feeling stronger, more energized?

Her watch beeped. She rotated her wrist and the time illuminated on in its face.

She shoveled the last of her meal into her mouth, put her plate in the sink to be dealt with later, and grabbed her leather jacket off the arm of her purple sofa before stepping into the empty linen closet beside it.

Then she waited in the dark, her back pressed against the cool wood of the closet's wall, and breathed. Her breath was always louder in the dark.

The darkness softened around her. Her apartment in St. Louis fell away and Florence formed in its place.

She stepped from the shadows to find Konstantine naked, his body damp, his hair soaking wet. She leaned against the frame of his closet, enjoying the look of him and the tattoos snaking up his arm, over his shoulder toward his chest.

He looked up then and saw her watching him.

"I have good timing," she said, not bothering to hide where her eyes had fixed.

"We already knew that," he said, a shy smile forming on his lips. "But I'm always happy to please you, *amore mio*."

She came toward him, stopping his hands so that he couldn't pull on his shirt.

"You don't want me to dress?" he asked, still smiling.

"No."

"What about you?"

Lou shrugged out of her leather jacket and the shoulder holster beneath, laying her guns across the chair in the corner. Then she pulled her shirt and bra off in one fluid movement.

When he saw her breasts, his smile wasn't shy anymore.

"I missed you," he said.

She laughed low in her throat. "I was here a few hours ago."

He pulled her down into the bed with him, taking deep, dramatic breaths of her skin, allowing his nose to trace a line from her stomach to her throat.

"It seems like much longer to me," he said.

She pushed her fingers through his dark hair. It was unruly these days, longer and thicker than usual. She liked it like this. Long enough to fist in her hands.

"You're home early," she said. "It's only four here, right? Or five?"

"*Sì.* I had a stressful day."

"Another gang war on your doorstep so soon?" she asked hopefully.

"No. Something else."

Her fingers hesitated in his hair. "Are you intentionally trying to build suspense or do you not want to tell me?"

"You know the new boy, Gabriele?"

Lou's stomach tightened. *He knows then.*

"*Her* name is Gabriella." When Lou said nothing to this, he lifted his head and searched her face. His eyes fluttered. "You knew?"

"I knew." Lou had known the second she'd seen her, though her disguise had been good enough.

Konstantine pouted. "Why didn't you tell me?"

"Was it my place to tell you?"

He came up onto his elbows, staring down at her. "Would you have told me if she were a threat?"

She gave him a warning look. "No. I saved you from Nico and Yamamoto just so you could be murdered by a child."

His expression softened. "I'm sorry, *amore mio*. I'm only confused why you would side with the girl and keep her secret. Did she ask you to?"

"No. I don't think she's seen me."

"Then why didn't you trust me?" he asked. "I thought we weren't keeping secrets from each other anymore."

She realized he was genuinely hurt. "It wasn't my secret. I don't need to tell you that young girls are just as vulnerable as young boys."

"You say that as if I won't help her because she is a girl," he said, his green eyes bright.

"Does she have as many options as Matteo?"

"Of course," he said, without hesitation. "I want her to go to school and get any job she likes."

"Are you going to let her sleep in the dorms?"

"I don't want a girl in the room with all those boys all night, every night. I am not prepared to see a thirteen-year-old pregnant."

"Is that what you're really worried about?" she asked him.

"No," he admitted. "No, I am more concerned that she is a spy, planted to watch me and to report what I do to whoever has bought her. Or maybe she will be asked to hide a bomb under my desk or something."

Lou's hand relaxed in his hair again. "Then follow her. Find out if that's what's going on. If it makes you feel better, I've never sensed that she wants to hurt you."

He rested his chin on her collarbone. "It doesn't mean she doesn't work for someone who does."

"How hard can it be to follow a little girl?" she asked.

He scowled at her, but the corners of his lips were turning up against his will. "Oh, if only I had your gifts, *amore mio*. I could be so much more productive in a day."

"I doubt it," she said, taking hold of him. "I would still be around to distract you."

He pressed himself into her palm, a soft breath escaping along her neck.

She traced him with a gentle fingertip. His body tightened against hers. "You're teasing me."

"No," she said. "It's only teasing if I have no intention of finishing what I've started."

He laughed in her ear, but already he was hardening in her hand, and her grip strengthened.

They removed the last of her clothing until nothing lay between them.

She was still holding on to him when his fingers slid between her legs and he found her.

His breath caught in his throat.

"You're very wet," he choked out.

"I missed you."

She rolled him easily, pinning him on his back beneath her. His eyes found hers the moment before she lowered herself onto him.

His eyes fluttered closed. "*Sei divina. Venere incarnata.*"

Konstantine had a habit of muttering in Italian when he was happy and caught up in his pleasure. She didn't mind. She appreciated the possibility that she could turn off parts of his brain with her touch alone.

She kissed him, careful not to interrupt the rhythm they built together. His hands mostly stayed on her hips, leaving only to slide up her back and grasp her hair.

Her speed increased. Lou felt like she was bearing down on him, and if that hurt, she couldn't tell given the delicious sounds escaping him.

"I'm—" he managed, but Lou went first.

She rode her waves, then his.

"*Amore*—" he begged. "Just a minute."

Reluctantly, she slowed, but she didn't relinquish him.

He chuckled, his cheeks flushed. "You are not finished."

"No," she said.

His eyes fluttered open, and she saw how brilliantly green they were. They always seemed greener when they had sex. She wondered if it was a trick of the light or her imagination.

After several beats of silence, his hands returned to her hips. "I am ready."

She laughed, low in her throat. "Are you sure? Last night, you gave up on me after the fourth round."

"I will manage," he said. "Though I would be lying if I said your increase in energy hasn't had certain *repercussions*."

"You were the one who said I needed to take better care of myself," she purred into his mouth. "Do you regret it?"

Now it was his turn to roll her onto her back beneath him.

"No," he said with a devilish grin, clasping one of her thighs in each hand. "I have no regrets."

3

Melandra Durand stood nervously outside the Treme Community Center, twisting the end of her long head scarf between her sweating palms.

"Just go in now," she said to herself. "Don't you be standing out here on the street for everybody to gawk at."

Her eyes slid over the beautiful building with its shining glass windows and painted mural. A mother with three little ones passed her on the sidewalk. The littlest was already in her bathing suit, a lifejacket gripped in one pudgy fist.

She seemed confused as to why Melandra wouldn't want to go in such a wonderful place.

Because I'm not here for a swim in the Olympic pool, baby, she thought.

Still, those credulous eyes were enough to spur Melandra forward.

With a deep breath, she started up the walk and entered the building.

It was full of life. Children laughing and screaming. The dull roar of conversation.

After a brief exchange with the receptionist, Mel learned that the meeting for the Association of Black Women Business Owners in New Orleans was in an upstairs conference room.

Mel followed the directions the receptionist had provided and approached the meeting as one might approach the gallows.

By the time she reached the door of the meeting room, her heart was pounding so hard in her chest she thought she might pass out.

She sucked in a breath and pushed open the door.

More than a few heads swiveled her way as she slid into the room, but to her relief, it wasn't a small meeting. Close to a hundred women filled the space, which was enough for Melandra to feel as if she could take a seat in the back and hide herself from the scrutiny of others.

She wouldn't have come at all, of course, if not for the invitation sent by Tamara Jones, the director of the association. She'd heard that woman's name in more than a few mouths from other shop owners in the Quarter. Apparently, she wielded plenty of power at City Hall.

The fact she'd sent Melandra a handwritten request to join today's meeting felt like an offer Melandra simply couldn't refuse, no matter how much she hated such things.

It was difficult to follow the meeting's conversation when Melandra's heart pounded as loudly as it did. She hardly heard anything as several of the women stood, approached the podium, said their piece, answered questions, then returned to their seats.

She caught snippets of their words: *fundraiser*, *last year*, *a million dollars*, *more important than ever*.

There was also something about the difficulty of hiring. Over ninety percent of the Black businesses in the city couldn't afford to hire employees, and Mel knew the truth of that. She had Piper, and she did what she could to keep the girl, but Lord knows it hadn't been easy.

The meeting adjourned and the women filed from the room. More than a few flashed her polite smiles and curious glances as they passed. Others stopped to speak to friends, forming little groups of conversation.

It occurred to Mel now that she looked too much like the fortune teller she was.

Her head scarf, her long, flowy dress, and gold bangles stood out in this sea of business attire and beautiful pantsuits.

She shrank from their stares, preparing to flee the room. But then she heard her name.

"Ms. Durand! Ms. Durand, up here!"

Mel turned and saw who'd called her. It was Tamara Jones. She wore a bright red pantsuit to match the color of her lipstick. Her gold eyes shone and her cropped hair made her face seem full of angles. Sharp and proud.

"Ms. Durand, thank you so much for accepting my invitation," she said. "I hope it wasn't too difficult for you to get away from your store."

"I've got someone covering it for me," she said, remembering the way Piper had burst in, wet-haired, from the supply closet five minutes before Mel had needed to leave for the meeting. She'd said something about the gym before Mel bid both her and Louie a rushed goodbye.

"What did you think of the meeting?" Ms. Jones asked, her smile still bright.

"A lot of great ideas," Mel said. *If only I'd heard a single one of them.*

"Good, good," she said, beaming. "We'll be counting on you to help with the fundraiser."

Mel's heart sputtered in her chest. "Yes, of course."

She didn't know what else to say.

"A hundred thousand dollars is a high figure, but it will be worth it considering the good we can do."

"A hundred thousand!" Mel almost choked. "Why not half a million?"

Tamara laughed. "That's the attitude I like to hear. Why *not* half a million? If this quarter goes well, perhaps we'll try for half a million next time."

"Can you remind me again what the deadline is for this?" Mel asked. "How long do we have to come up with the money?"

"*Come up with the money?*" Tamara cocked her head. "Now this ain't rent or a mortgage, Ms. Durand. You don't have to *come up* with anything. We only ask that you raise what you can. There'll be no penalty if we can't reach our goals. We have membership tiers for all levels. The lowest tier requires no funding at all."

The lowest tier.

Mel didn't want to be a member of the lowest tier. She'd felt that all her life people saw her as some scrap at the bottom of a bucket.

"Ms. Jones." Mel licked her lips and tried to draw breath into her tightening chest. "May I ask what you'd recommend for a fundraiser?"

"Let me see. Some people host galas or events in their spaces. Some people do sales promotions. Last year, Laquina Abbot did a drag show."

"And is Laquina Abbot a member on one of the lowest tiers?" Mel asked, wondering immediately if she'd just committed a faux pas.

Tamara laughed. "Oh no! Ms. Abbot is one of our highest contributors."

She must've put on one hell of a show, Melandra thought. Perhaps Piper's friend Henry was dancing at the wrong place.

"Whatever you choose to do, as long as you can submit

the money by April thirtieth, it will count toward our first-quarter fundraising efforts."

April thirtieth. My Lord.

Mel had less than a month. At least this wasn't happening during Mardi Gras. In no world would she have been able to run a fundraiser while the chaos of the season was upon her.

And yet, if Mel could do this, if she could earn herself a place among these women, they would be a powerful ally against economic ruin. The association had a strong network and connections that they used on the behalf of their members. They provided grants and loans to businesses in the community that were struggling.

The truth was Mel was tired of scraping and striving to do right by Fortunes and Fixes all on her own. She might not be as legitimate as these women. She didn't own a restaurant, bar, or a hotel. She didn't give tours or provide travel accommodations.

She just sold candles and merchandise. She read palms. How could she even compare to them?

Yet she had to try.

Tamara's hand grabbed Melandra's shoulder and squeezed. "Everyone's nervous their first time, but don't you worry, Ms. Durand. Your fundraiser will go better than you imagine, and I *can't wait* to celebrate with you."

Better than I imagine? Mel scoffed. It was hard to imagine anything better than a hundred thousand dollars.

ROBERT KING LOVED SPRING IN NEW ORLEANS, WHEN IT was still cool enough to enjoy the beautiful, sunny days. It was preferable to the summer, when the sweat seemed to pour from every inch of his body.

Enjoy it while you can, he told himself as he passed Jackson

Square, his fresh cup of Café du Monde coffee in his grip and a sack of hot beignets in the other hand.

An artist was setting up for the day, propping her colorful canvases against the black wrought-iron fence that lined the park.

King caught the scent of some sweet fragrant bloom, oleander maybe, as he crossed through the park to Royal Street.

Across from the cathedral, a brass band was almost ready to play their first song. One guy had a cigarette dangling between his lips as he removed his trombone from its case and assembled it. The girl beside him was trying to arrange the 1920s headband across her brow just so.

King nodded to them before the park slipped from sight and only the cobbled stone of Royal Street stretched before him. He spared a hello for the shop owners and residents he knew as he passed and marveled, if only to himself, how at home he had become here in just a few short years.

He'd moved around a lot when he'd been a DEA agent, and every place had felt different. In some places the people were quite cold and uninterested in welcoming anyone new. Others were warm and inviting. New Orleans had struck him as standoffish at first. A superficial party girl who was friendly when she saw you but never exactly called you up to get coffee on a Sunday morning.

Of course, King had been a depressed drunk when he'd first arrived in the Big Easy. Perhaps it wasn't the city that had changed but him.

Then again, how many times had Piper told him *the Quarter is not New Orleans?*

King stopped in front of 777 Royal Street and fished his keys from the pocket of his duster, cradling the bag of beignets in the crook of his arm while he did so.

He'd almost gotten to the key he wanted when the door

opened.

"Morning, boss," Piper called, holding it open for him.

"Morning, Genereux," he said, offering her the bag of beignets. "I didn't know you'd beat me here or I would've brought you a coffee. I thought you were at the shop this morning?"

She motioned to the steaming mug on her desk. "I was, but she sent me here."

He noticed that she didn't open the beignet bag. "Give me those if you're not going to eat them."

Her hand tightened on the bag.

"I'll have *one*," she said, fishing out a beignet and placing it on a napkin beside her mug of coffee. "But if I eat too much sugar I get really sleepy in the afternoon, and I've got a lot to do today."

"Can I give you a word of unsolicited advice?" King asked, taking his own seat at his desk.

"Of course." Her eyes were wide and attentive. Her eagerness always amused him.

"Don't make your work the most important thing. Enjoy what you can—be it a good beignet or a night with friends, whatever it is. When you look back on your life, it won't be how many bad guys you put away that made it special."

Piper dipped her head. "Duly noted, boss. I'll do my best not to let work suck the joy from my bones."

"Now," King said, "give me a status report on your cases."

"I'm almost done with the legwork for the cybercrime case you gave me. I'm sorry it's taken me a long time. Cybercrime is *hard*. I thought my eyes were gonna bleed, looking through all those transactions."

King didn't have the heart to tell her he'd given her the grunt work. Poring over thousands of transactions to see which were legitimate and which were perpetrated by criminals was the job the company had wanted to hire out for.

It was the sad fact for someone of her age and rank that the early years of her career were going to be mostly the work qualified investigators didn't want to do. And she'd be paid less for it.

"Yes," King said, infusing his voice with empathy. "But the experience will look good on your resume because the FBI has to deal with a lot of cybercrime these days. It's not all exciting field cases with guns blazing, you know."

"Bummer," Piper said. "Especially since I think I want to specialize in murder."

Of course you do. King fought to keep his face free of emotion. "What else?"

"I wrapped up the carjacking case and sent all of the paperwork over to the DA like you asked. I also tracked down the civilian footage of the armed robbery in Black Pearl that the police asked you to get. I emailed it to you this morning."

King opened his email and found it, along with about forty other requests for his services. Mostly from partners certain their beloveds were knocking boots with someone else. Who knew his decades of experience hunting the worst drug syndicates in the world would be reduced to this?

You're supposed to be retired, King chided himself. *You're almost sixty-three years old. You aren't supposed to be pounding the pavement like you're in your twenties anymore.*

Before he could fully succumb to his own nostalgia, the door to the Crescent City Detective Agency flew open.

Melandra entered like a whirlwind, her scarf askew on her head. The gold bangles on her wrist rang out like an alarm.

Piper's fingers froze mid-typing. "What happened? Are you okay?"

Mel put her hand over her chest, as if holding it there might steady her.

"Mel?" King said, the suspense building. "Are you all right?"

She shook her head, but still didn't offer more.

"Whatever it is, spit it out," King said. "We can handle it."

Was that excitement he was feeling now? That lift in his chest and the flutter in his heart? Were things about to get interesting just as he was feeling sorry for himself, and perhaps a little bored?

"I was just at the shop twenty minutes ago. What could've possibly happened in twenty minutes? You're right. It doesn't matter." Piper punched her fist into her opposite hand. "We've faced mob bosses, and drug lords, and your sleezy ex. Whatever it is, we've got this."

King appreciated Piper's enthusiasm, but the look in Mel's eyes concerned him. "We can't help if you don't tell us what's going on, Mel."

"I—" She took another deep breath. "I have to—I have to throw a party."

King blinked. "Excuse me?"

"I have to throw a party," she said again, her hand still at her throat.

Given the expression on her face, she might as well have said she had to have all her limbs amputated the next day.

A surprised snort escaped Piper. "A party?" You didn't say anything about a party this morning. What kind of party?"

Mel came into the room and collapsed onto the chair. "A party. A fundraiser. The more I think about it, the more I start to panic."

What followed was a barely comprehensible retelling of that morning's meeting with the business association for Black entrepreneurs. King had heard of the group. In fact, if he wasn't mistaken, he'd recommended that Mel reach out to them a couple of years ago, when she was having trouble keeping Fortunes and Fixes afloat.

Piper rubbed her hands together. "An impromptu party is the kind of emergency I can get behind."

"Hold on," King said, frowning. He wasn't sure he'd heard correctly. "You went to the meeting and they told you to come up with a hundred thousand dollars?"

"She didn't say it like that. She just said that all members needed to contribute to the fundraising efforts and that the money was really important and would do a lot of good. Plus, the more you raise, the higher the tier you can join. I don't want to be on the lowest tier."

"But a *hundred thousand* dollars?" King repeated. That didn't seem right. It was a lot of money to ask a new member to come up with. "Are you sure you went to the right meeting? This isn't a Ponzi scheme, is it?"

Mel's nostrils flared and her jaw set tight. After a slow exhale, she said, "No, Mr. King. I didn't wander into a pyramid scheme. Tamara Jones was there. I saw her with my own eyes."

"What happens if you don't raise enough?" he asked. "What's the penalty?"

"I don't know. I think you're just on the lowest tier, below everyone else."

"What's the deadline?" Piper asked. She was already scribbling notes on the pad of paper beside her coffee.

"I've got to turn the money in on the thirtieth of this month," Melandra said. "Something about getting the money in before the first quarter ended."

King sat back in his chair. He didn't like this. Was the association a scam? Were they taking advantage of hardworking businesswomen like Mel?

Where was all of that money going?

"Why are you rubbing your chin like that, Mr. King?" Melandra asked.

"I'm just thinking," he said.

"Okay," Piper interrupted, holding up her notepad full of scribblings. "I've got some ideas about the party."

"What is all that?" Mel pointed at the page Piper had written all over.

"I'm brainstorming. You want to hear my ideas or not?"

No, I want to know what's really going on here, King thought, but he had the good sense not to speak.

"I sure do," Melandra said.

"Okay." Piper steepled her fingers. "How do you feel about zombies?"

Mel leaned back. "Excuse me?"

"People like to dress up. We could have a zombie party in a voodoo shop. It'll be fun."

Mel's brows went up. "No."

Piper scratched out that line. "What about cats? Or it can be cats versus dogs. The team that has the most attendees wins a prize?"

"No. Did you hear what I said about the *hundred thousand dollars*?" Mel asked.

Piper's brow scrunched. "What about it?"

"I need to invite people who have money," Mel said. "Those kinds of people ain't gonna wanna dress up like dogs and cats."

"You're thinking classier." Piper pointed finger guns at her. "And I hear you."

A minute later, she tapped the paper again.

"If you want classy, how about historical figures or a masquerade?"

Mel arched a brow. "New Orleans does have an abundance of masks. It will be very easy for people to find one."

"And if the dress requirement isn't too expensive, they'll have more to donate. I think a masquerade would be a lot of fun." She turned to King. "What do you think?"

I think I need to start digging.

4

The killer stood in front of the stove, humming a lullaby. His shoulders were relaxed, his heart lifted. He didn't even mind the leather bit in his mouth, the muzzle that remained fastened at the back of his head. He was happy to have such a beautiful kitchen to work in, such elegant plates and cooking utensils at hand.

The oven dinged at the same time, and he bent to remove the roast. He checked it with his knife. The flesh split easily and the aroma was heavenly. He'd cooked it just right. He was drooling around the leather straps.

Satisfied with how the meal was coming together, he admired his work. The platter was arranged beautifully, artfully, in the pattern of a rose at the center to match the floral design tracing the edge of the china.

He was still humming when he carried the platter into the dining room and placed it in the middle of the table, before taking his seat.

He was lord and master of this house now.

His subjects were obedient, if not loyal. The girl was on the right, her head held upright by the rope tied across her throat. Without the bindings they would have slouched in their chairs, and he couldn't have that.

Impeccable manners were to be observed while at the dinner table.

The mother was opposite the daughter, on his left. Her jaw was slack, her eyes gouged out. He had made a mess of it, he was afraid, but he wasn't to blame. She had refused to hold still. At least he had done his best to put her hair back in place.

Oh well. Live and learn.

The father's eyes were open, unseeing, the cavern of his chest a bloody mess.

"Given the sort of man you are," the killer said, taking a slice of the roast and placing it on his dinner plate, "I thought you might want to see what was going to happen to you."

The killer admired his plate and the table he had set. The roast, the fingerlings. It was all so beautiful. He said a small prayer of gratitude for the meal and reached for his fork and knife.

It was time then, the killer knew.

He reached up behind his head and found the metal buckle. With eager fingers he pulled the leather strap free, and the muzzle fell away from his face into his hand.

He opened and closed his jaw in anticipation. Almost as soon it was free of its restraints, sharp teeth grazed the killer's lower lip.

He tasted blood.

LOU SAT UP IN BED. SHE'D BEEN DOZING, KONSTANTINE breathing softly beside her, when she'd been pulled to consciousness. It had been her compass, she was sure of it. Yet now, it was still again. Perfectly at ease.

"What is it?" Konstantine asked, lifting his head from the

pillow.

At the sound of his voice, Octavia, the British Blue, leapt onto the bed, meowing. Konstantine stroked her soft ears, but his eyes remained fixed on Lou.

"*Amore mio?*"

She checked her watch. "I need to go."

"Is there trouble?" he asked.

Maybe. She threw back the covers. "I'm supposed to meet Piper in twenty minutes."

Octavia flopped onto her side and stretched luxuriously, shamelessly seizing Lou's place.

Konstantine, however, did not look nearly as pleased.

"I'll be back," she told him, hoping that would soothe him.

"Be careful," he said.

"Am I ever not careful?" Lou bent and kissed him, tapping Octavia on the nose as she did. The cat batted her hand away, trying to sink her claws into Lou's skin.

"Yes," Konstantine said, his green eyes looking brown in the shadowed bedroom. "*Often* you are not careful."

She didn't dignify this with an answer. She only pulled on her clothes and leather jacket, stepped through the shadows, and was gone.

The night was damp and chilly. It was hard to tell the hour given the fact that Bourbon Street rarely stopped its revelry. No matter the time of year, the bars stayed full, the drinks strong, and the music loud. Lou found Piper standing on the street outside the Wild Cat, talking to Henry, who had a large bag slung over one shoulder. He looked ready to go into the club, which meant he was probably putting on a show tonight.

Lou stuck to the shadows until their conversation ended.

As soon as Henry left Piper, Lou appeared at her elbow. "Hey."

"Hey!" Piper said. She checked the clock on her phone. "You're early. I was going to go home and change."

"You can if you want."

Piper waved her off. "It's fine. I need to be back in an hour anyway. Henry wants us to come to his show tonight. He needs feedback on his new routine. Is an hour enough?"

"Should be," Lou said, and pulled her through the dark.

Lou was grateful to find that her compass, at least at her urging, was still in working order.

When she stepped into the world again, they were in a Los Angeles bar. Nearly all of the women were blond and large-breasted. The men were no less plastic with their slicked hair and full lips.

"Are you trying to destroy my self-esteem?" Piper asked under her breath. "Why is everyone here so beautiful?"

"Tell me who has guns," Lou said, motioning for the bartender to take their order. The woman was dressed to kill. A red skirt cut across her thighs and clung to her curves. Her nails gleamed in the overhead lights and her smile was perfect. Lou had never seen teeth so straight and white.

"What can I get you?" the bartender asked, her fake lashes fluttering at the question.

"Two beers," Lou said.

The woman arched a brow. "Any particular brand? You don't seem fussy."

When Lou's mirrored shades did nothing more than reflect her own face back at her, Lou expected the woman to look away. Instead, she tilted her head a little and stuck her breasts out farther, clearly enjoying the sight of her reflection.

"Two Coronas," Piper said, and slid a twenty-dollar bill across the bar. The woman took it and sauntered away.

Once she was gone, Piper took Lou's arm and bent toward her ear conspiratorially.

"Okay. I'm thinking those guys over at the table are the

bad news bears."

"Guys at the table," Lou repeated. "Be more specific."

"The ones against the wall there, by the bathrooms."

"Why them?"

"Because of the position they chose in the room and because of how they're sitting. There are eight seats, but they've all chosen one side of the table so they can watch the doors."

"You watch too many movies," Lou said. "People with guns usually sit wherever the hell they want."

"I'm wrong?" Piper asked, her face falling. "I was feeling pretty good about the one in the blue shirt."

Piper was right. That one did have a gun.

"Partial credit," Lou said.

"Why only partial?"

"He has a gun, but he's not the one you have to worry about." When Piper started pouting, Lou added, "He's a bodyguard. He'll make a move to protect the rich kid beside him, but he won't start trouble. I want you to know who in this room will pull a gun *first*."

It was a subtle distinction, but an important one. True, it was impossible to know how a situation would unfold. People were unpredictable—Lou had learned that firsthand. People with guns could be even more irrational. But she wanted to teach Piper the game of probabilities, how to scan a room, and what to be aware of. These were the things that would improve her chances of staying alive when a situation turned deadly.

"How do you know he's a bodyguard?" Piper asked, doing her best not to stare.

Lou could see the earpiece from here. And he wasn't being subtle in the way his eyes kept sliding toward the kid at the end of the table, looking him over. Either they were lovers or he was charged with keeping him alive.

Of course, it could be both.

The bartender returned with the two beers but no change.

Piper took a sip of her beer then said, "Worst in the room, worst in the room, worst in the—*Ah!* Too easy. It's Mr. Polka."

Lou clinked her beer against Piper's. "Good eye. He is, in fact, the worst in the room."

"Who is he?"

"He's the son of Miguel Devantes."

"Ah, yes. Of course. Good ol' Devantes." Piper nodded sagely. "Can you remind me who that is again?"

"He runs one of the largest drug cartels in Mexico."

"Why is he in this swanky place then?"

Lou nodded at the blonde with very plump lips laughing like a horse beside him. "His girlfriend is an American model."

"This was too easy. I want a challenge, *Louie.* I want to be the most qualified rookie to ever walk into Quantico. Give me something hard."

Lou flashed her a devilish grin. "Careful what you wish for."

They put their unfinished drinks on the bar and crossed the noisy room to the bathroom.

The three girls gossiping in front of the mirrors looked them up and down as they entered. The shortest of the three, one with an upturned, piggish nose, sneered.

But before they could say something snide, Lou turned off the lights and stepped through the dark to the sound of their screams.

When Lou turned the light on again, the bathroom was very different. It was a quarter of the size of the posh one they'd left behind, and where there had been a marble counter and soft lighting, now there was a single dull bulb that hissed and flickered above an empty towel dispenser and a stained sink.

"Oh man," Piper whispered. "Is it too late to back out now?"

"I thought you wanted a challenge."

Piper puffed her cheeks. "If this bathroom is any indication of where you've brought me, I already know it's going to be a challenge."

Lou held open the bathroom door and urged Piper to step out first.

The crowd looked rough. That's why Lou had chosen it. But Lou wasn't going to walk the girl into an actual lion's den for a mere training demo. She just wanted the place to *look* like a lion's den. Besides, it was so dark, Lou could slip from anywhere in the room.

And it was fun to watch Piper squirm as she tried to cross the room casually, past the groups of hulking bikers in spiky leather jackets and women with sharp stares. She looked ready to run by the time she reached the bar and took a seat.

To her credit, she maintained her cover and tried to blend in as Lou had taught her. Even if Piper's ears were a bit red by the time she motioned for the bartender.

"What can I get you girls?" the bartender asked. She couldn't have been more different than the glossy model they'd left back in Los Angeles. This woman was at least forty years older and she was missing her front left tooth.

"A beer, please," Piper said. "Whatever you've got is fine."

"And you?" she asked Lou.

"The same."

Once she'd walked away to get their drinks, Lou turned her attention back to Piper.

"Stop wiping your hands on your jeans and tell me who would be the biggest threat to you here. Who would you need to keep your eyes on?"

"I can't!" Piper hissed.

Lou couldn't suppress her smile. "Why?"

"I'm scared to look! What if I make accidental eye contact with someone? Why are they all so big and burly?"

"How do you know they're big and burly if you won't look?"

"It's a presence," Piper whined. "I feel a *presence*."

Lou placed a twenty on the tabletop for the bartender when she returned with the drinks.

"Who?" Lou pressed.

"How am I supposed to guess who would pull a gun on me first when everyone looks like they'd kill me?"

"You *said* you wanted a challenge." The bartender delivered their drinks, and Lou took a sip of the new beer before tipping it toward Piper. "Come on. Who do you think the wild card is?"

Piper took her beer, and between sips, she dared to look out over the room, at the men playing pool and the women gathered in groups along the wall. Lou watched her dismiss the guy at the jukebox and people sitting in the booths talking.

"I don't know. It's too hard. All of these people genuinely terrify me. I—Wait." Piper's words broke off when she turned back toward the bar. "No. *Really?*"

Lou watched Piper struggle to keep her face calm and placid. She was getting better at masking her true feelings, Lou could give her that.

Piper leaned forward and whispered, "The bartender. She's the biggest baddie in the room."

A corner of Lou's mouth lifted. "Why?"

"She has a shotgun behind the bar." Piper's thumb picked at the beer's peeling label. "That's a big gun."

Lou squeezed Piper's shoulder. "Good work. She *would* be the one to keep your eye on."

5

D ani Allendale couldn't find Piper. She'd gotten the text telling her to head to the Wild Cat and get a good table before Henry's show. That was twenty minutes ago, and now Dani was sitting alone in a crowded gay bar, where every forty seconds she had to convince someone that *yes*, in fact, she did need the extra chair, and then contend with the dirty looks that followed. .

"Look who it is," a voice called.

Dani's stomach twisted even before she looked up. "Hello, Scarlett."

Scarlett stood on the other side of the table, her black curls falling in perfect ringlets around her pale round face. Her blue eyes were made brighter by shimmering eyeshadow, false lashes, and winged eyeliner. Dani wondered if the mole on her face had been penciled in or if it was real.

"Oh, so you *do* know my name," Scarlett said with a derisive laugh. "I'm surprised. You don't really look all that smart."

"But she does look like she *eats*," the skeletal blonde beside Scarlett said.

The girls laughed. Dani considered which witty retort she could use that they might understand and had just decided to not dignify them with a response when someone shouted to her left.

"Be gone, demons!" a man called out. "I see you starting shit! I'm gonna give you some when I get over there."

Henry, well over six feet tall in his heels, marched toward her table, elbowing his way through the crowd.

"Let's go," the skeletal blonde said, tugging on Scarlett's arm.

"I'll see you around," Scarlett said, and knocked over Dani's glass. Dani managed to dodge the flood of alcohol, at least. The childish act reminded her of her cat, Octavia, and Dani suppressed a laugh.

"Oh you think that's funny—"

"Come *on*! I'm not getting my ass beat for you tonight." The blonde finally managed to pull Scarlett away.

"Yeah, you better get out of here, you freaking losers." Henry pulled out one of the empty chairs, his full attention on Dani's face. "Don't you dare! Don't you fucking *dare* cry in this club. This is not her victory."

"I'm not crying. I'm laughing."

Henry pursed his lips, the glitter on his face catching the light and sparkling. "Oh. Well that's okay then. What did she say to you?"

"Apart from implying that I'm fat and ugly? Nothing at all."

"Christ. That bitch. I'm gonna stomp on her Achille's heel with my stilettos the next time I see her."

Dani placed a hand on his arm. "I appreciate the offer, but if she knows that she's gotten to me then she's won, right?"

"You are *so* classy. No wonder Piper loves you."

"Does she?" Dani asked. The question was out of her mouth before she could stop herself. She hadn't meant to let her insecurity show. Maybe Scarlett was getting to her more than she thought. Why, though? Dani had dealt with girls like that all her life. Competitive and possessive girls were the norm in the elite circles she grew up in.

Henry tilted his head. "Look, I'll be straight with you—no, not straight. Girl, you know I can't be straight if I tried, but I'll be *honest*."

Dani didn't think Henry could say anything worse than Scarlett had, and at least his intentions were good. "Go on."

"It's true that Piper used to be a bit of a, well, *slut*." Henry wrinkled his nose. "I guess that's not feminist. Should we say a player?"

Dani's stomach turned again.

"She had half of these Quarter groupies in love with her, and the other half willing to give her any time of day—or night."

Dani frowned. "I'm not sure I want to know what you're trying to tell me, Henry."

"I'm trying to say that I've seen Piper with a lot of girls, but I've never seen her look at any one of them the way she looks at you."

Dani's face warmed even though she suspected he might be lying for the sake of cheering her up.

Henry must've known he was on the right track because he began twirling one of the blond curls from his wig. "I'm serious, and it's not just how she looks at you. She talks about you differently, and I know I'm not the only one who's noticed, which is why all these girls are hating on you right now. You've managed to do what not one of them could."

"I haven't married her," Dani said, even as a little voice in her mind whispered, *Yet*.

"No, but you're living together. She openly refers to you as her girlfriend, when the most they got was a night or two in Piper's bed."

"She calls Scarlett her ex."

Henry rolled her eyes. "She calls everyone she hooked up with her ex. Piper doesn't really know what *ex* means."

Dani could do without the image of Piper in Scarlett's bed. The very thought of their lips touching—let alone anything else—made her blood begin to boil.

"I know Piper," Henry said, and there was much conviction in his voice. "Once she's made someone her person, she's loyal. Once you've got her, you've *got* her. Do you hear what I'm saying?"

Dani laid her hand over Henry's and squeezed. "Thank you. I appreciate you trying to cheer me up."

"I mean, let me be clear. If you ever wanna go to the praline shop where Scarlett works and confront that bitch, *I am down*. I'll pick me up some saltwater taffy while I'm there."

This earned Henry a laugh, and he reveled in it.

"I'm serious. Don't you think for a second that she's got anything on you, or that she's going to somehow manage to pry Piper away from you. P can be impulsive, but she's not an idiot."

The music changed and Henry turned, cocking his head. "Oh, that's my cue. I gotta get backstage. Here's your girl anyway. Emphasis on the *your*, my dear."

Smiling, Dani turned to see Piper pushing her way through the crowd, patting a few shoulders and calling a few hellos as she made her way through the crush.

Once she saw Dani, her face lit up.

She plopped down in the seat Henry had vacated. "Hey, babe. Sorry I'm late."

Piper leaned across the table and kissed her. Her lips were soft and sweet. Dani tried to lose herself in the kiss and let the last of her insecurities and fears melt away.

She would have managed it if she hadn't opened her eyes

and spotted Scarlett watching them from across the room, her gaze cold and murderous.

KONSTANTINE DECIDED TO FOLLOW THE GIRL HIMSELF. HE didn't want to give the job to one of the boys, who might give the game away, or to Stefano, who might be too heavy-handed in his approach.

No, it was best that no one in the group suspected Gabriella of anything until Konstantine himself could confirm her guilt.

Her guilt of *what* he had yet to determine.

She was lying to him, of that he was sure. It was true that she arrived at the church in the mornings and walked to school with Matteo and the others. She seemed to be following the terms of their agreement though she still wore boy's clothes and kept her hair hidden under the cap as before.

Konstantine let the children have a head start. It was easy to fall into step a few blocks behind them. The boys were so loud and boisterous as they cut through the piazza toward the school that not one of them noticed much of anything, let alone that their master was close on their heels.

Outside of the school, Konstantine confirmed the first lie.

Gabriella had assured him that she was going to school. And yet, she'd remained on the street outside and waved goodbye to Matteo. She didn't go into the building. She earned a couple of curious looks from parents dropping off their children and teachers who stood near the door, but no one stopped her as she ran back into the busy Florentine streets.

Konstantine again let her take the lead, keeping a safe distance from her. Her first stop was Ponte Vecchio, where she bought a sweet roll the size of her head. She ate it on the bridge overlooking the Arno River. Then she walked along the riverfront, looking at the shops and cramped streets, gazing in windows at the trinkets for sale.

He'd almost given up chase, half believing that perhaps she really was nothing more than a little girl who hated school, when something changed.

Until that moment she'd seemed rather happy. The picture of a child exploring the city until the clock in the piazza began to chime. He watched her freeze in the middle of the square and turn toward the clock as if its ominous toll rang out for her. With each strike of the bell, a great weight seemed to settle onto her small shoulders. After the eleventh chime struck, the air filled with resounding silence.

She walked slowly away from the piazza, heading north, her shoulders slumped.

Konstantine remained close, watching her weave her way through the day's foot traffic until she got further and further from the city center. They were almost thirty minutes from the Duomo at the heart of Florence when she turned down a little road. By the time he'd reached the mouth of it, she was gone.

He waited. She had to have entered one of these buildings, and he didn't want to run the risk of passing her and exposing himself. It was five minutes before she reappeared, stepping out onto the road again with a small paper bag in one hand.

As she started up the street toward him, Konstantine ducked out of sight, pressing himself into the shadows the way he'd seen Lou do so often. He remained hidden until she passed him.

There was no way to get closer, to see what sort of place she'd just left and what threat it might pose to him, without giving up his plans to follow her. But he made note of its location so he could return later.

Could there be a rival gang forming in his own city? A separate faction that hoped to undo him from the inside out? He didn't think so. He'd taken many precautions after Nico's coup against him.

Was it a police sting then? Someone hoping to gain enough evidence to prosecute him? That seemed unlikely too, considering how many of the officers he had befriended—and paid handsomely.

Konstantine was expecting another long walk, perhaps back across the city toward its center, but instead she headed farther north, toward the little neighborhoods that clustered on the outskirts of town.

He had to give her a great deal of room when she took the overpass. It was out in the open. There was no cover for him there. No alley to duck into or obstruction to hide behind. She would have needed only to turn around and look at him to know he was following her, so he let her disappear from his sight completely more than once.

But he always found her again.

The last time on a quiet street. The daily market was wrapping up for the day. The woman who sold fruits and vegetables and flowers was carefully packing up what she had not managed to sell. She eyed Konstantine suspiciously as he cut across the street in pursuit of the girl.

It was on this last cramped road that Konstantine saw Gabriella stop yet again before a doorway. She knocked for a long time. She shouted up at the windows.

"*Sono io! Gabriella!*" She carried on this way until the heavy door creaked open and a rough hand pulled her inside.

"Is there a reason why you're following little girls around?" the woman asked, her hands on her hips.

"No," Konstantine said, trying to hide his irritation at being seen. At least this woman did not know him.

"*Allora vattene prima che chiamo la polizia*," she said. "Go on."

Konstantine let himself be shooed, lest he make trouble for himself. But the feeling of unease he carried didn't relent, even after his long walk back to the church.

6

King stood outside the police precinct, trying to decide what he would say when he went inside and who he should talk to. He couldn't very well ask anyone about the business association without raising a few eyebrows. In fact, maybe he shouldn't start with the police at all. What if they had a few cops in their pockets? Cops weren't immune to bribes. King himself had never accepted money under the table, but his longtime partner Chaz Brasso certainly had. He'd been so deep in a senator's pockets that he'd been willing to kill King—and had tried.

Detective Dick White stepped out of his car and began crossing the street with a cup of coffee in hand.

As soon as he saw King, he lit up. "Hey, Robbie, how you doing?"

There goes my chance to change my mind, he thought. He couldn't pretend he'd never been here with White staring him down.

King extended his hand. "Not too bad, White, how are you?"

White took it, gave it a firm shake. "Not a complaint in

sight for once. It makes me nervous. I'm due for some bad luck."

"I hear you."

"What are you working on these days?" White asked, putting one foot on the step above King's and leaning his weight on it. "Nothing as exciting as a teenage girl threatening to shoot herself, I hope?"

"No," King said with a relaxed smile. "Though I would like to ask you a couple questions, if you have a few minutes to spare."

"Is this about a case?" White asked, his interest piqued.

"An unofficial consult," King said. It was best not to lie if he could help it.

"By all means, ask away."

"Have you gotten any complaints about the Association of Black Women Business Owners?" King asked.

"*No*," White said, with a great deal of humor in his voice. "Are you kidding me? You're talking about Tamara Jones. She's the closest thing to a saint we've got round here. Apart from the ones running round the stadium. Jones's put a lot of blood, sweat, and tears into that association. That woman is a bulldog for her ladies."

White's unrestrained praise for the group and its leader made King hesitate. "No complaints of money going missing? Or that the members were being exploited in any way?"

White's good-natured smile wilted at its edges. "Where's this coming from, King? I know Tammy. She's good people."

I've overstepped, he realized. *I'm going to do real damage if I don't fix this.*

"I don't doubt it," King was quick to say. "It's just that Mel has joined up and I wanted to make sure it was a smart choice for her and all. She's already got a great deal of admiration and faith in Ms. Jones, and I wanted to make sure it was well placed. Forgive an old fool for being overprotective."

White's scowl softened. "Nothing wrong with checking up on things when you need to, but take it from me, Jones is good. She does a lot for this city—and not just the ladies. I respect the hell out of her. You're not going to find any dirt on Tamara Jones."

King put his hands up in front of him in surrender. "Like I said, I meant no offense."

"You're not from here, so you're forgiven," White said. "Besides, you and I both know there's plenty of corruption in this town. It can't hurt to check the list twice where there's money involved."

King slapped him on the shoulder. "On that we agree."

LOU FOUND KING IN HIS OFFICE. HE WAS LEANING BACK IN his chair, squeezing his stress penguin while the poor creature's eyes bulged and contracted. She pushed her mirrored shades up on her head and arched a brow.

"Having a bad day?" she asked.

He turned, starting at the sound of her voice.

Someone is lost in thought.

"I'm all right. Piper went over to Fortunes and Fixes to help Mel measure the shop."

Lou had known Piper wasn't here, but didn't say so.

He added, "Mel wants to throw a fundraiser and raise some money for this *club* she's joined. She wants to know how much square footage she's got so she can get a permit from the fire department to have the event in the shop."

"That doesn't tell me why you summoned me," Lou said.

"Right." He put the penguin on the desk, perching it on its block of fake ice, and then reached into his drawer. He pulled out a folded sheet of paper and handed it across the desk to her.

She read each name in turn. "What did these five do?"

"Menner, Stanley, and Cooke are pedophiles who got their convictions overturned. Bates and Howe killed eight children between them, all under the age of ten." When she didn't reply, he said, "I noticed that you were favoring sick bastards who preyed on kids, so I thought I'd pass these along in case you were interested. Was I wrong?"

"No." Lou slipped the folded sheet of paper into the front pocket of her jeans. "You're not wrong."

He nodded, but his gaze was distant again.

"If you've nothing else, then I'll leave you to it," Lou said, sliding her mirrored shades back over her eyes as she turned to go.

"There's one other thing," he said, seeming to catch himself. "I wanted to say how impressed I was by your dedication."

"I don't know if dedication to *murder* is worthy of admiration," she said with a wan smile.

"I'm talking about what you're doing with Piper. I see you girls working hard and I just wanted you to know that Lucy would be proud. I can't tell you how many times she complained to me about you not taking care of yourself."

Lou's heart ached at the mention of her late aunt. Lucy, her sole source of love and comfort after her parents had been killed. Lucy, the would-be bodhisattva who did her best to turn her murderous niece into someone loving and kind. Lucy, who had died of cancer, lost to a disease that Lou, despite her many gifts, had had no power to stop.

"I know she would be," Lou said. "I have few memories where she isn't trying to feed me or get me to do yoga."

"At least she never made you go to a naked yoga class with her," King said, taking the penguin off the desk again and pointing it at her. "*That* was an experience."

"No," Lou said. "I can't say that she did."

. . .

THE KILLER SAT AT HIS DESK, HIS PEN POISED ABOVE THE paper. He reread his last lines again.

Three hundred and seventy-five degrees was too hot. It dried out the flesh and made the roast far too stringy. I am not sure what I expected. A far better experience would have been possible if I had not rushed. If I had cooked the roast at three hundred, for perhaps two hours—three? Longer?

His pen tapped against the page. His hand went to his mouth, but he found his cheeks smooth and uncovered, the lips exposed.

He hadn't put the muzzle back on yet. It wouldn't be necessary for a few days, until the beast's hunger stirred to wakefulness again.

A father's heart was all that could ease the restlessness.

I don't know why it's got to be the heart, the killer wrote, his hand moving smoothly across the page, unhurried. *But it's always got to be the heart. Nothing else works.*

He tapped the page with the end of his pen, daring to look up and meet his eyes in the mirror. He couldn't hold his gaze for long. Instead, his eyes slid down, to the scar that consumed half of his right cheek and encircled his jaw. He traced the discolored skin, pinched and disfigured.

His hands began to shake at the memory of the creature throwing itself down on top of him, called by the scent of his blood. Of the feeling of its jaws clamping down on the side of his face. His own scream ringing out in his ears as he begged for his mother.

With his mother's screaming in his ears, he saw his own wide and fearful eyes in the mirror.

It didn't matter. The screaming went on and on.

The whole world seemed to ring with the sound of it.

What do I have to do to stop it? What do I have to do?

7

B y the time her lunch break rolled around, Dani felt
terrible. She hadn't slept at all the night before. She'd
tried not to toss or turn. She couldn't even sit up
because Piper was such a light sleeper, any movement on her
part would have woken her.

Instead, she'd lain on her back in their bedroom and
stared at the ceiling, her irritation hot in her guts and
limbs. Every time she closed her eyes, she saw Scarlett's
face.

After a useless morning behind her editorial desk at *The
Herald*, Dani decided she wasn't going to lose another night of
sleep over this woman. This wasn't high school. This wasn't
some telenovela drama full of manipulative and backstabbing
women trying to ruin happy homes.

This was her life.

And *she*, Daniella Viviane Allendale, never ran from a
problem.

Or at least this is what she had told herself in the hours
leading up to her lunch break, when she resolved to go and
see Scarlett at the praline shop. An hour for lunch should be

enough time to make it from St. Charles down to the shop to visit Piper's ex.

Not really an ex, she reminded herself, thinking of Henry's assurances. *Just someone Piper slept with. A lot.*

Her mind warred with itself back and forth as the streetcar rumbled along its rails. When it finally hooked a right on Canal, Dani hopped off and began the remainder of the journey on foot.

She stayed off Royal Street. Piper would either be at the detective agency or Fortunes and Fixes, and either way, Dani didn't want to run into her. She didn't want to have to explain why she'd decided to spend her precious lunch break talking to Scarlett. Worse, what if she wanted to join her?

At least it wasn't rainy today, nor was it too hot, which meant she could maintain some semblance of dignity in her appearance.

It had been Henry who had confirmed the girl was working today and had sent Dani the address, offering one last time to meet her for a joint attack.

But no.

That wasn't Dani's style. She handled her problems directly, like a mature woman, unless reinforcements were absolutely required.

While Scarlett certainly annoyed Dani to no end, she didn't strike fear in her. After being tortured for sixteen hours by a Russian mob boss and having her finger cut off, a catty girl was hardly a threat. Or so she kept telling herself.

Dani would be lying if she said her stomach wasn't in knots by the time she entered the praline shop. It reeked of spun sugar as she slowly moved through the store's center displays and shelves toward the counter. She'd spotted Scarlett almost as soon as she'd entered.

Today her black hair was pulled up off her neck, exposing a slender milk-white throat. A black choker stretched across it. A few ringlets had been pulled down to frame her face and she wore enough mascara to make her eyes really pop.

She wore a plaid jumper beneath the apron that all the shopgirls wore.

Dani hated, more than a little bit, how pretty the girl was. Would it have killed Piper to choose ugly lovers, if only for the sake of her self-esteem?

Don't do that to yourself, she thought. *There is no reason to compare yourself to her.*

And yet she couldn't stop. They were both curvy. They both had round, feminine faces. Scarlett's eyes were blue and her hair black. Dani had dark brown eyes and brunette waves. They both had full lips, though Scarlett's top lip was a smidge thinner than Dani's. And Scarlett had a cute hoop in her nose that Dani's face wouldn't ever have been able to pull off. Not without her mother having a stroke.

Dani's nerves intensified on her way to the register, and she stepped off to the side at the last minute to gather herself. She needed an opening line. A good one. A strong one.

She grabbed a box of the pecan hash and a small bag of saltwater taffy. At the last second, she also grabbed some pralines.

Then she went to the counter and laid them down in front of Scarlett, making sure the pecan hash was on top.

Scarlett looked up and her gaze darkened.

"It's Piper's favorite," Dani said, ignoring the drum of her pulse in her ears. "The pecan hash. She said it was good here."

Not a lie. Though when Piper had told Dani this, Piper had yet to make it clear she'd learned how good their pecan hash was because of Scarlett.

Scarlett's mouth hardened. "I know."

"While I'm here, I thought we could talk." Dani's voice was strong, at least. Cool and level. She could thank her years of investigative reporting for that. A good reporter couldn't let their emotions show in their voice when they wanted people to divulge their secrets. They had to seem collected, nearly indifferent, no matter what might really be going on beneath the surface.

"Go ahead," the other shopgirl behind the counter said. She was a short, mousy redhead. "I'll cover you for fifteen."

Scarlett's eyebrows went up and stayed up. The other girl was already bagging Dani's purchase and returning her debit card to her.

"I could use a smoke anyway," Scarlett said.

"You know Margorie hates it when you smoke in the apron," the second girl called.

Scarlett flipped her the bird and walked out of the shop. That's when Dani noticed that Scarlett's left hand had been bandaged.

Dani took her shopping bag and thanked the mousy girl.

On the street, Scarlett fished a packet of cigarettes and a lighter out of the front of her green apron.

"Look, Scarlett. I don't know you well, and you don't know me—"

"You're Daniella Allendale, the only daughter of some rich-ass immigrants from Mexico who live in some Mandeville mansion."

They immigrated from Honduras and Cuba, actually.

"You graduated from Tulane and now you're working at *The Herald*. There's also a bunch of shit all over the web about you winning some competitions—music, dancing, horses— your basic rich-girl shit. So I'd say you're a typical overachieving, thinks-she's-better-than-everyone-else bitch. Am I right?"

She did her homework, Dani thought. Though not well. Clearly she'd done a few intensive internet searches, but if she'd *really* dug deep and had wanted to screw with Dani, she would've mentioned her hospitalization after Dmitri Petrov's torture, or her personal leave from work and school for psychiatric reasons. Dani couldn't believe for a second that Scarlett would miss the chance to call Dani crazy if she could.

When Dani didn't answer, Scarlett exhaled a thin stream of smoke to the sky. "You're not from here. You'll never understand her or what she's been through. Do you know what her mom did to her? Do you know about her dad?"

"I do," Dani said reflexively.

Don't, she warned herself. *You have nothing to prove.*

"It sucks for her that you're not even that pretty. What does she see in you?"

"Maybe she was just tired of all the typical, boozy Quarter groupies and wanted to settle down with someone she could build an actual future with."

God help me, I sound like my mother.

Five minutes in and she'd already let her composure slip.

"I didn't come here to fight," Dani said, doing her best to regain her neutrality. "I came to make a deal with you."

Scarlett snorted. "This will be cute."

"I want you to stop bothering Piper and me as long as we're together—"

Scarlett snorted again and picked a piece of stray tobacco off her tongue. She had to switch her cigarette to her bandaged hand to do it. As soon as Dani began looking at the hand, Scarlett slid it into her apron, out of sight.

"In exchange for the promise that should Piper and I ever break up, I will pay you the same respect. I won't do anything to try and break the two of you up"—*as if she would ever go back to you. If she leaves me for you, I'll kill her*—"or, you know, call you a bitch in a club when I see you or shoulder-check you every time you're on the street with a cup of coffee."

The other cashier poked her head out of the shop and flashed an apologetic smile. "Scarlett, I need you to watch the register while I go to the bathroom."

Scarlett shrugged at Dani as if to say, *What can I do?* "Time's up."

"Do we have a deal?" Dani asked, coming up on her toes before she could force her heels back down. She was trying not to seem too eager. "Or should I continue to expect childish behavior from you for the foreseeable future?"

"Sure." Scarlett's grin was too wide, and she twisted her boot on the cigarette butt, grinding it into the pavement. "Whatever you say."

8

———————

Lou pulled the sheet of paper from her pocket and looked at the names again. The sunlight filtering through the park's trees danced prettily across the page while children screamed and laughed from the jungle gym behind her.

Where to start?

King hadn't included any information except the men's names. She didn't know what time zone they were in or if they might not be alone. All she could do was look at the list and wait for her compass to give her a better sense of where to go first.

As her eyes fell on the name Bates, a sharp tug hooked through her navel.

"Bates it is," she murmured, and walked toward the large shadows collected beneath the live oak in front of her.

She stepped into the darkness, and while it was thin, it was still enough to pool along her skin and offer her a door to the rest of the world.

When she put her foot down again, she was in a supply closet that reeked of bleach and something bitter. She shoved a mop handle out of her face and found the doorknob.

Outside the closet lay a sea of cubicles. Slowly, she snaked her way through the aisles, letting her compass guide her through the maze of corporate conformity.

Lou was working her way toward the center of the maze when a man stood, a plastic badge swinging from his neck. Lou's compass fixated on him. As he began walking her way, the compass's tug grew stronger.

She followed him to the bathrooms, noting as he moved his height, the way his weight settled more to his right side than his left. How his hands, large, hung loosely at his sides. His hair was too short to grab. But she could grab him by the belt, she thought.

It's why she loved belts.

It was easy to move a man around as she pleased when she got a good hold on one.

Just before he entered the bathroom, Lou grabbed the collar of his dress shirt with one hand and the leather belt with the other.

He'd only just begun to turn toward her, a snarl on his lips, when she pulled him through the dark.

When the world reformed again, they were at her lake in Alaska, miles of wilderness stretching in all directions around her. A flock of birds in the tree took flight at their sudden arrival, a pounding of black wings escaping in every direction.

The frogs that were just beginning to wake to the spring-time ceased their croaking and fell silent. One jumped into the water, leaving a trace of ripples on its otherwise placid surface.

The man stumbled but did not fall, though his shoes were far too nice for this terrain.

Is he the right one? she asked her compass. *Did he hurt the kids?*

Because while she trusted King, it never hurt to check.

The compass gave a resounding *yes*, its pulsing current remaining strong within her.

Too bad for Bates.

"Who the hell are you?" he asked, his eyes taking in the placid lake. The evergreens stretched as far as the eye could see. He fussed with the plastic badge hanging from his neck. "Where did you take me?"

It was always interesting when she brought them to the lake in the light of day. They were much more likely to show confusion around what was happening to them. When she brought them at night, with the moon high above and the cold prevailing, they often thought they were dreaming, that Lou was a phantom or apparition of some kind.

But Bates's chest was heaving on the verge of panic.

His eyes were too wide and grew even wider as Lou pulled the Beretta from the holster hidden under her leather jacket and pointed its unflinching eye at the man before her.

"W-wait."

The crack of the gun cut off the rest of his words. He dropped like a rock, his eyes open and unseeing, fixed on the blue sky above. As blood slid across his forehead and dripped from his temple at the water's edge, Lou looked at the list of names again.

She'd wait to drag the bodies across until she had the others. It wasn't her favorite thing, hunting in wet socks. If she crossed the waters to La Loon now, she would either have to go home and change them between kills or hunt with cold, shriveled feet.

The very idea irritated her.

No. The bodies could wait. No one was going to find them out here with hundreds of miles of evergreens and untouched terrain stretching on all sides.

She'd always known that both her Nova Scotian and

Alaskan lakes were remote. But thanks to Piper, she finally knew just *how* remote.

Very.

It had been Piper's idea to drop a pin the last time she was at this lake and then look up its location using internet maps. Lou had done that and discovered that the nearest town here in Nova Scotia was over two hundred miles away. It was even farther between her Alaskan stronghold and the next town.

For that reason, Lou didn't worry about a wayward human discovering this place.

It was more likely that a grizzly or a wolf would get to the corpses and make a mess of things before she got back. As she looked at the list once more, her eyes fixed on the name Menner.

Lou's compass whirled to life again.

Menner had been fishing, overlooking the coursing stream where he stood wearing camo waders and a matching hat. He was very confused to be moved from one embankment to another. He'd sputtered to find his river was now a lake. He hadn't even gotten a look at Lou before she put a bullet through the back of his head, his fishing pole falling from his grip into the water.

Lou had fond memories of fishing with her father when she was a child. They were one of the rare childhood memories involving water unmarred by her complete panic.

She remembered the careful way her father showed her how to slide a worm onto a hook. She even remembered how she felt a little sorry for it before her line was tossed into the water and the worm disappeared beneath the shimmering surface.

She decided she would keep the pole for now. She pulled it from the water and left it propped against the nearest tree.

Menner remained face down beside Bates as she went to get Cooke.

Cooke had his head under the hood of a car, looking at an engine.

The place smelled of hot oil and burning rubber.

Lou waited until the other mechanic stepped out of the garage to answer a trilling phone before she approached him and grabbed the hood of the car. She brought it down on the back of his head and Cooke cried out, howling.

As she lifted the hood with one hand, she took hold of him with the other. The stench of grease and a hot engine burned her nose as she pulled him toward the shadows collected along the garage's wall.

He was still howling when the lake swelled up before them.

Then he saw the bodies. He stumbled from her grip.

"Oh shit." That was all he managed to say before Lou put a bullet in his brains too.

She waited for her compass to select its fourth victim, but nothing happened.

It remained still. Wherever Stanley and Howe were now, Lou couldn't get to them easily. And if her compass thought it was best to wait, she would wait.

Lou shrugged out of her leather jacket and threw it over a boulder to keep it dry. Then she grabbed Bates's nice leather shoes and pulled him into the water.

Lou waded out until the cold water was breast high, and then she sank, dipping her head below the surface. When she first told Piper that she had to sit at the bottom of a dark lake, holding on to a corpse in order to dispose of the body, Piper's face had blanched.

You do what now? the girl had said. *That's going to be a hard pass for me.*

It had been difficult for Lou to explain that she didn't find it terrifying, sitting under the water's surface with a loose grip on a corpse. There was something soothing about the cold water, about the anticipation of crossing over to her world.

But as the waters warmed notably, shifting from pale gray to red, Lou admitted if only to herself she had not always had such peace with her gift. She recalled quite clearly how scared she'd been of the water when she was a child. Back then the water took her against her will. She couldn't control when she slipped through it.

No, she thought. *I thought I was scared of the water, but it had never been the water.*

She'd been scared of her power.

Of her inability to master it.

Of the beast that waited for her on the opposite shore. She hadn't bonded with Jabbers yet. The creature was twice her size and something from her nightmares.

Now Lou was comfortable with nightmares.

With the water red, Lou knew her crossing was complete. She kicked to the surface of Blood Lake, breaking through with a grateful gasp.

And there was the beast in question.

Jabbers sat on the sandy shore, her weight on the last two of her six legs, her haunches bent and extending to either size much like a cat's. Her belly was pale compared to the black scales that covered her body, limbs, and back. Her eyes were yellow and slitted like a serpent's. The tongue and mouth when she yawned as white as a cottonmouth's. Her muscles rippled with anticipation at the sight of Lou, and she let out a small chuffing sound, not unlike a tiger's.

Lou dragged Bates's body to the shore—it had lost a shoe somewhere in its travels—and dropped it at Jabbers's feet.

The beast's throat groaned and clicked with happiness as it pushed its head into Lou's outstretched hand, knocking her back a few steps with its strength.

Lou smiled. "There are two more."

She waded out into the waters.

"I'll be back," she assured Jabbers.

More pleased chuffing came between great sniffing snorts as the beast inspected the offerings.

The last thing Lou saw before she slid beneath the red waters of this alien lake was Jabbers's white, slug-like tongue dragging across Bates's face, lapping at the blood drying across his forehead and temple.

On the second trip, Lou managed to get both Menner and Cooke across, but she couldn't surface with Cooke.

Once the blue-gray waters were replaced by red again, signaling her shift from one world to the other, Lou realized her error. Menner's waders had filled with water and their weight was now pulling her down toward the bottom of Blood Lake. It didn't matter how hard she pulled, she couldn't heft him and maintain her control of the second body.

She relented and let Menner's corpse sink to the dark depths below, making it to shore only with Cooke in tow. Jabbers had already ripped into Bates, having done away with his nice office clothes and half his organs, and seemed equally excited to see Lou carrying another gift for her. Lou thought that was a grin she was seeing, beneath all the gore.

"I had to leave the other one in the lake," she told her, pointing a thumb over her shoulder. "If you want it."

Because while there were already beasts in the waters that could eat a corpse—Lou had nearly been eaten herself by the strange orca-like creatures that sometimes came into the shallows—she also knew that Jabbers could swim. She'd seen her stretch herself out on the lake's surface and glide like a water bug, and also dive deep for her prey.

Jabbers chuffed again.

Lou couldn't be sure what this reply meant, or if Jabbers even understood her words.

While Jabbers ate first Bates then Cooke, Lou regarded the monstrous landscape. The bruised color of the sky gave the impression of perpetual twilight. And if she needed any evidence that she was no longer in her own world, her own time, she need only look at the twin moons hanging in the sky. They appeared content to rest just above the hazy smoke-yellow mountains for all eternity.

The stench of sulfur that hung in the air was as thick as ever, but Lou hardly noticed. Her mind was fixated on her own body.

Usually after a hunt, she noticed the energy depleted from her body. After all, even though the taking and killing of the men wasn't especially strenuous, it still required quite a bit of strength to haul them from one world to another before dumping them on this shore.

It was different now.

Lou had never felt stronger.

She was wet, but not the least bit winded. She'd exercised, thrown Konstantine around for a few hours, and still had it in her to bring three bodies to La Loon without even breaking a sweat.

Was this the reward for taking good care of herself? This renewed stamina and sense of invincibility? She couldn't deny that for years she'd rolled her eyes when her aunt Lucy had insisted that she eat regularly, sleep more, and drink water. She thought these instructions had only been something Lucy had felt compelled to say, now that Lou's parents were dead and Lucy had taken charge of her.

But now, after a few weeks, she could hardly deny the results.

A rustle behind Lou made her turn away from the view to find that Jabbers had flopped over on her back and was rolling in the undergrowth, scratching herself in the oil-black grass the way a dog might.

That's when Lou noticed the change.

Jabbers's stomach was quite swollen.

It had been impossible to see the swelling when the beast sat on her haunches. Six legs had a way of obscuring the underbelly beneath.

"You're pregnant," Lou said.

Lou remembered the other beast that had visited Jabbers months ago—or at least it had been months on Earth. It was hard to say how much time had passed here in La Loon.

The smaller creature had been fiercer, more aggressive than Jabbers. Or perhaps that was only Lou's perspective since it had been a very long time since Jabbers had taken a bite out of her. Jabbers had challenged her mate on Lou's behalf, succeeding in buying Lou the time she'd needed to escape to safety.

Since she'd left in a hurry, Lou hadn't been sure if the mating had been successful.

Now she knew it had been. Unless something else was wrong with Jabbers, some illness that caused stomach swelling, perhaps. But seeing Jabbers roll around in the grass like a dog made her inclined to think not.

"Are you going to be a mother?" Lou asked her, her hand still resting on the beast's swollen belly, which rose and fell with each of the beast's great breaths.

Jabbers released a soft cooing sound.

Lou took that as a yes.

"Well," Lou said with her own deep sigh, "I hope they like me as much as you do."

9

K ing was outside the marquee at exactly 6:30 with two tickets in his hand. He'd been wondering if he should go inside the cinema and check out the seating situation, or maybe get in the popcorn line to save time, when Beth turned the corner and lifted a hand in greeting.

"Hey," he said, holding a ticket out for her.

"Sorry I'm cutting it close," she said. She came up onto her toes to kiss him on the cheek. It was the most affectionate Beth ever got in public, a kiss on the cheek. King understood. She was the DA and a lot of people knew her in town.

A lot of nosy people, she would've added.

"I got held up. Oh, but they don't look too busy, do they?"

Beth wore a cream-colored pantsuit. Her braids had been pulled back and tied at the nape of her neck. At her scalp, he could see the gray hair growing through. Her black-framed glasses hung around her neck, secured by a golden chain, and her smile was as bright as ever.

"Nah, we should have plenty of time to get popcorn," King said, holding the door open for her.

"And a pretzel," she said. "I've been thinking about one of those big soft pretzels all day."

Even though there were only two kids working the concession stand, they'd gotten their popcorn, soda, and Beth's pretzel in record time. They even made it to their seats with seven minutes to spare.

"It's why I like this theater," she told him. "It's smaller, cozier. And when you come straight after work like this, it's not as busy as the later shows."

He could only nod since he was shoving a fistful of buttered popcorn into his mouth. When she reached for her own handful, he saw her nails. They were long and purple. He was fairly certain they'd been turquoise just two days ago, when he'd seen her last.

"Your nails look very nice," he said.

Her grin brightened. "Thank you, Robbie. I got them done yesterday. And I've finally got my hair appointment. I can't wait. I need it done."

"I don't know what you're talking about. You look beautiful to me."

She tilted her head. "Such a charmer. But enough about me. How was your day?"

She put on her glasses and glanced at the screen before turning back to him.

Oh, just trying to figure out if my best friend has been roped into a scam, he thought. Aloud, he said, "Just work."

"Anything of note?" she asked. Because Beth liked interesting cases as much as he did.

It couldn't hurt to ask. "What do you know about the Association of Black Women Business Owners?"

"That's Tamara Jones's baby," she said. "She's poured her heart and soul into building that organization."

He tried to keep his expression neutral. "So, no complaints? Nothing suspicious or under the table?"

She frowned, her pretzel stopping halfway to her mouth. "Heavens, no. Ms. Jones is a wonderful woman. I trust her."

King tried to remember if it had been Tamara Jones who had told Mel to come up with all of that money.

"What's this about?" Beth asked, adjusting her glasses on the bridge of her nose.

"Mel went to one of their meetings this morning and it seemed like they wanted her to come up with a lot of cash," he said, adjusting the popcorn bucket on his lap. "I just wanted to make sure they were legitimate is all."

"You can rest easy. I've never known Ms. Jones to lead anyone astray." Beth finished off her pretzel. "And if Mel were to make some new friends, I can't think of anyone better than Jones and the rest of those ladies. They're good people."

"You knew about the fundraising then?"

"Of course," she said. "No organization can run without funds, Robbie. Especially not an organization whose sole purpose is to give away money. Let Melandra do her part. She'll be rewarded with great connections and a strong support network. You'll see."

"I hope you're right," he said as the lights in the room began to dim and the previews started on the screen.

But all throughout the movie, his stomach churned and his mind wrestled with the idea.

Something about what Beth had said was getting to him.

Halfway through the movie, Beth's phone began to vibrate in her purse. She pulled it out, checked the number, and excused herself after giving King a brief squeeze on his arm.

She was gone for almost five minutes, King's attention only half on the movie, half on the door she'd disappeared through.

When she returned, she had a noticeable pep in her step.

His curiosity ate at him until after the movie ended and they found themselves outside on the street in the damp spring air again.

"Was it a good phone call?" he finally asked her. "You seemed like you got some great news."

"It was my son," she said, taking his hand in hers. Another unabashed display of affection, right here out in the open.

She really is in a good mood tonight, he thought.

"He proposed to Rita," she said, her grin bright. "They want to get married in July."

"Three months isn't much time to plan a wedding," King said.

She waved this away. "They've been together a long time. They know what they want and they're both teachers. It's easier to get the wedding and honeymoon done in the summer when there's no school."

King laughed as she practically danced up the street in the direction of her apartment. King had taken the streetcar to the theater because he knew this was the plan. First a movie then a walk back to Beth's place for their customary night of sex.

He should be pleased.

The movie hadn't been disappointing, even if it had been a rather bland crime drama.

The night was beautiful, and Beth could not be happier.

Yet something weighed on his heart.

"You'll probably be busy for the next three months then. Will you head to Orlando to help with the preparations?"

"Oh *no*. Not at all," Beth said with a laugh. "I won't be steppin' on nobody's toes."

"You're his mother. I don't see how you'd be stepping on anybody's toes." In truth, King had no idea what role parents played at their children's weddings. He had no children of his own and the closest substitute would be Lou, who he'd semi-inherited through his marriage to Lucy. But he suspected the world would end and zombies would inherit the Earth before Lou had herself a white wedding.

"The bride knows what she wants, and she comes from a big family with parents, stepparents, and half a dozen sisters and half sisters. They'll do the heavy lifting. I'll do a chore if she gives me one, but otherwise, I'm quite content to enjoy the show from my seat. And hopefully soon, I'll be a *grandmother.*"

She practically crowed her excitement. He tried to be happy for her, tried to be as excited as she was by the prospect of her having grandchildren, despite what their birth would mean.

Beth had told him more than once that she would retire from her position as DA and move from New Orleans to Orlando once these hypothetical grandchildren were born.

That she would leave him behind without so much as a backward glance, which was unfortunate, because he'd grown really fond of her.

She took his hand and squeezed it.

"Don't you worry, Robbie. There's no reason to look so glum. I'll be here to help you," she said.

He was unable to hide his confusion. "Help me?"

"With the fundraiser," she said as her Prytania Street townhouse leapt into view with its soft pink façade and welcoming porch light. "You're going to help Mel with her fundraiser, aren't you?"

King's stomach clenched again, but he forced a smile. "Yes. That's my plan."

LOU STEPPED OUT OF THE SHOWER, INTO THE STEAMY bathroom. Her hair dripped onto her shoulders. She'd only just wrapped her hair when her compass spun to life.

Great timing, she thought as she pulled on clean cargo pants and a black sweater.

She quit trying to towel-dry her hair and shrugged on her leather jacket. She also slid on her mirrored shades.

She realized she didn't need them once she was out in the rainy night.

Lightning cracked open the night and the roar of thunder rumbled in her chest as she stood on a dark sidewalk.

Glad I didn't bother with drying my hair.

It wouldn't have done her any good.

The blustery wind pulled at her clothes as she surveyed the empty street, trying to let her eyes adjust to the low light. There was also the customary tension in the air, a restless electricity she often felt before a strong storm.

Yet the neighborhood was sleepy. Most of the windows were dark, with only a few porch lights spilling out onto the sidewalks running along the side of the road. The streetlights themselves resembled black lanterns. Their glowing halos of light momentarily illuminated the rain as it fell to the pavement

Lou waited. She couldn't see him yet. But she could feel him.

Where are you?

The first movement that caught her eye was a cat. It marched up the walkway leading to a house, its ears back and head down. It was obviously upset to have been caught in the storm. It yowled before diving into a bush against the house, out of sight.

Where are you?

Her compass was tugging her forward. She took one uneasy step, then a second.

Nothing moved but the falling rain and the trees ruffled by the wind, their branches creaking.

Yet her compass was insistent, and Lou knew better than to mistrust it.

Someone was here in the storm with her.

Waiting, like she was. She stood very still.

How many minutes passed? Five? Fifteen? It was hard to say.

Lightning spiderwebbed across the purple sky above her head again and another great crash of thunder vibrated Lou's body—and that's when she saw him.

A tall, hulking form, nearly as one with the darkness as she was.

Lou guessed by the shape and size of the figure that it was male. Of course, there were always exceptions. But Lou rarely saw women that bulky, even when they did manage to grow that tall.

Now that she'd fixed on his location, his details stood out in stark relief.

He stood wrapped in a rain-soaked trench coat. Water ran off the brim of the hat hiding his face. The shadows beneath that brim were complete. Lou couldn't see his eyes. No mouth. There wasn't even the suggestion of a nose.

If not for the buttons on his jacket—and Lou realized now that it had been his buttons that had caught the lamp-light—she wasn't sure she would have spotted him at all.

There it was again, the sparking of light, though this time it was too high to be the buttons. Something on his cheek? Did he have a piercing on his face, maybe?

Lou was about to go to him. She could pluck him right out of the darkness where he hid and figure out his crimes later.

But as she stepped forward, the force of her compass died away. Her footsteps faltered.

Her gut said no.

Why?

She watched as he turned and walked up the street away from her, rain hitting his shoulders. He stuck to the shadows, just beyond the reach of the streetlights above.

Don't you want me to take him? she asked her compass. *Isn't he a killer?*

Her compass did not move. It didn't spin to life.

Whatever it had been seeking was no longer within reach.

10

I *wasn't alone tonight,* he wrote. His hand hovered above the page. *I'm not ever alone because of the beast in me. It never lets me forget it either, but this was different.*
This was the first time I felt somebody before I saw them.
I felt her.
I thought she was a ghost.
Old neighborhoods are full of them.
And I know I'm haunted. Nobody's got to tell me that.
They're all in me, these ghosts. They'll be with me forever, I guess. Especially if the beast keeps collecting them.
But forget about that. I know what I felt.
Her.
Her.
Her—
I did not see her at first—how didn't I see her?
She's gotta be friends with the dark too. I saw that myself. I saw the way it touched her. It curls around her. No, not curls—a caress.
It loves her.
I've only ever seen it do something like that a long time ago. There

*was another woman who came right to me right after I—But that
was a long time ago.*

*What is this feeling? I feel like I'm going everywhere at once. It's
almost like how I lose to the beast, but this is better. I don't feel weak
with this one. I feel strong.*

Really strong.

Am I excited? Why does she make me feel like this?

It's got to be her. Nothing else has changed.

As soon as the beast knew she was there, it hid.

How did she do that? Was it some power or is it scared of her?

Scared of her! Can you imagine? What the hell is she?

*If she can master the darkness, if the beast inside me hides
from her—*

Could she—

"I'm going to die," Mel said. She put both of her
hands on her head scarf and groaned. "Pitch my body in the
river and let's be done with this."

"Come on. Don't be like that," Piper said. "It's a party, not
your funeral."

"Says you!" Mel said. "You don't have to figure out a clever
way to get a hundred thousand dollars from strangers."

"I thought we were doing the masquerade. It's a great
idea."

Mel was rubbing her temples furiously, her bangles
tingling musically with each rotation of her wrist.

"Walk me through the masquerade again," she said.

"Okay. Picture this. Fortunes and Fixes stuffed to the brim
with people in masks, eating snacks, drinking, chatting it up,
and you and I wandering the room telling fortunes and
reading palms. Or if someone wants a private reading then we
can go behind the curtain."

"How many people are we talking?"

"Fire code says you can get up to two hundred and fifty people in here at a time. And not everyone will be here at once anyway. They'll come and go throughout the night," Piper said, opening the pricing gun and adding the fresh roll of price tag tape to the dispenser. "Let's say that we can get a thousand people—"

"A thousand people!" Mel cried.

"Yes, if we're lucky a thousand people, and we'll ask for a fifty-dollar suggested donation at the door—though they'll be welcome to give more. That's fifty thousand right there. Of course, I'd think it was a huge success if we can get just five hundred in here."

"Fifty thousand does not a hundred thousand make," Mel said.

Piper rolled her eyes up to her. "*Again.* You don't need to buy these business ladies with a hundred thousand dollars, Mel. I'm telling you. You're amazing. They'll like you anyway."

Mel's mind filled with the image of Tamara Jones in her beautifully pressed pantsuit and how small and ugly she had felt beside her in her flowing skirts and bangles.

They might change their mind. They might not let me join at all.

"Fifty dollars for a private party is a good mark. This Tanya Jones—"

"Tamara Jones."

"Sorry, *Tamara* Jones is not going to turn her nose up at your money even if you only show up with five thousand bucks. It's going to be *okay*."

What if Mel didn't raise enough? What if she wasn't invited to be a full member of the club? Would she be back to struggling and striving on her own every time a crisis hit her shop forever?

What if nothing ever changed?

It's not really about that, she admitted, if only to herself. Mel had weathered many a storm on her own. She didn't need anyone else to save her.

She *wanted* this. She wanted to, finally at long last, feel like a part of New Orleans.

She'd lived in the city for many years, and Melandra's Fortunes and Fixes had become a staple in the Quarter, yet she still felt like an outsider.

Mel chewed her lower lip. "Why in the world would anyone pay fifty dollars to hang out in my shop when most days they can drink and wear a mask in here for free?"

Piper pointed the pricing gun at her. "Because not only do they get to hang out in this super-cool shop, but it will be an after-hours, *private*, *exclusive* event. Secondly, they get my punch. It's an *amazing* punch and I never share it with randos."

"I don't think they're coming here for your punch," Mel said, one eyebrow raised.

"Just shows that you've never had my punch." Piper huffed. "But even if they don't know about the punch, they're getting their fortune told and they have an excuse to dress up and drink. We could up our game by handing out a souvenir too. Maybe a choice of a crystal or a sugar skull as long as supplies last. It's a steal, man."

"Maybe I should just donate the money myself," Mel said, holding her thumbnail between her teeth. She was already doing the math in her head of how much she could take out of her savings without ruining herself.

"No, if anything, your money is going to the inventory loss for souvenirs. You can write it off as a tax-deductible business expense, too. I say we use the unpolished stones that you never set out anyway because you don't think they're pretty enough. No one is gonna know the difference. It would be better if we hand them out in little bags with 'Melandra's Fortunes and Fixes' stamped on it, though. That's marketing right there. Maybe you'll get people coming back to the shop. Win-win."

Mel couldn't handle this right now. It was hard enough trying to think of how she was going to lure a thousand customers to her shop for a single night when she did good to hit that number during a Mardi Gras weekend.

"You're doing that thing where you stop breathing and turn red." Piper put an arm on her shoulder. "Stop it. It freaks me out."

"Sorry." Mel forced herself to exhale slowly. "I just don't know how this is going to work."

"It will work. I don't mean to brag, but I'm *great* at planning parties. Why do you think Henry's always asking me to come to his shows at the Wild Cat? Because *I* know how to pack a room. It's a gift, really."

Mel barely heard the girl over the pounding of her own heart. She needed to calm down. Why was it that every time she thought about this stupid fundraiser her heart went off like a shot?

"I'm going to print up the flyers tonight and pass them around the Quarter. I've settled on the last Friday—"

Mel whirled on her. "Why?"

"Because that's a good night for a party. Fridays are a little quieter than Saturdays, so less competition. It's far enough out that people can plan for it, and if the money is due Tuesday, then we'll have the weekend to count up how we did. Plus, there will still be time for any last-ditch efforts if we need them. But I don't think we will."

Mel was biting her lip again, looking around the shop and trying to imagine how in the world Fortunes and Fixes was going to pull this off.

"Suze at du Monde already said she'd take some of the flyers, and so will Zeke across the street. Henry's going to circulate them at the Wild Cat, and I've got a few friends who work around the Quarter who will take some. I haven't asked King yet, but that's because all his friends are cops and I wasn't sure if that's the crowd you wanted to invite."

Mel frowned. "Why is everybody willing to hand out flyers for this?"

Piper threw up her hands. "It's a party! Everyone loves a party. Geez, have you never *been* to a party?"

In truth, Mel couldn't remember the last time she was at a party. It had been many years.

Her niece had had a birthday party back home, but that was ten—no twelve—years ago.

Piper frowned at her. "Why don't you let me take care of inventory and you look up prices for the little personalized bags that are big enough to put a crystal in. Come on."

Piper pushed her behind the glass case and opened her laptop browser.

"Here we go. It's the internet. The internet is great at distracting us from things we don't want to think about."

The storage closet opened and Louie stepped into the shop, her eyes hidden behind mirrored shades.

"Lou-blue!" Piper called. "What are you doing here?"

Lou's hand hesitated on the closet door. "I thought someone needed help."

Piper whirled on Mel. "Your freaking out made Lou come. *Mel!* You're sending distress calls about a *party*. If Lou can feel you, imagine what vibes you're sending out into the universe right now. Aren't you always telling me to be positive? That it's a requirement for good outcomes?"

"I'm sorry." Mel pressed her fingertips into her temples and tried to exhale another slow breath. "I'll try harder."

"Where's Lady?" Lou asked.

"With King," Mel said. "When I'm agitated it only works her up."

Lou pushed her sunglasses up on top of her head. "Why are you upset? What's going on?"

Piper put a hand on her hip, pointing with the pricing gun as she spoke. "There's no mobsters or death threats here. Mel just *thinks* she's dying, but really we're planning a party. Apparently someone is *very* party phobic."

Lou looked as if she wasn't sure what to do with her hands without a dog to pet. "What kind of party?"

"Mel wants to join this club for business ladies and needs to raise money to get in. *I* think they'll let her in even if she doesn't raise a hundred thousand dollars."

Lou's brows arched. "A hundred thousand dollars to join a club?"

"Right? I'm about to call Tamara and ask her what's up with that."

"Please don't," Mel begged. She was holding on to the edge of the glass cabinet where the laptop rested to steady herself. "I don't want her to think I can't handle this."

I already feel horrible enough.

Piper gave Lou a look that Mel couldn't quite interpret. Did they think she was crazy? She felt a little crazy.

"I keep telling her that we can throw a great party, but she's been in panic mode this whole time. I don't think she realizes how cool this shop is."

"I could rob a bank," Lou said with a hint of a smile. "If it comes to that."

"No," Mel said, tilting her head. "Please do not sidestep your way into a bank vault for me."

"Wait." Piper lowered her voice and leaned toward Lou. "Can you do that?"

"I have. I needed to pay off the contact who gave me Benito Martinelli."

"Damn." Piper looked impressed. "If I ever need to abscond to the Bahamas on a whim, good to know I've got not only the free travel"—she pointed at Lou—"but the funds too."

Mel's head was killing her. She felt like her skull was going to split in two. Worse, she was sweating.

She *hated* when she stress-sweated.

"Can you girls go for a coffee or something? I need a minute alone." She pressed her cool hands to her face.

Piper placed the pricing gun on the cabinet and gave a little salute. "Whatever you say, boss. Come on, Lou-blue. Let's go see what the big guy is doing. No, this way. Step away from the closet. We're *walking*. It's literally around the corner. It'll take two minutes."

Lou released her hold on the storage closet door and followed Piper out into the day.

For a moment, all Mel could do was stand there, listening to the ringing silence.

She kept breathing, kept forcing air in and out of her nose, slow and deep.

"I can do this," she whispered to herself.

She pulled her tarot cards from her pocket. The battered but beautiful cards that had been brought from Haiti after the revolution. They'd been a gift to her great-great-great-great-great-great-aunt Josephine Beloit by her mother Simone to mark their newfound freedom and independence. It had been Grandmamie who'd given the cards to Mel not long before she died.

With the old, battered cards in her hand, a steadiness settled into her muscles and bones as it always did. The power of generation after generation of strong women welling up inside her. Finally, her breath evened out. Her heart steadied.

She shuffled the deck.

"I can do this," she whispered again, and turned over the first card. "Please show me how."

11

K ing had been searching the internet for information on the women's business association when news of the horrific murders in Boise began filling his screen.

He was deep into the description of how the family had been found. They'd been discovered sitting around the dining room table. Their bodies were strapped to their seats, the mother's eyes gouged out. The father's heart was missing. The bodies of the teenage daughter and toddler were somewhat spared. Apart from the blunt-force strikes to their heads which killed them, they had no markings or trauma on their remains. One news outlet had gone so far as to call it *merciful*.

The bell above the Crescent City Detective Agency rang out, breaking the spell the gruesome story held over him. He looked up.

Piper and Lou stepped into the agency, and Lady was on her feet a heartbeat later. Tail wagging, she sauntered up to the girls and pressed her nose into their extended hands. They fell on her, scratching her ears and back while Lady grunted, tongue out.

"What are you doing here?" he asked, turning his computer away from them. He frowned at Lou. "Did you just use the front door?"

He wasn't sure he'd ever seen Lou walk into this office off the street. She always used the storage closet with its joke of a name plate, *Lou Thorne*, fixed beside it as if it were her private office.

"Right?" Piper snorted. "She's slumming it with us normal folk today. I'm so proud of her."

"I thought you were at Fortunes until two," he said.

"I was supposed to be, but Mel kicked us out. I'm guessing she wants to have her freak-out *alone*."

King's stomach dropped. "Why is she freaking out? What happened?"

"Nothing. It's just about the party." Piper slid to the floor when Lady flopped over and offered her belly. In her baby voice reserved only for animals and infants, she added, "She's worried about nothing. *Absolutely nothing.*"

King wasn't sure he wanted to tell them that he had his own misgivings and had also wasted half the morning neglecting their cases so that he could conduct his own investigation into Jones and her association.

Lou's gaze was fixed on him.

"What were you looking at when we came in?" she asked.

Reluctantly, he turned his computer so she could see the news report.

"They found a family in Boise," he said.

"*Boi*-zee," Piper repeated. When she saw their looks, she said, "What? It's a funny word. I'm tired of no one having a sense of humor today."

Lou was bending down to look at the story. She arched a brow. "He eats them?"

"It's not clear if he ate the mother's eyes or if they were

just missing," King said. "But he definitely ate the father's heart. There were traces of it on one of the dinner plates."

"Jesus. That's *sick*." Piper made a gagging noise.

"Are they sure the killer is a man?" Lou asked.

King shrugged. "You're right. I don't know if they have evidence to support that or if it's an assumption."

"Is this the first family they've found?" Piper asked.

"Staged like this around the table? Yes. That's why they're calling him the Hammersmith Cannibal. That was their last name, the Hammersmiths. But there might have been other killings. A few of their older cold cases look like they belong to the same killer."

Lou only stared at him, obviously waiting for him to give her more details. But this wasn't King's case. He knew well enough that these details couldn't be treated as fact. Not all journalists had Dani's penchant for accuracy. Or morality, for that matter.

"A couple of years ago they found a graveyard outside of Boise with half-eaten corpses, hearts missing from the men's chests," King said. "The crude way the bodies had been torn apart, they'd thought it was wolves because the remains had been gnawed on. Now they're not so sure."

Piper wrinkled her nose. "Not so sure they were gnawed on?"

"No, not so sure they were wolves," King corrected.

"They've got a lot of wolves in Idaho?" Lou asked.

"They've got wolves, yeah." King met Lou's stare. "Are you going to check it out?"

She had that look on her face. If she hadn't pushed her sunglasses up on her head, King wouldn't have noticed anything at all. But since he could see her eyes now, he knew she was touching base with her compass. Her head was turned ever so slightly to the left as if she were listening to something.

"Probably," she said at last.

"I'd rather you not interrupt an active investigation that could lead to closure for the families, but if you want to step in and make sure no one else gets hurt before he's caught, I'm all for it."

Lou said nothing to this, and King knew he should let it go.

Instead, he asked, "How's it going with the list I gave you?"

"Three out of the five are taken care of," she said, watching Lady and Piper roll around on the agency floor.

"Did you run into any trouble?"

"No," she said.

He nodded. "Good. Let me know if you do and if there's anything I can do to help."

Offering to be Louie's backup always felt a little ridiculous. Then again, he'd been of use to her once, in a Tuscan shootout between Konstantine and his rival Nico. King had successfully cut the power and set Lou free to shift through the darkness again.

She'd even thanked him for his help, after she'd destroyed Nico and burned the entire villa to the ground.

King closed his laptop. "All right. Let's talk about this party."

DANI'S AFTERNOON HAD BEEN UNEVENTFUL. AFTER speaking to Scarlett, she'd spent the remaining hours of her workday fact-checking the articles that crossed her desk as well as inspecting other possible leads for headlines they could run. Everything was faster now that they published mostly online and had reduced their paper circulation to the Sunday edition only.

She'd been trying to work out if the story about the

cannibal killer could wait until then, or if they should go ahead and put something on their website about it. It might be better to report the facts once they actually had them.

She also made a note to tell Lou about it. It seemed like a case that would interest her, if she didn't know about it already.

Dani stepped off the streetcar into the Quarter. She was almost home and her feet hurt, but instead of walking to Royal Street and their apartment, where Piper was making spaghetti, meatballs, and cheesy garlic bread for dinner, she passed the agency and walked in the direction of the parking garage where she kept her car.

She'd left a notebook in there, if she could call it a notebook. In truth, it was more of a massive binder that held all the contact information for her connections across the country. She wanted to see if she knew anyone in the Boise area who could give her more information on the cannibal case. As of yet, no one was coming to mind, but Dani took extensive notes. She might know someone who knew someone who knew someone.

When the elevator opened on the third floor of the parking garage, she pulled her keys out of her leather messenger bag and smashed the fob.

Her taillights flashed, and she stopped dead just five feet short of her vehicle.

"Oh no." The words escaped her as a thin whine. She took a few steps forward, hesitantly. "Oh *no*."

Slowly, Dani circled the SUV, inspecting it from hood to rear bumper.

She reached out and touched the closest gouge with her finger, and her heart sank.

Her eyes weren't deceiving her.

Someone had keyed the *hell* out of her SUV. And not just an innocent, presumably *accidental* scuff of paint.

No.

It looked like someone had dragged a crowbar from one end of the car to the other several times over.

Sometimes the marks even went up and down, as if they'd tried to carve the very metal off its frame.

If that wasn't insult enough, her two front tires had been slashed.

Her blood began to boil, bubbling over like a tea kettle.

"Why not bust out the windows while you're at it?" she said to the empty garage.

Because that would've set off the alarm and they'd been having too much fun.

Dani's first instinct was to blame Scarlett.

But Scarlett had been at work all day. Dani had seen her there with her own eyes.

Then again, the last time Dani had seen her car in good condition was when she checked on it a few days ago, before the incident at Henry's show. It was possible that Scarlett and her friends had keyed the car then, and Dani was just now seeing it.

Wouldn't Scarlett have said something today if she'd been responsible? Wouldn't she have made at least one snide, suggestive comment to take credit for the act?

Or was that why Scarlett had tried to keep her bandaged hand out of sight?

Had she hurt it trying to slash Dani's tires?

The petty part of her certainly hoped so. But now Dani couldn't remember if Scarlett's hand had been bandaged at the bar.

She didn't think so. Maybe they'd visited the garage after the show.

Maybe while Dani was lying in bed with Piper that night, Scarlett and her friends had been going to town on Dani's SUV.

Dani had other questions, too. How did Scarlett know that this was where Dani kept her SUV? Or even that this was Dani's vehicle. Has she seen Piper and Dani in it? It was possible. As to how they found it, it might simply have been a matter of deduction. Street parking was hard to come by in the Quarter. This was the garage closest to where she and Piper lived. It made sense that she would look here before anywhere else.

But what if it hadn't been Scarlett at all, just an ill-timed act of vandalism? Property damage was definitely a problem in the city. Maybe she should give the girl the benefit of the doubt and not blame her right away. Bitterness and a bandaged hand were hardly iron-clad evidence.

Too bad this garage didn't have cameras, or Dani could've searched for footage of the incident.

Maybe it wasn't her. You don't know.

She tried to keep an open mind as she unlocked the door and found the interior at least was untouched. She reached across the seats and got the notebook she'd come for.

She didn't want to report the incident to the police, even though vandalism was a crime. Too many people knew her at the local precinct. Word might get back to Piper about what really happened.

No. It's better if I handle this on my own.

Dani opened her phone and dialed a number.

"Yes, hello," she breathed into the phone. "I'm going to need a tow truck, please."

12

L ou was curious about the cannibal in Idaho.

Idaho.

She couldn't even think about the state's name without hearing a jingle from her childhood about potatoes.

She tried to refrain from making a joke about *meat* and potatoes as she waited for night to fall.

It wasn't enough to wait until the sun had set in St. Louis. Idaho was two hours behind her. So she padded around her apartment, drank coffee, and ate dinner—chicken and broccoli tonight—and watched the bravest of boats cut a path up the Mississippi River in defiance of the ruthless April wind.

Once she was certain full dark had fallen even in Idaho, she gave up her view of the Arch, with the artificial spotlights encircling it, and stepped into her converted linen closet.

On the other side of the darkness, she found herself in a cave. Or at least she thought she was in a cave. Stone walls surrounded her on all sides, with the exception of the packed-dirt floor.

She reached into the pocket of her cargo pants and pulled

out her phone for its flashlight. Once its beam clicked on, it was clear she was standing in the middle of a crime scene.

Everything had been carefully marked off, tagged, and flagged with yellow police tape.

Lou looked about the cave and was reminded of Jabbers's lair in La Loon, with its throne of bones piled against one wall.

Yet she was disappointed to see there were no remains here. If there had been bones or bodies, then the police had taken them away for processing. All that was left was some blood splattered on the floor and walls, and drag marks along the ground.

Lou followed the tunnel out into the open air. There was still a thin seam of purple on the horizon as she regarded the landscape. It was shrubland as far as the eye could see. Short bushy spats of green punctuated the sandy floor. Not desert, exactly, but also not the lush paradise she'd been expecting. She supposed she did not know much about Idaho.

The air was cooler than she expected too. She wondered what the elevation of this place might be and dropped a pin using her GPS watch to look it up later.

This view of the nighttime scrubland reminded her of Colorado, actually. She'd hunted plenty of gunmen in Colorado, and this sparse greenery was just like it.

It's very remote. How did you get out here? she wondered, and imagined the killer driving a vehicle out to this empty stretch of nowhere before leaving his evidence in the cave behind her.

The cave itself would've been easy to overlook from a distance, like little more than a collection of boulders. How had he found it?

How had he known about this place?

Lou turned back toward the cave. The tallest boulder was no more than an inch above her head. In fact, she had to stoop a bit to keep from splitting her skull on the edge of a rock.

Was he short? Or could it be a woman? Or had he ducked down to enter the space?

Maybe he even crawled into the dark on his hands and knees. Though that didn't explain how he'd gotten the bodies inside.

Maybe he dragged them in with his teeth. Like a wolf.

The cave faced away from the tire tracks in the dirt. They weren't very visible now as the last of the light faded away. But they were deep enough to give Lou the impression of which direction the vehicles had gone. She had a sense that Boise was back that way. West.

She knelt and used her phone's flashlight to examine the grooves cut into the earth.

Lou wanted to talk to Dani and figure out what she knew about this case. No doubt this story would've crossed her desk by now. If she hadn't made ten calls about it already, Lou would be surprised.

Howling struck up in the distance. A deep longing unleashed on the night.

Wolves.

Had to be. The coyotes that Lou was used to sounded much more frantic in their calling. More yippish than this throaty harmony.

She turned off her flashlight and returned her phone to her pocket.

Take me to the one who did this, Lou told her compass.

She wouldn't take him while the investigation went on, but Lou wanted to see him. To know who she was up against, and more importantly, to imprint him clearly on her compass. How else could she keep an eye on him and make sure he didn't hurt anyone else?

It was dark enough around her now that when her compass clicked into place, she needed only to take a step forward. To lift her foot from the desert floor and into a crowded room.

She hadn't been expecting that.

A guy with a plastic cup of beer bumped into her and swore. Foam sloshed over the edge of his cup and wet her boots.

"Watch where the f—Shit." His words sputtered when he saw her. "I didn't see you. Sorry."

He was younger than she was. His soft baby face and big doe eyes told her that he couldn't be more than twenty-one, and had probably bought the beer by the skin of his teeth.

Not him, she knew. The open, goofy expression on his face conveyed nothing more sinister than his mild intoxication. He wasn't her killer.

She turned her attention to her compass again and found it was pulling her to the left, around the man, deeper into the crowd.

"Hey, is this your first time at La Casa?" he asked her. "Are you—"

She pushed past him, parting the crowd the way a shark's fins cut through water. A slow, steady glide as she became one with the current.

People were laughing and shouting over each other, a hundred conversations all fighting for the same space. She also heard music coming from a distant room somewhere behind her, a mingling of live drums and a pitchy voice floating her way.

Her attention fixed on a door in the farthest wall. A circular window in its middle made it look like a porthole in a ship. In fact, now that she looked around her, quite a bit of the decor was borrowing from a nautical theme. Fishing nets, plastic anchors, and if Lou wasn't mistaken, that was a one-eyed pirate with a hook for a hand sitting perched above the long bar.

"Miss!" someone called. A rough hand grabbed Lou's shoulder.

Lou turned and seized the wrist in a hard grip. Her other hand was halfway to her gun.

A terrified girl stood frozen in front of her, her voice stuck in her throat.

Lou released her.

She cradled her wrist and blinked her eyes several times before managing to speak. "I'm sorry, but you can't go in there. That's for staff only."

"What's back there?" Lou asked, nodding at the door beside her with its porthole window.

"The kitchen. Just the kitchen."

Lou thought of King's descriptions of how the family was arranged around a dining room table. Kitchen staff? Could it be that her killer cooked at this place? Or did he just have access to a few professional knives?

"What's the name of this place?" Lou asked.

"La Casa del Diablo, ma'am," she said, still holding her wrist and looking up at Lou with a wounded expression.

Lou softened her stance. "What city am I in?"

The girl frowned. "What?"

"What city is this?" Lou asked again. "Is this Boise?"

"Yeah, it's Boise. Ma'am, do I need to call someone for you? You seem confused."

"No," Lou said, and glanced through the porthole window once more. There was a lot of light in the kitchen. It was probably why she hadn't been able to slip back there and was delivered instead to the throng of drunk and swaying bodies. "I just need the bathroom."

"It's over there." The girl pointed. "Down that hallway."

Lou thanked her and turned away.

The house of the devil, she thought as she pushed open the bathroom door. She met her own expression in the mirror.

"How fitting," she said, amused by the killer's sense of humor. If it could be called humor.

No one heard her chuckle as she reached up and turned off the bathroom light.

13

Dani thought she was slowly losing her mind. She took a deep breath and said, "Say it again."

Piper adjusted the Spanish workbook in her lap.

"*Yo quiero comprar un sombrero*," Piper said, looking up from the workbook. "*Cuánto está el sombrero?*"

"We don't have to say '*yo*' in this context," Dani said. "It's implied in the way you conjugate the verb."

Piper cleared her throat. "*Quiero comprar uno sombrero. Cuánto está el sombrero?*"

Dani refrained from rubbing her temples. "Do you want to buy *a* hat, *one* hat, or *the* hat?"

"What did I just say?" Piper asked.

Dani shoved her plate of half-eaten spaghetti and forgotten garlic bread away.

"First you said *a* hat. Then you said *one* hat. Both times you changed it to *the* hat when you asked the second question, as if you already have a hat in mind. *Do* you have a hat in mind?"

"I don't know, babe. I'm just reading the sentences."

Piper turned the book toward Dani so she could see the cartoon drawing of a man pointing to a hat above the woman's head.

"Try '*Quiero comprar un sombrero. Cuánto cuesta?*'"

"Can you say that more slowly? Wait, wait! I know this one. *Repetir, por favor. Gracias.*"

Dani wet her lips. "*Quiero comprar un sombrero. Cuánto cuesta?*"

"*Quiero comprar—*"

"Roll your *R*," Dani interjected.

"*Quiero comprarrr—*"

"No, not that *R*. The first one. Put your tongue on the roof of your mouth. It's like the two *T*s in 'otter.'"

Piper frowned. "How do two *T*s make an *R* sound?"

Dani demonstrated.

Piper repeated it. "Otter."

Piper was right. The way Piper said *otter* required zero rolling of the tongue. Dani sighed and demonstrated again, saying it faster and faster until the sound began to roll together.

"Babe, that's sexy. Do it again."

Dani didn't want to do it again. She wanted to take a shower and maybe some aspirin for this horrible headache building behind her eyes.

Who'd you piss off? the tow truck guy had asked her when he'd taken a good look at her trashed SUV.

Every time Dani thought about it, her blood warmed several degrees and threatened to erupt out of the top of her head.

Piper's eyes slid to Dani's dinner plate. "Are you still hungry? You didn't eat much of your dinner."

"Can we just stop here for the day? I think I'm getting a migraine," she said.

The disappointment on Piper's face was evident, but if

Dani didn't get away right now she was going to say something she regretted.

"Of course. No problemo," Piper said, closing the workbook. "Why don't you go ahead and go to bed early? Your sumatriptan is in the nightstand."

Dani made the effort of leaning forward and brushing a kiss across Piper's lips even though kissing was the last thing on her mind. She wanted to scream. Maybe punch Scarlett in the face.

It's not Piper's fault, Dani reminded herself. *She has no control over Scarlett's behavior. And this is what Scarlett wants, to drive a wedge between us. I* refuse *to let that happen.*

But even the shower, with all its wonderful high pressure and hot water, wasn't enough to drive her thoughts of Scarlett away. She kept replaying the conversation she'd had with her at the praline shop, searching each moment for a hint or sign that she'd known about Dani's car.

And there was still her bandaged hand.

When Piper slid into bed just before midnight, she whispered, "Are you still awake?"

Dani considered a fake snore, but Piper was too smart to fall for that. "Yes."

"How do you feel?"

"I've been better," she admitted, though she didn't credit the majority of that terribleness to its true perpetrator.

"Is it about your SUV?" Piper asked, proving that despite Dani's best efforts, Piper remained her usual insightful self. "How long did they say it would take to fix the belt thingy?"

The belt thingy. Because Dani hadn't wanted to tell Piper that she thought Scarlett had trashed it. She didn't want to give Piper any reason to have to go and talk to her at all. So she'd lied and said that the timing belt needed to be repaired.

"A week," Dani said. "That's it."

"You can afford the repairs, right?" Piper said. It wasn't

really a question. "If not, I can give you some money. And we don't even use the car for weeks sometimes."

Here she was trying to ease Dani's mind over a problem that didn't exist.

"I know," she said, her affection for Piper swelling. Dani took her hand and squeezed it. "The world won't end."

But that wasn't the point, was it?

It was that Scarlett had figured out how to get to her, how to push her buttons. And Dani had yet to learn how to do the same.

She *hated* not having the upper hand.

"I'll be okay," Dani said, turning toward her.

Piper brushed kisses across Dani's cheeks. "I'm sorry you had a bad day, baby."

Dani snuggled in closer, breathed her in, tried to let the scent and warmth of Piper fill her up so that no room for Scarlett remained.

I'm here. Not her.

Me.

"Thank you, baby," she whispered into the dark, and wrapped her arms around her.

LOU SO OFTEN FOUND KONSTANTINE IN HIS APARTMENT overlooking the Arno River or in the old church that served as the headquarters for his gang that it was strange to find him like this. But here he was in an alleyway with Lou at his back, looking down on him in surprise. She stilled for a moment, one hand on the stone wall beside her as if to steady herself.

Was he hiding from someone? Was he in the middle of an attack?

He could not look more suspicious, crouched down as he was, his gaze fixed on the building across the alleyway.

She put her hand on his shoulder. "What are you doing?"

He jumped. "Che cazzo!"

He wouldn't have fallen back and put a hand over his chest like that in the middle of a firefight.

Her body relaxed.

He swore again.

"What are you doing out here?" She checked her watch. "It's not even six in the morning."

That explained why the streets were quiet and the air so cold.

"I am watching for her," he said, bringing himself up to his full height.

"For who?"

"Gabriella," he said, keeping his voice low. "She has to come out for school soon."

"You're hiding in the street, looking for a *child?*"

"I took your advice and followed her. She came here. She's inside that house."

Lou checked her compass.

The pull in her stomach tugged away from the house, toward the city center behind them where the Duomo loomed in the sky. Konstantine's church was in that direction.

"She's not in there," Lou said.

He frowned. "I've watched it all night. She went in but didn't come out. She has to be in there."

Lou felt her compass whirl and click before settling on a new location. "She's not. I think she's back in the dormitories."

He frowned and started up the walk. He passed the shuttered window. "Is there another exit in the back?"

She arched a brow. "I don't automatically know how many doors a building has."

That wasn't how her compass worked.

He came up onto his toes. "I think there's a garden."

He began pulling on the wall that ran from the side of the building to the corner of the street as if to hoist himself over it.

"Stop. You'll hurt yourself." She grabbed his arm and pulled him down. "I'll take you."

She encircled his waist and together they slipped. There was still enough darkness on the street at this hour where the close-cut buildings crowded each other, throwing their shadows over one another on the cobblestones.

When the world reformed around them, they were in an enclosed garden.

The wall covered three of the four sides, with vines and plants growing up the stucco unchecked. It looked like no one had tried to pull it down in years. The grass too was high, reaching the top of Lou's boots and trailing across her calves like fingers.

Konstantine pointed at the window.

"She could've crawled out of there." Now he pointed at the gate stuck into one part of the wall. "And I wouldn't have seen her."

"Do you think this is the lair of some secret rival?" Lou asked. In truth, she didn't understand his suspicion of the girl.

She was a child. She posed no threat to him. But Konstantine's cautiousness had kept him alive this long in a game where someone wanted to kill him and take control of his fortune every day of his life.

If he was going to show respect for Lou's compass and ability, the least she could do was return the favor and acknowledge that he couldn't afford to be as cavalier about these things as she could.

"I'll take you to her," she said. "Assuming you're done here."

"I am." Konstantine slid his arms around her, taking

possession of her waist.

She enjoyed it. She liked to feel the weight of his body against hers.

When the world reformed, they were in the church just as she'd suspected. At the end of the hallway, Matteo stood outside the restroom adjacent to the dormitory where they slept.

His eyes were only half open, his hair mussed and sticking up at all angles. His pajamas properly wrinkled. He looked ready to fall asleep on his feet. No surprise, given the hour.

Then he blinked and seemed to see Lou first. Then Konstantine.

His eyes snapped open. "Good morning, sir! Good morning, Signora Strega."

He spoke in English for Lou's benefit.

She ruffled his hair.

"Matteo, what are you doing standing here outside the bathroom? Why aren't you in bed?"

Matteo opened and closed his mouth like a beached fish.

Before he could formulate what was most certainly a lie, the bathroom door opened and Gabriella appeared, her close-cut hair and skin damp from the shower.

She looked ready to run as soon as she saw Konstantine.

Before she could, he asked, "Where did you sleep last night?"

She licked her lips.

"It's my fault," Matteo said. "I asked her to stay here with me."

Konstantine arched his brow and turned on the boy. "Did you? And did she tell you that I told her she couldn't? That I didn't want her sleeping in a room full of boys?"

Matteo didn't look nearly as surprised as he should have.

"She did," Lou said.

"She is my friend," Matteo said in his shy, halting English.

"When did she get here? This morning?"

Matteo muttered a number under his breath that Lou didn't catch.

Konstantine swore. "Four hours and I was looking at nothing. Back to bed, both of you. I'm too tired to beat you now."

They scurried, darting into the dormitory and easing the door shut.

Konstantine rubbed his forehead with a closed fist. "*Amore mio*, take me to bed, please."

She hooked one arm around his waist. When the world reformed, she pushed him onto the bed and motioned for him to take off his leather jacket.

He shrugged out of it and handed it over.

Then she knelt and began to undo his boots. He looked down at her.

"When you look up at me with those eyes you make me think of certain things, *amore mio*."

"I thought you were tired," she said.

He laughed. "I am. I *really* am."

She pulled off his boots and his pants and threw a pair of his silken pajamas at him.

"No shirt?" he asked.

"Are you cold?" she asked.

"No."

"Then no shirt for you."

She climbed under the covers with him as he chuckled.

She didn't point out that he really must be tired if he didn't want to shower first. Konstantine was nearly religious about showering before getting into his bed.

"I'll wash the sheets tomorrow. Or today," he muttered, as if she'd asked him about it aloud. "Later."

"*Sleep*," she commanded. She could get what she wanted from him when he woke up.

"Aren't you worried she's going to kill me?" Konstantine said, his eyes closed and dark lashes fanning over his cheeks.

"She's a girl," Lou said.

"She's thirteen. You were twelve when your parents died," he reminded her. "Isn't that when you decided to kill Angelo?"

It was true that Lou had been twelve when her family was killed. But as miserable and heartbroken as she had been after Angelo Martinelli walked into her life and murdered her parents, Lou had not yet been a killer.

That had come years later.

"No. I didn't decide to kill them until I was older. Sixteen. Maybe seventeen."

"We don't know if someone is using her. Some of my enemies strap bombs to the chests of children," he said quietly, half asleep now. "We can't dismiss this danger just because she is a child."

"I'll keep an eye on her," Lou said gently. "Now *sleep*."

Twined in her arms, with his head on her shoulder, he finally did.

ON HIS BREAKS, THE KILLER OFTEN SAT IN THE DINING AREA and watched the families eat. The dining area was quieter than the open bar area beside the kitchen. There, drunken fools would talk too loudly, drink too much, and could even be heard over the bothersome roar of the kitchen's chaos.

The dining room, however, was mostly free of that. The families that came to La Casa del Diablo were drawn to the place for its playful theme and great seafood. He knew the seafood was good because he made those dishes himself. The children liked La Casa del Diablo because of the pirates that hung from the corners of the room and seemed to grin down on them jovially.

There was also the added benefit of their very own pirate hat and eye patch to wear while they ate. They needed only ask a hostess for these tokens, and the hostesses were always more than happy to oblige.

Today the killer sat at his table alone, nursing his frozen lemonade and a basket of fried calamari as he watched families move about the room. He was the only single. The other tables contained two couples and several quartets and quintets.

He counted them once. Twice.

He ate slowly, without hurry.

He was on the third round of counting when he saw them.

This family sat to one side of the room beneath the high windows. The mother was turned in her seat, trying to fasten a bib over her child's chest. The child was old enough that it could tear the flimsy paper barrier off with a single furious swipe of its hand, and it seemed to revel in doing so.

The father, opposite her, was drinking his beer and largely ignoring the exchange.

The killer watched the father finish his beer and order another from a passing waitress carrying a tray of dirty dishes.

He was halfway through the second beer when the mother got so exasperated that she snapped at them both.

That's when the killer saw what he was looking for.

The flash of anger in the man's eyes. A cold look of disdain.

The way the woman flinched back when he turned that look on her.

I see you, he thought, his heart lifting with anticipation.

He popped another piece of calamari in his mouth.

He'd already finished his basket and his frozen lemonade by the time the waitress brought the family their check, signaling the end of their meal.

As soon as the waitress was gone, the killer brushed fried

crumbs from his oily hands and crossed the dining room to the family.

"Hello," he said. He flashed a smile first at the father, then at the mother, whose food was mostly untouched. Her face was red and her forehead damp with sweat.

The father eyed him warily.

"I'm the chef here at La Casa del Diablo," the killer said brightly, his smile on full display. "I was wondering how your meal was today?"

"The fish was a little dry, to be honest," the father said over the rim of his beer before he swallowed down the rest of it, emptying the glass.

"Dennis!" the mother cried. She turned to him, her cheeks redder than ever. "Please ignore him. I thought it was very delicious. Thank you for your hard work today."

He fought the urge to let his eyes slide to her plate.

Very delicious? And how would you know when you barely ate anything?

The father, already bored with the exchange, was pulling his card out of his wallet to pay the bill.

"I can take that for you, sir," the killer said, extending his hand.

The father threw the card down, and the killer lifted it along with the bill, feeling the weight of the card against his fingers.

"I just need to see some ID, sir," he said.

When the father produced his driver's license, the killer smiled. "Thank you."

At the register, he wrote down the father's full name and address on a napkin while the card processed.

Then he slipped the address into his pocket before taking the card and the signature slip back to the table.

14

L ou rolled over with the aim of slipping from the bed without waking Konstantine. She did not succeed. His arms enveloped her and pulled her close to him, holding her against his chest, his knees pressing into the back of hers.

He made a sound that could be mistaken for human speech.

She snorted. "What was that?"

"Please don't go."

She let her fingers trace first his forearm, then his elbow. "I thought you wanted me to keep eating on schedule. Are you trying to sabotage my efforts?"

"It's cold," he growled into the back of her neck. "You're warm. Stay in bed with me."

Lou tried, managing no more than thirty minutes before she grew too restless in his arms to lie there any longer.

Reluctantly, he released her. "What will you do today?"

"I want to see Dani about a cannibal in Idaho."

He rubbed the sleep from his eyes. "I don't believe you've told me about a cannibal. In *Idaho*."

She told him of the news story and the cave she'd found. She even shared her theory that he worked in the kitchens at La Casa del Diablo.

He listened, his fingers counting the vertebrae in her back while she spoke.

When she finished lacing her boots, he said, "There are certain cultures who believe that if you consume someone's flesh or blood, that person becomes part of you. Their spirit will live on within you."

Lou turned so he could see her arched brow. "Don't tell me you have an interest in cannibalism."

He stretched his arms over head. "No. But all this talk of eating is making me hungry. Have breakfast with me before you go."

He trailed his fingers down her exposed arm.

"Please. I'll make you a coffee," he begged.

How could she resist that pout? "Say no more."

Ten minutes later, Lou had her coffee in hand and the apartment smelled like bacon. He was singing while it sizzled on his stove. Evidently pleased with its progress, he began whisking eggs into a pan.

"One American breakfast coming up," he said, sparing her a smile before pouring the eggs into the greased pan.

"What about you?" she asked.

"*Two* American breakfasts," he corrected. "Though that isn't how they say it on the television."

She slid her arms around his waist while he stood at the stove and let her cheek rest on the plane of his shoulders while he worked. She did this only because he'd told her how much he liked it—when once she'd spontaneously hugged him from behind.

"Would you like another coffee?" he asked.

She didn't miss the way his nose wrinkled slightly at the word *coffee*.

Italians loved their espresso, and the fact that he had to add water to hers to make it resemble something like the brewed coffee she was used to must have felt like sacrilege to him.

"Will it kill you to make another?" she asked. "Will it crush your soul?"

"Only a little," he said with a dramatic tone. "I will survive."

They ate breakfast while the Florentine sun poured through the front window overlooking the courtyard and listened to the bustle building in the streets.

When Lou cleared her plate she found Konstantine watching her with a cautious look on his face.

"What?" she asked, her hand tensing, half reaching for her gun.

"How do you feel about living together?" he asked.

Her hand stilled. After a beat, she said, "We practically live together now."

She couldn't remember the last time she'd slept in her own bed. For a while she'd been using her mattress in front of the large, picturesque window only for naps. But even that had ended. Part of the problem was simply how comfortable his bed was. He must've spent a fortune on his mattress as it was far superior to her own—and hers had not been cheap either.

"But what if we made it official? What if all of your things were here?"

She snorted. "Your apartment is too small for all of my *things*."

She wasn't talking about her furniture. Lou had few personal possessions. Clothes and some books. A few photographs and two paintings that she loved. She'd acquired more cooking utensils and glasses in the last two months, but even those were limited.

Her real *things* were the guns, knives, and ammunition that made up her secret arsenal.

"We can find a bigger place," he said. "If you want to pay for half so it feels like yours, I could be talked into that too, though you know I don't expect anything."

She almost laughed. Konstantine was a very rich man. He didn't need money from her, but he knew her well enough that she might use it as an objection.

"We could make a home. Together," he said. His hand had flexed toward hers but stopped.

He thinks I'll run, she thought.

Something in her guts twisted. She was certain that her face had not betrayed her, and yet he looked away.

"Just think about it. I'm not in a hurry." He returned his attention to the last of his breakfast. "It was only an idea."

Only an idea my ass.

She knew what she saw. Him—pulling back to protect her —or himself.

After finishing off the last few bites, he stood and took their plates to the sink.

Still, she remained frozen even after he returned and bent for a kiss.

She tilted her chin up to meet him halfway. She could still do that much, at least.

"I'm going to shower now," he said. "I assume you will leave once you finish your coffee?"

"That's the plan," she said.

He kissed her again. "I will see you tonight then, *amore mio*."

She stayed in her seat long after she heard the bathroom door click shut and the shower running.

She couldn't say why she felt frozen in place, looking around the apartment as if she had never seen it before.

We could make a home together.

But she liked Konstantine's apartment. And she liked the view of the Mississippi River from her own apartment in St. Louis. She didn't want to give either up.

Or so she told herself.

But inside, she wondered if it was something more.

Lou stepped from the alley just as the St. Charles streetcar trilled past. She watched as it built momentum, heading in the direction of the French Quarter, away from the Garden District where she now stood.

She walked the block between the dark alcove where she'd entered this part of the world to Dani's office. The small offices of *The Herald* were housed in a single-story, squat brick building that looked as if it had been erected sometime in the seventies, with its burnt-orange panels and flat roof. The small sign above the door could have been ignored, and undoubtedly often was, by passersby on the street.

It said simply *The Herald* and had two old-fashioned newspaper dispensers affixed to the concrete out front. They were empty of papers.

Lou pulled open the door and walked into the office. She passed the receptionist with a nod. The fox-faced girl with bright red hair and brown eyes gave Lou the same curious stare she always did.

"She's in her office," she said, half rising from her seat.

The door to Dani's office was open, so Lou knocked on the metal frame, waiting for permission to enter.

Dani looked up from her desktop computer and her eyebrows rose. "Hey. Come in. Shut the door."

Lou did as she was told and took a seat in the chair opposite Dani's desk.

"Your receptionist was giving me that look again. What did you tell her?"

"That you're an informant and just to let you in whenever you show up. No questions asked." Dani pulled her glasses off her face and laid them lenses up on the desk. She began to rub her eyes.

Lou saw the dark circles under them. "Is this a bad time?"

"No, I need to take a break anyway. It feels like my eyes are bleeding. I've been combing the feeds for info on this cannibal all morning. Did you know about him? It's a train wreck."

"King told us about it. What do they know?" Lou rolled her shoulders in her leather jacket.

"Not nearly enough," Dani groaned. "I was about to call you, actually—I was wondering if you could scope him out."

"I did," Lou said. "He works in the kitchen at La Casa del Diablo in Boise."

"The house of the devil." Dani snorted. "Fitting for a monster."

She scribbled something down on the notepad in front of her. Lou noted how her hands shook.

How much coffee did you have today?

"I'll get the names of the kitchen staff and see if any of the deceased have a connection to the place. King will be happy you didn't just snatch him off the street. I was wondering if you would."

Lou didn't bother to tell her she'd tried to get a lock on him twice but her compass had run interference, or at least, it had changed its mind. Maybe there was more to this killer than they realized.

"I'll let you know if I learn more," Lou promised, and rose to go.

Her hand had only just touched the handle when Dani said, "Wait!"

Lou turned back.

When Dani didn't say anything after a considerable pause, Lou asked, "*Yes?*"

"I just—*ugh*. I don't even want to talk about it. It's stupid. But if I don't say something to someone, I'm going to lose my mind. I've brought it up with my therapist, but she just keeps going on about my fear of losing someone I love, and this is *not* that."

Lou released the handle and went back to her chair. She didn't want to sit, but she didn't think this was the time to stand over Dani, so she perched on the edge of the seat instead.

Mention of her therapist had brought old memories back to Lou.

She'd met Dani just after Dmitri Petrov had nearly killed her. She'd never known a Dani that wasn't contending with her PTSD.

Yet dark circles and shaky hands weren't the usual symptoms Lou had come to expect from one of her episodes.

When Dani was struggling with her PTSD, she was more prone to shallow breathing. Dilated or constricted pupils. Sweat on her brow. Panic attacks.

"I'm here." Lou pushed her glasses up onto her head and waited. "I'm listening."

She was rewarded for her patience when Dani finally said, "It's so dumb, but Piper's got this ex, Scarlett. Have you ever met her?"

THE SECOND PIPER'S MIND WANDERED—THIS TIME BECAUSE an idea for Mel's fundraiser popped into her head—Bane punched her in the face. Again.

"*Oww.*" Piper staggered back, holding her sore nose. It wasn't broken. The punch hadn't been hard enough for that, but even with the thick boxing gloves, getting hit did *not* feel pleasant.

At all.

"Am I not presenting enough of a challenge for you?" Bane said, smacking her gum. "Do I need to get my baseball bat?"

"No, sorry," Piper groaned, her voice nasal from where she was pinching her nose shut. "I got distracted."

"Like I didn't know," she replied, popping a bubble.

Bane was lean, having the rail-straight body of a boy. Her flat chest only emphasized this boyish look, but her hair was pulled up in a messy ponytail on the top of her head and the Monroe piercing on her face caught the light and shone.

She'd recently dyed her hair from pink to blood red, and it made her dark eyes stand out more.

Bane hit her boxing gloves together. "Your mind has been wandering all morning. What's wrong with you? Trouble with your friend?"

Piper ignored this, the way she ignored all references and questions about Lou. Bane never pushed her. And nobody pushed Bane.

That in and of itself was interesting, considering that Bane looked like she could blow away in a strong wind and some of these guys were three times her size.

If Piper didn't know better, she'd put money on the fact that Bane wasn't the only member of Konstantine's gang who hung out at the City Park gym. She was starting to think they all did, the way they paid Bane a great deal of deference and left Piper alone.

Almost every time she saw the weird power dynamic play itself out, she thought, *What's up with this kid?*

Whatever it was, the fact remained that Bane had saved Piper's ass twice. But maybe she'd only done that because she was interested in Louie.

Or maybe if Bane really was one of Konstantine's people,

she was just following orders. It's possible the Italian stallion told her to keep an eye on things in New Orleans. It wouldn't surprise Piper. He'd seemed like the protective type. Regardless of whether Bane was calling the shots or Konstantine was, it was hard to tell what their true motivations were.

"I'm gonna punch you again if you don't tell me where your head's at," Bane said.

This wasn't a threat. It was only delivered in that matter-of-fact way that Bane had about her. And she wasn't wrong, exactly. If Piper didn't start focusing, she was going to get hit again.

"Girl problems," Piper said.

"I didn't know you had something like that going with her." Bane's grin was mischievous. "Does she wear a lot of leather in the bedroom too?"

"Lou's not my girlfriend," Piper said. *Shit, I said her name again.* It wasn't the first time Piper had let it slip. "I'm talking about Dani. The one that dropped me off last week."

"Right, the one with the nice ass," she said.

Piper's expression hardened.

Bane held up a gloved hand. "Relax. I don't swing that way. I'm just saying she's got a nice ass. You can appreciate the merchandise even when you don't shop in the store. Don't *you* think she's got a nice ass?"

"Yes, but she's also really smart," Piper said cautiously. "She's very accomplished. And—and professional."

Bane arched a brow. "Yeah, as opposed to the rest of us amateurs out here."

"You know what I mean."

"Okay." Bane shrugged. "I don't hear a problem."

Piper rubbed her brow with her gloved hand. "It's just that I'm trying to learn Spanish and she said she'd help me and usually it's fine, but last night she was mad at me, and I don't know what I did."

"Did you ask?"

"She said she was tired," Piper said. But now Piper couldn't be sure if that was exactly what was said. Had Piper asked? Did she say explicitly, *What did I do?* Or had she just assumed it had been about Dani's SUV, even though she knew stuff like that never bothered Dani?

Dani was a problem-solver. She could take a crisis in stride.

"So she's mad but she didn't tell you why." Bane adjusted the straps on her gloves. "Then something's going on and she doesn't want to get you involved. Maybe it's a work thing. Or maybe she's got problems with another bitch. She loyal?"

"Of course she's loyal," Piper said defensively.

But that didn't mean there wasn't a girl involved.

Scarlett.

Piper had seen Scarlett pass their table when she'd arrived at the Wild Cat. And from a distance, it had looked like Scarlett had said something to Dani, but by the time Piper got to the table, they were gone.

"Why do you want to learn Spanish?" Bane asked. "Why not Italian?"

"Dani does speak Italian, but King thinks that Spanish will be more attractive on an FBI application. Anyway, maybe I've been asking too much of her. She does have a lot going on at work. What if she doesn't have time to teach me Spanish but she's too nice to say."

Bane turned and yelled over her shoulder, "Juan! *Juan*, where the hell you at?"

A sweaty guy looked up from the floor. "Nah, Bane. Come on. I just went six rounds with Venice. I'm tired."

"I don't want to fight you."

"Then what do you want?" he whined.

"Get over here or I'll punch you harder than Venice ever could."

Juan pulled himself off the floor and crossed the room to them. He stopped just short of where Piper and Bane stood in the middle of the gym. He gave Piper the barest of nods.

"Aren't you Mexican?" Bane asked.

"Puerto Rican."

"Whatever. You speak Spanish?"

"Does Juan Angel Luis Colón speak Spanish?" he asked with a snort.

"That's what I asked, didn't I? Do you or don't you?" She pointed her gloved fist at Piper. "She needs a Spanish teacher."

Juan frowned at her. "I'm no teacher, man. I can teach you some dirty words, if you want, but like good grammar and shit, nah. I ain't got the patience for that."

Neither does Dani, Piper thought sadly.

"I got a sister though. She actually wants to be a teacher. I bet she'll do it."

Piper perked up. "That would be great. Is twenty dollars an hour enough?"

Juan's brows went up. "Twenty bucks an hour. Man, forget my sister. I'll teach you."

"You just said you can't do it. Don't try scamming her." Bane elbowed him in the gut. The air left him in a grunt.

When he recovered, he said, "I'll talk to her tonight when she gets off work."

Piper tapped his gloved fist with her own. "Thanks, man."

"There," Bane said. "Your problems are solved."

She started jumping up and down again, carving a half circle around the spot where Piper stood.

"Now. Pay attention or I'm going to knock your ass out."

15

L ou sat in the laundromat, a magazine open on her lap. Her head was tilted down as if looking at the glossy photographs spread there. But she didn't see them. Her gaze, hidden behind her reflective shades, was fixed on the man. He was pulling his wet clothes from the industrial washer and moving them to the dryer positioned below it.

If he had looked up, he probably would've thought she was just another patron waiting for her clothes to dry.

At the end of their conversation, after Dani had confessed that she was at a loss for the best way to handle Scarlett, Lou had sought to distract her with a task. One call from Konstantine had helped them along with a list of all the employees of La Casa del Diablo—there were twenty full-time employees and another forty part-timers.

From this, Dani was able to construct a list of possible suspects.

"I'll get pictures and you get a good look at his face," Dani had said at the end of their conversation, and it had pleased Lou that her plan had worked.

It seemed luck was on their side because Lou also believed she'd found the killer.

Here in this brightly lit laundromat.

While the traffic rolled past the glass storefront and students sipped their six-dollar lattes and laughed outside the café next door, Lou's eyes tracked the man across the room.

After he moved his clothes to the dryer, he took a seat across from her.

Then he pulled a piece of paper from his pocket and smiled.

What have you got there? she wondered.

This thought was lost almost the minute she realized something was wrong with his face.

It was partially hidden by his long shaggy blond hair. Even more so by the scruffy stubble that grazed his jaw and chin, trying to form a beard and failing.

But the hair wasn't the problem, exactly. It was the way the beard had grown on his face. It was patchy, and when he turned his head just right, she was almost certain she was looking at some kind of scar that stretched over his jaw and down to his throat.

A bell chimed, signaling someone's arrival.

When he glanced up to see who was coming through the door, Lou got a better look at his neck.

Yes. There were definitely scars. Though it was hard to see from here what might have caused them.

A fire? An accident?

It wasn't like she could walk up and ask. At least, that's what she thought.

He must have felt her eyes on him because his head snapped toward her suddenly. His gaze met hers, and then he was out of his seat.

That's when Lou knew she had a problem.

Shit.

Lou didn't move immediately. She shifted imperceptibly, reassuring herself that the gun beneath her leather jacket was still there, still within reach.

She could feel it when she breathed in, her chest resisting the holster's compression.

The killer sat down in the seat beside her, his shaggy hair falling forward into his face.

"Hey," he said, his smile on full wattage. His piercing blue eyes fixed on her. "What's your name?"

"Go away," Lou said.

"Funny name," he said. "I just want to say hi. You look familiar. Have we met before?"

"I'm not interested in your pickup lines," she said.

"Why? Do you have a boyfriend?"

Yes, she thought. She closed the magazine and considered striking him with it.

He cocked his head, his smile widening even more. "Is that a no?"

You think you're the only one who can ask questions? "What happened to your face?"

There was something in his eyes then. A flash of emotion tinged with fury, but it passed too quickly for her to be sure of what she saw.

"Oh this? You mean my scars, huh?" He tilted his head away, exposing his throat to her. "I was attacked when I was a kid."

"Attacked by who?" she asked.

"By *what*," he said, his smile mischievous.

When he did not offer more, she did not ask. Was he lying? Did he think the lack of clarity would intrigue her?

"You don't seem appalled," he said, those blue eyes searching her face.

His gaze was strange. If Lou didn't know better, she would've said that he could actually see her eyes. That was impossible. The whole reason she wore mirrored shades was so people were forced to contend with themselves. But he wasn't distracted by the reflection.

He smiled as if he'd seen her work all of this out. "Most people are horrified when I show them my neck like this. They clam up. But not you."

He hadn't come toward her, and yet her hand itched for her gun.

She didn't like how close he was. She could smell him. His shampoo, the musk of his cologne, and even that hint of fried fish, which was detectable even over the powerful scent of laundry detergent and fabric softener.

"Maybe I'm right about you," he said. "Maybe you're different."

She couldn't help but arch her brow.

"Are you sure we haven't met?" He turned his head like a bird, examining her. "There's something *so* familiar about you."

He placed a hand on her knee.

Lou moved without thinking. One hand covered his, clamping down on it hard enough that a single twist would have broken all his fingers and maybe the wrist, too. Her other hand had made it inside her leather jacket, closing around the butt of her gun before she could stop herself.

She'd gotten it out of the holster but hadn't fully brought it into the light.

Don't, she thought. *You can't blow his brains out here in a laundromat half a mile from a campus with witnesses all around. Konstantine is good at covering for you, but he's no miracle worker.*

His fingers tightened on her knee. "Do you have something for me? Under your jacket?"

He leaned toward her. He *smelled* her.

She released his hand and stood. The magazine fell to the floor.

Don't leave him, her mind begged.

Take him to an alley.

Take him to the lake.

Take him anywhere *and put a bullet between those cold blue eyes.*

But she didn't listen.

She walked out of the laundromat with his soft chuckle in her ear.

"Until next time, then," he said, bending to pick the magazine up.

As she passed the glass doors, she saw he was still watching her from his seat, his gaze never wavering.

His smile never faltered.

K ONSTANTINE WANTED TO KNOW WHAT IT WAS ABOUT windows. Who had taught Gabriella that she could simply throw herself out of one whenever she liked? That morning when Konstantine had led the children to school, he'd left Gabriella little choice but to walk into the building with the others.

She had moped and dragged her feet for most of the journey, even while the boys had loved the attention. They loved to be seen with Konstantine anywhere, this much he knew.

They chatted happily as they made their way to the steps of the Scuola Bilingue di Firenze with Konstantine at their helm. Then he'd touched each boy affectionately on the head before they passed the school's marble columns and disappeared into the building.

"Are you going to wait here for us?" Gabriella had asked.

He smiled at this, knowing she must have already been trying to plan her escape from the moment he'd invited himself along.

"*Sì*," he replied. "I have business in this part of the city today. I'll be back when school is over."

At this, she reluctantly retreated into the building.

Only Konstantine did not leave to do any business. He went to the café next door and ordered an espresso. Then he chose a seat with a good view of the school.

He had only to wait an hour before he saw first a leg, then another, come through a first-floor window. He wasn't entirely sure if the creature who'd leapt out was Gabriella until she stood and brushed the grass from her clothes. Then he saw her stern little face and the triumphant way she snatched her bag off the ground before running off into the streets.

Konstantine threw back his espresso and followed her.

Unlike the first morning, the girl didn't have time to stroll about the city looking at the food stalls and souvenir carts aimed at the tourists.

Instead, she went straight to the place she'd visited before.

He watched her disappear inside again, and a few minutes later, she reappeared with another brown paper bag in her fist.

This time Konstantine waited with his back in the alley until she ran past him before following her out of the city center and over the bridge to the suburbs again.

He wasn't surprised when she returned to the same house she had before. At least today there wasn't a market vendor to yell at him or imply that he was a pedophile.

"*Sono io! Gabriella!*" she called up at the building.

Konstantine thought he heard the gruff voice of a man before the front door snapped shut behind her.

He decided not to watch the house this time. She would leave whenever she wanted, after she performed whatever malevolent task she was meant to perform in order to undo him.

Don't be too angry with her, he thought. *She's a child.*

Whatever reason she had to turn on him, he was sure it was much more about what she aimed to protect, rather than any true malevolence against Konstantine himself.

He doubled back, retracing his steps until he found her first stop again, and called Stefano to join him.

Fifteen minutes later, Stefano strode into the alleyway, cupping his hand around a cigarette. He held it between his lips as he reached into his jacket and passed over a gun to Konstantine.

"I've got my own," he said through pursed lips.

Konstantine took it. "You stay here and make sure my exit is clear."

"You don't want me to come in with you?"

"I don't know the situation yet," Konstantine said. "What if they are our rivals?"

Stefano scoffed. "You have no rivals in this city, *fratello*."

"If I am not out in ten minutes, come and get me," Konstantine said, patting Stefano on the shoulder. Stefano took up his post against the stone wall as Konstantine slid the gun into the waistband of his pants, at the small of his back.

Then he crossed the threshold and found himself in a shop.

It was a small, dim place. He suspected this was so because there were no windows on either side of the shop and the window by the front door faced only the alley, where there wasn't much light to gather.

Konstantine's eyes swept the shelves and clear glass cases and saw only an endless parade of bottles.

It wasn't just a shop, it was a pharmacy. Or at least, it *looked* like a pharmacy.

"*Come la posso aiutare?*" a man called out. "How can I help you?"

An old man hobbled forward into the light. His eyes were

set deep in his face, his glasses thick. A sheen of cataracts had formed over the once blue irises, giving them a cloudy look.

"My niece Gabriella just came to see you," he said.

"*Sì*, I know Gabriella," he said.

Konstantine searched his face for some visceral reaction to the girl's name, but there was none.

"She picked up something for us and has already lost it climbing over a wall. It dropped into the sewer."

The man shook his head. "That child. Someone needs to tell her she's a lady. Or she could be one. One day, with a bit of practice."

Konstantine forced a polite smile. "I've come for another. For its replacement."

"Very well. I will check if I have any more," the man said.

The man disappeared behind a black curtain and Konstantine's hand went to his gun. For all he knew, the old man would reappear with a rifle. Cataracts or no, surely he could fire at him.

But he didn't return with a gun. Instead, he held a blister pack of tablets in one hand. "This is all I've got, and I'll only give you this if you also settle her account," he said in Italian. "I try to be a patient man, but I am running a business here."

Her account?

"That's no problem," Konstantine said. "*Quanto le devo?*"

"*Quaranta*," the old man said, and slid the blister pack of unmarked pills into a brown bag just like the one he'd seen Gabriella with twice before.

Konstantine opened his wallet and fished out two twenties. "Anything else?"

The man seemed pleased by this, accepting with a liver-spotted hand. "No, *grazie*. Thank you for settling her account."

On the street, Konstantine frowned down at the unmarked pills.

As soon as Stefano saw him, he took one last drag on the cigarette and threw the butt down to crush it beneath his boot. "*Allora? Come è andata?*"

Konstantine showed him the pills.

Stefano inspected the packaging over his shoulder. "She's a mule then? She's carrying drugs around the city for someone? What is it? Fentanyl, maybe?"

"I don't know," Konstantine said, turning the package over in his hands. "But I know who we can ask."

Lou could admit to herself, if no one else, that she was taking her frustration out on Stanley. She recognized what she was doing the moment she tore him, King's fourth target, from his recliner and dragged him screaming down the hallway of his dingy duplex. When she'd left the killer at the laundromat, her blood had been simmering. She wasn't sure what it had been about the way the killer had approached her, the way he'd sat down beside her, spoke to her as if he wanted to flirt or strike up a friendship. All of it had grated along her skin, and she'd been irritated that her only course of action had been retreat.

Retreat.

It was something that Louie Thorne rarely resigned herself to.

When Lou found Stanley—the second-to-last man on King's list of irredeemables—sitting in front of his television with a beer held loosely in his grip, it was a wonder that her gun wasn't already in her hand. That she was able to simply seize him under the glow of the television's blue light instead of shooting him on the spot.

There was something about seeing him like that that had taken her back to Gus Johnson, her very first kill. She couldn't be sure if it was the recliner, or even the look of

Stanley himself. He bore a resemblance to Gus Johnson, even down to the way his glasses caught and reflected the television's light, his mouth parting in surprise.

Gus Johnson had been her father's partner. He'd sold her father out to the Martinelli crime family in hopes of saving his own skin. It had bought him time—time for Lou to grow up and become far more dangerous than the Martinellis could ever dream of being. She'd been just seventeen when she'd plunged her father's knife into his neck.

She'd gotten better at killing over the years.

It was why she didn't stab Stanley in the living room.

The fallen beer pouring out on the stained carpet would be the only evidence she'd leave behind as she pulled him through the dark.

When the night broke open around them and the temperature fell noticeably, Lou didn't let go of Stanley. She shoved his back against the rough bark of a tree. The smell of pine was all around her, but it wasn't enough to blot out the stench of blood when she pulled the blade from her forearm sheath and rammed it into his guts.

Again. And again. And again.

He cried out, his hands wrapping around hers as if he could push her away or slow her down. His glasses were askew on the bridge of his nose.

He whimpered.

Disgusted, she pulled the knife out of his guts and snatched the glasses off his face.

Stanley slid down the front of the tree, the last of his breath burbling between his bloodied lips.

It's not Stanley who's gotten under your skin, a calm voice warned. *It's not Stanley you're killing now.*

The cattails and long grasses clouding the edge of the lake swayed gently in the breeze.

Lou washed her hands in the lake and replayed the laundromat scene in her mind. Her in a chair. Her watching him behind mirrored shades. Him seeing her and coming straight to her, unafraid. Not an ounce of hesitation in him as he sat down beside her. As he looked at her, as he spoke to her.

Had it been the same man on the street that night in the rain?

She'd seen nothing metal on his face today. There was no piercing. Hadn't something glinted in the night when she'd seen him in the rain? Was she sure it was the same person?

She thought so.

Though he had been different each time. His—what would Lucy call it? His *energy*?

Yes. His energy had changed.

The man standing on the street in the dark had been like her. Cold. A killer. She recognized that in him almost immediately.

In the laundromat the cold had been gone. He was arrogant, entitled, boyish, and at the edge of his charm there had been a sharpness.

She finished rinsing her blade in the lake and returned it to its sheath before grabbing Stanley's collapsed body and dragging him into the water.

Something was different about him, her mind said again as she thought of those cunning blue eyes and that stiff smile. Lou just wasn't sure what.

16

He had been so excited that he'd forgotten a load of his clothes at the laundromat. He'd retrieve them later. He'd call John, one of the guys who worked behind the counter, and explain that something had come up. John would take care of it.

She looked at me. She looked at me and asked about the scars.

The killer's heart was soaring. Had anyone seen him so clearly before? So quickly?

It had been the same for him too. As soon as he'd seen her in the laundromat, he'd known it was her. She looked different by the light of day. Even light fell on her hair and body differently. He thought it was almost repulsed by her, the light.

But the darkness loved her. It clung to her, caressed her.

I like her, too, he thought with surprise. He could not remember the last time he'd liked anyone.

I want to know her. Maybe we could be fri—

The beast inside him stirred. Perhaps it was his excitement or perhaps he wasn't being careful enough. Whatever it was, it had begun to rise up and overtake him.

No! he thought. *Not now!*

He dashed for his bedroom, went to the vanity, and threw open a drawer. He managed to get the leather bit between his teeth and the muzzle over his face, buckling it roughly at the back of his head.

Then he threw himself into his bed and pulled the covers over his head as if the softness and the dark might also serve to soothe the beast.

Not her, he thought. *She's like us. Not her. I found someone else for you. He's perfect. Forget about her!*

The beast within him only growled, its hunger growing.

The growling took him back to all those years ago.

To the sound of his father's tires speeding off into the night while he sat hunched on the ground, in pain, crying.

That had been the first time—well, it had been a lot of firsts, actually.

The first time he'd seen that much blood.

The first time he'd been in that much pain.

The first time he'd heard wolves howling in the distance.

He'd run then. After the fading red taillights kicking up dirt.

"Don't. Don't leave me here," he'd screamed at those lights. "I'm sorry, Daddy! Don't leave me!"

But begging hadn't saved him.

It never did.

I GOTTA PULL MYSELF TOGETHER, KING THOUGHT, AND threw the notepad and pen he'd been holding down onto his desktop. That was the fourth follow-up call he'd gotten today on cases in which he'd had no progress to report.

That wasn't like him. He was punctual. He was focused.

He was a *professional*.

He looked at his mess of a desk—his desk was *never* messy

—and frowned. Piper's served as a sharp contrast since she'd already left for the day. The clean tabletop seemed to mock him, amplifying his feelings of confusion.

"I need a refresh," he said to the empty room. "I'll quit for today and begin again tomorrow."

The bell above the agency door dinged, and Dick White strode in.

He wore a pressed dress shirt tucked into his dress pants and his shoes reflected the light filtering through the front windows and glass door.

"Hey, Dick," King said, standing and offering his hand in hello.

King knew he *looked* composed—of that he was certain, even while his mind raced, trying to remember if he owed Dick something.

Evidence, maybe? A testimony? Did he have some open and unfinished case—

"Maybe this is a bad time," Dick said, releasing King's hand and glancing at the clutter on his desk. "You look like you've got your hands full."

"Not at all," King said. He was waiting for Dick to say something, anything, to give him a clue as to what this visit was about. When the other man didn't answer right away, King asked, "What can I do for you?"

"I know it's strange for me to turn up in the middle of the day, but I came to see if you wanted to grab a drink with me. I could use a friend."

King's shoulders relaxed. *Not about work.*

"I'd be more than happy to join you, though don't be disappointed when I get a soda. And maybe some onion rings."

Dick snapped his fingers. "That's right. I forgot you were cutting back. Will it bother you if I have something stronger?"

King grabbed his duster off the back of his chair and slapped Dick on the shoulders. "Not at all. Just let me—One second here."

He tried to pack up most of the desk and turn it into some semblance of sanity before locking the agency behind them.

Ten minutes later they were seated at Bennigan's, over-looking Jackson Square. A duo—a woman playing an upright bass and a young man with an accordion—spun a tune and tapped out a rhythm with their feet.

King didn't push Dick to talk. Instead, he placed his order for onion rings and a cherry soda, thanking the waitress when she brought both.

Dick was about halfway through his beer when he said, "I saw a kid die today."

King's heart ached sympathetically. "I'm sorry. That's always hell."

"We were at the row houses down by the river, and this kid—Lord help me, Robbie—he couldn't have been more than thirteen, fourteen. He stepped between Hanson and his brother and took the bullet. Hanson's gun should've never gone off. He's on leave for that and might never come back, though we're so short-staffed they'll probably let him. It happened too fast. How did we get from talking to shooting just like that?" Dick snapped his fingers. "How?"

King didn't answer. There was nothing to say.

Instead, he told him about the drug raid in St. Louis where they'd broken into a meth lab. The inhabitants started firing through the walls, and King's squad had returned fire for almost ten minutes before the shooting stopped. When they combed the wreckage, they found the bodies of two little girls, six and eight, pumped with bullet holes. King had gone to a therapist for years over that. And he still had night-mares from time to time of the littlest girl sitting up, fishing a bullet out of her chest, and offering it to King with a haunting, *Is this yours, Mister?*

It didn't matter even a little bit that he had never fired his gun that day.

Dick swore after King relayed the dream to him. "Jesus Christ, man."

"Some things are hard to live with," King finished. "You might want to find someone to talk to."

Dick clinked his beer against King's sweating soda glass. "I did."

King laughed. "Someone *professional*."

Dick changed the subject to other things. Happenings at the precinct—the cases he was allowed to talk about, anyway. He also gave King an update on his wife and kids. They'd exhausted nearly every subject and Dick had drunk his way through four beers before an easy silence settled between them.

It was something about the silence that encouraged King to clear his own mind.

"Have you ever been wrong?" King asked.

Dick snorted. "You're going to have to be a lot more specific with your questions, Robbie. I'd say I was wrong today. I handled that situation *all* wrong, but I doubt that is what you have in mind."

"No, nothing like that." King wiped his greasy fingers on a paper napkin. "Have you ever had a hunch about a case and you start digging but everything is shipshape. Not a hair out of place. Did it turn out you were wrong?"

Dick considered this, his eyes on the passersby beyond the big window.

A couple had stopped to throw money into the open bass case in front of the playing duo. The accordion player stopped playing long enough to tip his Fedora at them as they ambled away.

"Not about a case," Dick said. "But—"

King turned toward him. "But what?"

"I've been wrong in my relationship." Dick ordered another beer, waving his latest empty at the waitress.

"You'd better slow down or your wife is gonna blame me," King said.

"I'll cut myself off at six," Dick said. "That's my limit."

King didn't want him to get distracted. "Tell me about when you were wrong."

"My wife had started acting differently. Sneaking around. Going places and not wanting to tell me where. If I pressed her, she'd lie. Naturally, I thought she was having an affair."

King arched a brow. "She wasn't?"

"No," Dick laughed. "She had a dance class. *Samba*. Women only. Well, all women unless you counted the one gay guy running the class. Sometimes after the class she went out with those girls, and they had a drink or two or even dinner. My point is, she wasn't cheating. She just didn't want me interfering."

"Why?" King frowned. Dick didn't seem like the kind of guy to be controlling or abusive.

"Because she knew I'd get jealous." Dick laughed.

King about choked on his onion ring. "Jealous?"

"And I'm not too proud to admit I was. Sheila's my best friend. We have a good marriage. I married her because I love to be around her. But she wanted a life of her own too. I thought I would be fine with that until I saw her out there having fun without me. And she knew me well enough to know I'd struggle with it, so she just told me she was shopping or going to yoga or whatever. Anything that kept me from thinking she wanted to be with other people who weren't me."

"So what happened?"

Dick accepted the beer from the waitress and thanked

her. "I pouted. I sulked. She put up with it. And when I officially got over myself, I started taking her dancing once a week, and we've kept that up ever since. The night varies, it has to because of my schedule—I hardly need to tell you that —but it's been almost eight years and once a week I *still* take my wife dancing. I love every minute of it."

"A happy ending," King said.

"What about you?" Dick asked.

"Oh, my wife was certainly having an affair," King said with a laugh.

Dick licked beer foam from his lips. "No, what are you wrong about? Or what do you *think* you might be wrong about?"

He'd already mentioned the women's association to Dick, and he'd been firm in proclaiming Tamara Jones to be the epitome of upstanding citizenship. He saw no point in flirting with disaster again. Even if he did want to express his frustration in not being able to find even a speck of dirt on that woman's name.

"I'm not sure yet," he said. "But maybe I'm just jealous that someone wants to spend time without me too."

Dick gave him a long, hard look and then seemed to decide something. "Whatever it is, my advice is to be direct. Confront the situation head on and resolve it. Sometimes us detective types look for problems where there are none. Don't be making mountains out of molehills."

King polished off his onion rings in deep thought.

Be direct, he thought. It was good advice. But good advice was always easier said than done.

DANI'S EYES FELT LIKE THEY WERE COVERED IN SAND BY the time she printed the last employee photo from La Casa del Diablo. It was nearly eight and she had no one to blame but herself. When five o'clock had rolled around and she was only halfway through identifying the employees, Dani had made the decision to stay and finish her task while she was still in a good flow state.

She'd called Piper to give her a heads-up that she was on her own for dinner, and Piper being the sweetheart that she was had given her a pass with no questions. She'd even offered to bring Dani dinner, but Dani had declined, fearing that any interruption might set her back.

It was dark and her head was pounding by the time Dani turned off the last of the lights and stepped out into the warm April night. She pulled her keys from her bag with the intention of locking up *The Herald*, but her hand faltered on the handle.

She dropped her keys to the pavement.

She took one step back from the building, then two more.

She blinked several times, but her eyes were not deceiving her.

"No," she groaned. "*Come on.*"

Daniella Allendale is a WHORE

WHORE had been written in all caps on the agency's window in white soap marker, so that it shone even brighter in the streetlight.

Dani had fixated on the word because it was far larger than the others, but now that she was getting over the shock of seeing it, she noticed the remaining, smaller script.

Her ruined car, she'd told herself, could've been a coincidence. This, in contrast, could not be clearer.

"That bitch," she said, and shoved open the door to *The Herald*'s offices. She threw her messenger bag in the receptionist's chair and went to the cleaning supply closet next to the restroom. She got the mop bucket and filled it at the sink with warm, soapy water.

Before the suds could reach the rim of the bucket, and

despite her best efforts not to let anyone get the best of her, furious tears had begun to flow down Dani's cheeks.

Lou had just stepped from the shower when the chord of rage shimmered through her. Not fear, not danger. *Rage*. She arched a brow, surprised. She couldn't remember the last time her compass had registered this level of fury in someone, other than herself.

At least it's not mine this time, she thought.

She dressed, towel-dried her damp hair, and said her good-byes to the starlit and shimmering Mississippi River before stepping through her linen closet.

When she put her foot down again, she was on the sidewalk. A ring of orange light thrown by the streetlamp claimed the concrete inches in front of her boot.

She spotted Dani immediately.

It would've been hard to miss her. How often did one see a woman slapping at a window with a soaked mop, furious grunting escaping her?

"Hey," Lou said, crossing beneath the streetlamp to meet her. "What are you doing?"

Lou tried to read the message that had been on the window, but there weren't enough letters left to make a coherent phrase. There was only *Dan lendale WHO*.

"Dani?" she said. "I got your call."

"Shit." Dani plunged the mop head into the soapy bucket and wiped her brow. "I didn't mean to call you. Or I did. God, I don't know."

"What's going on?"

When Dani rolled her eyes up to meet Lou's gaze, Lou saw her tear-stained cheeks and the ruined mascara.

"I'm just pissed off," she said, her lip quivering. "And I hate that I'm pissed off, which is making me *more* pissed off."

"Do I need to kill someone?" Lou asked plainly.

Lou had been joking, making an attempt to make things easier on her, but the look on Dani's face stopped her. She looked ready to say yes.

"I told you I tried talking to Scarlett like an adult, but I guess that was naïve of me. She's—bullying me, I guess, for lack of a better word. First she screwed up my car and now she's graffitiing the windows all because she wants me to leave Piper."

Dani had told her that Scarlett was giving her a hard time. But she hadn't been clear that things were this bad. Lou tried to remember if she'd met Scarlett. She thought she had. One night Lou had come looking for Piper and had found her in a bar. When the girl had seen them together, her stare had been a cold challenge before a very drunk Piper had lied and said Lou was her cousin.

Lou was almost certain they were talking about the same girl.

Dani plunged the mop into the soapy bucket again. "I'll be damned if I give her the satisfaction, but it's awful. It's really awful. And things were finally settling down and going so well. We just got my mother to get over herself and now this bitch comes along. It's exhausting."

"I could hold her and let you get in a few hits," Lou said.

"It's tempting. I can't tell you how many times a day I imagine grabbing a fist full of those dark curls and just—" She shook her balled fists in front of her face. After a moment she seemed to realize that she was only working herself up again and forced a long, slow exhale. "I will *not* stoop to her level. I won't do it. If she makes me compromise my integrity, then she wins."

"Is Piper worth it?" Lou asked.

"Of course she's worth it!" Dani spat venomously.

Lou was unable to hide a devilish grin, and that, at least, earned her a laugh.

"Oh *god*." Dani covered her face with her hand, still laughing. "Do you see what I mean? She's turning me into a crazy person."

"If we're not going to take Scarlett out tonight, what do you want to do?" Lou asked. "I'm free for a while."

"Eat? I haven't had dinner and I can't go back to the apartment looking like this. If Piper sees me, she'll ask me too many questions, and I can't lie to her."

"Why would you have to lie?"

Dani wiped her brow. "Because she'll feel like she has to do something about Scarlett, and I just know that Scarlett will use that as an excuse to be close to her. I can't stand the idea of them in the same room together."

"Give me that." Lou took the soaking mop from Dani's hands and scrubbed at the last of the lettering on the window.

When Lou finished, Dani took the bucket back inside, rinsed it out, and returned it to the supply closet. While she worked, Lou brought her clean clothes. Piper hadn't been in their apartment, so it had been easy to slip in and out without being noticed.

Of course, it begged the question of where Piper was at this hour.

Once she'd gathered up their things, Dani said, "Do you mind if we walk back to the Quarter? I know your way is faster, but I could use the air."

"I don't mind," Lou said. "I like walking."

And it was true. Sometimes when she couldn't sleep, Lou would walk the cities of the world for hours until her feet grew sore and her back ached.

They were almost to the Quarter when Lou asked, "Are you sure you don't want me to hurt her? Even a little."

"No," Dani said with a huff. The lines in her face had relaxed, at least. "But I swear to God, if she does one more thing to piss me off, I'll probably ask you to bury her somewhere."

Lou smiled. "You know that I don't bury them, right?"

"Even better." Dani stopped walking and pointed at a fried chicken place off Canal Street. "Have you eaten yet? I can just grab something to go if you don't want to sit down."

"We can sit." Lou opened the door for her.

They chose a table near the door, in view of the street. Clusters of tourists with Mardi Gras beads hanging thickly from their necks wandered past the windows while Dani and Lou placed their orders.

"I saw him," Lou offered, hoping to take Dani's mind off Scarlett. "I know what the cannibal looks like."

Dani stopped sucking down her sweet tea, eyebrows arching. "Oh. Then look at these and tell me which one he is."

She pulled her messenger bag off the empty chair beside her and rummaged for a folder.

Once she'd found what she wanted, she pushed it across the table to Lou. "There were only two employees who I couldn't find IDs for, so I hope he's not one of them."

Lou opened the manila folder and discovered a mound of faces looking back at her.

She moved the pictures from side to side, one after another, until her hand froze. "This one. This is him."

She pushed the open folder across the table toward Dani, who flipped the page over and read her own handwriting scrawled there. "Alan Rathers. Huh. He's not the one I would've put my money on. I was almost certain it was William Gray. Look at this guy."

Dani's fingers sorted through the printouts until she found another man's photo. The eyes looking back at her were black and hollow, the full mouth slack.

He was quite the contrast to Alan.

"I guess this is what they mean when they say it's someone you don't expect," Dani said. "Rathers looks charming. A little like a nerd but still charming."

"He can be," Lou replied before stopping herself.

Dani put her hands on the table. "You *spoke* to him?"

"Briefly."

When she didn't add more, Dani waved a hand. "*And?* What did he say?"

"Nothing interesting." Lou didn't want to share that he'd shown interest in her, that he had tried to pick her up. Or at least, Lou thought that was what was happening.

Dani looked doubtful but didn't push her. She turned her attention to her notes on Rathers instead. "He's been working at La Casa for almost five years. In the kitchen. Doubt he learned how to cook a heart there."

"What will you do next?" Lou asked her.

"Keep digging and try to find a contact I trust in Boise. We could also go there and look through the local archives for any information. Some of it will be impossible to get our hands on. No doubt the authorities are all over this, but I don't think they know it's Rathers yet." Dani gathered up the papers and stacked them neatly before returning them to the folder with Rathers's face on top. "Now that I know who he is, at least I can target my search better. Thanks for that."

Lou was spared from saying more by the arrival of the waitress.

Their dinner of fried chicken, mustard greens, and biscuits was placed on their table, and the waitress refilled Lou's coffee and Dani's tea.

They didn't talk while they ate. Dani and Lou had both ordered a second round of biscuits, which they buttered and added honey to. After Dani had sucked the last of the stray honey off her thumb, she said, "Can I ask you for a favor?"

"I already told you I'd kill her," Lou said.

"No, not that. Hopefully it won't come to that." Dani shook her head. "It's about Piper."

Lou waited, finishing the last of her black coffee.

"Can you please *not* tell Piper anything? Don't tell her about my car or about what Scarlett wrote on the window at work."

"What did she write on the window?" Lou asked over the rim of her ceramic cup.

"'Daniella Allendale is a whore,'" she said, and laughed bitterly. "Which is amusing because I bet she and Piper have had five times as many lovers as I have. I can count on one hand the number of people I've slept with and I don't even need all my fingers—"

She broke off, her face turning red.

Lou arched a playful brow. "You were saying..."

"I've only been with two other women besides Piper. That hardly makes me a slut."

"Third time's a charm," Lou said.

"Just promise me you won't tell her," Dani begged. "She'll only get worked up. I want to handle this, and if I can't come up with anything good in a couple of days, I'll ask for your help. I promise. Please?"

"I won't say anything," Lou said, and this seemed to satisfy her.

Yet Lou's mind kept turning back to *Daniella Allendale is a whore*, remembering the way Scarlett had looked that night on the street beside Piper.

Give me a reason, Lou thought. *Give me just one reason to hurt you.*

17

Konstantine sat in the waiting area of Isadora's clinic, his hands resting on his knees. Stefano was beside him, sipping the espresso that the receptionist had offered him upon their arrival. Konstantine didn't understand how he could stand to drink it in this place.

It smelled sterile, unnatural, despite the effort to fill the brightly lit room with cheerful chairs, vibrant green plants, and drawings made by Isadora's children.

He heard heels clicking against the floor a full minute before the door connecting the clinic to the reception area was pushed open and Isadora appeared.

He rose, as did Stefano, each paying her the respect she was due. She'd saved both of their lives and the lives of the people they cared about more than once. If that wasn't a reason to stand and show deference, Konstantine wasn't sure there was one.

"*Quale sarebbe il problema?*" she asked. "You both look healthy to me."

"We are well, thank you. There is no emergency today."

"Which is what Julia told me. What brings you then?"

Konstantine extended the blister pack of pills toward her. "I'm wondering if you can test this for me?"

She took the pack and turned it over in the light. "Test it? Why?"

"I want to know what it is," he said.

"I don't need to test it to tell you what it is. It's Dilti-azem," she said simply. When his face showed no recognition of what that meant, she added, "*È una medicina per il cuore.* Chest pain, high blood pressure. *Qualche volta viene usata per trattare cardiopatie.*"

"You're sure?" She gave him a stern look and he immediately apologized. "*Chiedo perdono.* Of course you are sure."

She held the pills up to the light again. "This was made by a pharmaceutical company, not on the street. The packaging is sealed. It hasn't been tampered with and it's properly labeled, see—*vedi?*"

She pointed at the numbers inscribed on the white pills.

Not a street drug. A simple medication for someone with heart problems. Konstantine continued to contemplate the possibilities of why Gabriella would have need for such a drug, let alone run up a tab for it, long after they thanked Isadora and began their walk back to the church.

Stefano knew well enough not to interrupt his friend while he was lost in his thoughts.

So it was Konstantine who spoke first.

"Perhaps I'm only half right," he admitted. Because if he couldn't admit his doubts to his closest friend and confidant —apart from Louie herself, of course—then who could he confess to?

"About Gabriella?" Stefano asked.

"Maybe she really is only a child with a secret, but not the secret I suspected."

Stefano pulled his cigarettes from his pocket, paused long enough to light the end with his lighter, cupping the flame in order to protect it from the wind. He took a deep inhale, the end of the cigarette glowing red.

After he exhaled, he said, "We were both children with secrets when we went looking for Padre Leo."

Konstantine nodded, his eyes on his shoes. That had been right. He'd come to Padre because he wanted to protect his mother. Stefano had come because he was the eldest of seven children—six brothers and a sister—who had no one to look after them when their grandmother died. So he worked for Padre to support his siblings. All of them grew up, went to college, got good jobs, and made families of their own. It was never clear to Konstantine if Stefano's siblings knew the price he'd paid for their security.

"Do you want me to find out more about her family?" Stefano asked. "We have the address of where she goes. I'm sure there are records."

The church came into view then, the piazza quiet as they approached. Only a single disgruntled pigeon took flight, annoyed by their arrival.

"No," Konstantine said, slapping Stefano on the shoulder. "I will handle it."

MEL USED THE BOX CUTTER TO OPEN THE LAST PACKAGE TO find yet another collection of souvenir bags. These were also a beautiful royal purple with gold lettering, *Melandra's Fortunes & Fixes* printed in script across the face of each.

Piper bent and pulled one out of the box to inspect it. "Oh, these are pretty! Look, the gold shimmers when you turn it in the light. Why didn't we get these sooner—I love them."

"Don't you worry," Melandra said wryly. "We'll have plenty for a long time."

There were almost five thousand bags between the three

inventory boxes. In no world was Melandra going to be able to throw a party with five thousand people in attendance. She was going to be stuffing crystals in these bags until the day she died.

Don't be so melodramatic, she told herself. Besides, it seemed that Piper was being morose enough for the both of them. Sure, she was trying to be encouraging and positive about the party. That much was clear. But Mel hadn't missed the way the girl's smile was quick to fade. How her excitement wilted at the edges a second too soon.

Finally, Mel couldn't take it anymore. "What's wrong with you?"

"Nothing," Piper said, her hands still elbow deep in the boxes. "I'm great."

Mel arched a brow and gave her a look. "If you think this party is a bad idea—"

"No," she said, her shoulders sagging.

"Then what's going on?" Mel asked, this time more slowly, gently. She was using a version of her fortune teller voice. The one that she sometimes used to get young girls or broken-hearted men to confess to their real fears. It was always easier that way, when those seeking advice were honest with her—and themselves—about why they were really there. It helped her see the messages in the cards more clearly.

"I think Dani is mad at me for something," Piper said.

"Did you do something?"

"I don't think so. Or maybe I've just been annoying? I don't know, and it's *killing* me. Last night she bailed on dinner with me and said she was gonna work late, but then she went and ate fried chicken with Louie. Why didn't they take me to get fried chicken?"

The level of sadness on Piper's face didn't match her quandary about chicken, but to Mel's credit, she didn't laugh.

"You know Lou could've just done her slippy thing, so it

wasn't like it was out of the way or that they'd have had to wait on me. So it's got to mean they didn't want me around. Or at least Dani didn't, and for whatever reason, Lou didn't fight her on it."

It was moments like this that Melandra didn't feel like she'd missed out on having girlfriends. The drama, the lack of communication, the general difficulty that came with just trying to get more than one human being on the same page about something.

If you don't wish you had friends then why are you working so hard to win over Tamara Jones? a small voice accused.

Mel shoved this down and turned her attention to Piper. She squeezed the girl's upper arm reassuringly and said the only thing she knew to say. "Let's look at the cards."

And why not?

They'd helped her well enough earlier when she'd asked them about the fundraiser. There had been mostly wands and threes—pointing to expansion and working with others. It was the reason why Mel had finally surrendered to the idea of ordering the personalized bags. The cards told her it might not turn out the way she expected, but help would come from an unexpected source and she should continue on her present path.

So here Mel was, with her *five thousand* stamped bags, waiting on a miracle.

But the real reason why the tarot worked, and Piper knew this as well as she did, was that it helped to get the querent's mind in the right place. The work can't begin, the solutions can't be found, when the battle still rages within.

Mel pulled her battered tarot deck from inside her robes and went to the glass countertop.

As she shuffled, she nodded at her little shrine against the adjacent wall. "Light some lemongrass for Mother Mary."

Piper did as she was told while Mel summoned her powers

of concentration. She tried to put the fundraiser out of her mind and hold Piper first and foremost in her vision.

What doesn't she see? Melandra asked the cards. *What does she need to know?*

By the time Piper had found a stick of lemongrass incense for the holder in front of Mother Mary's statue, lit it, and returned the step stool to the closet, Mel had laid out the cards.

The Queen of Wands.

The Queen of Cups reversed.

The Six of Cups.

The Five of Wands.

The Two of Swords reversed.

The Lovers reversed.

The Moon.

The Devil.

The Four of Wands reversed.

Death reversed.

Mel looked at the ten cards and tried to soften her mind at its edges and let any messages that wanted to be let in, *in*. Piper chewed on her thumb.

"Stop that," Mel told her. "I'm trying to focus."

"Sorry. I'm nervous." Piper released her thumb.

"Half of the cards are reversed," Mel said. "You or someone else is resisting change, creating disharmony. Stagnation."

She tapped the Six of Cups. "It might be a person or situation from your past that's causing this disharmony in your present."

Mel then tapped the Moon and the Lovers reversed cards. "Confusion, illusions, not seeing things clearly adds to this tension and conflict. I believe Dani is the Queen of Wands."

"She usually is, yeah," Piper said, her thumb halfway to

her mouth. One look from Mel made her shove her hand in her pocket instead.

"Then who is this Queen of Cups reversed? An old lover? She would be someone insecure, clingy. Emotional."

"That sounds like Scarlett. I think she's been giving Dani a hard time when I'm not around, but Dani won't talk to me about it. She probably thinks it'll make the situation worse if I get involved, but I *know* Scarlett. If I don't say something, she's going to keep pushing her to see how far she can go. That girl has an issue with boundaries."

Mel tapped the reversed Two of Swords. "You've been going against your intuition on this. If your intuition has been telling you to take care of it before it gets out of hand but you're listening to Dani instead, where will that get you?"

Piper rubbed the back of her head. "Yeah, okay. I see what you're saying."

Mel moved on to the Five of Wands and reversed Four of Wands. "The conflict in your home will continue unless you deal with the devil in your midst."

Mel lifted the Devil card and looked at it more closely. This was the one card in the deck that she'd drawn with her own hand. She'd redrawn it with her ex Terry's likeness, giving him the broad black hat, the shell necklace, and crow feather earrings. In her version of the card, you couldn't see the eyes hidden beneath the tipped hat, but you could see the menacing smile.

Exes who didn't know how to leave well enough alone were the worst. Mel understood this and sympathized with Piper's position.

Piper tapped the reversed Death card. "Is Lou going to get involved?"

Mel examined the card more closely, closing her eyes to see if any feelings or impressions rose up in her. But there was nothing but darkness behind her lids.

She laid the card down again. "I don't think so. It might signify Scarlett's fear of change and letting go, or serve as a warning that if you don't take care of this, it will break the two of you apart. You and Daniella. Letting something like this fester will decay your relationship beyond repair."

Piper bit her lower lip hard enough that all the color left it. "I don't want that to happen. Dani is the best thing that ever happened to me."

"Then you'd best fight for her," Mel said, breathing deeply of the lemongrass in the air. "And do it now."

PIPER DIDN'T NEED TO BE ASKED TWICE. WHEN MEL SAID that she wanted a coffee, that she was feeling the sleepiness of the long afternoon, Piper had volunteered to run down to Café du Monde and grab coffees for them both.

She took her time, weaving her way through the Quarter's foot traffic, listening to a brassy showtune floating her way from some side street. She recognized the melody but couldn't remember which movie she'd heard it from. The sky was darkening, turning gray. Storm clouds were on the horizon.

Fight for her. That was Mel's advice.

Yet a little voice made her hesitate. *Maybe it's just supposed to go this way. Maybe we're not meant to be together. I always knew she was too good for me. Maybe this is the universe's way of telling me that I can't have what I want.*

That's bullshit, she thought. And this proclamation was in Dani's voice. *That's utter bullshit and you know it.*

Maybe this was what Mel meant by *fight for her*. It wasn't necessarily that she had to beat Scarlett down in the streets or something. It was simply that Piper needed to make up her own mind, a hundred and ten percent, and get on board with the idea that not only was Dani the one she wanted but Dani was the person she deserved.

It was a hard pill to swallow, and her insecurities played in the back of her mind even after she reached the front of the ordering line at Café du Monde and got their coffees to go. At the last minute, Piper ordered some beignets too. She'd been trying to cut back on her sugar, and she already put three heaping scoops into her coffee whenever she drank it.

All this girl trouble had her craving sweets or some kind of comfort food. So it was either the beignets or it was Mama Kannie's baked mac and cheese for dinner—or maybe it would be the beignets now *and* the baked mac and cheese for dinner.

I'll regret it at the gym tomorrow, she thought. *Assuming those two are still gonna work out with me.*

The morose thought twisted her heart as she took a bite of her first beignet, a white puff of powdered sugar escaping into the air with each melancholic bite.

Piper sat down on a bench outside Café du Monde and watched the horse and buggies line up on the street outside the park.

Fight for her. *Fight.*

Piper pulled out her phone and searched her contacts for Scarlett's number. She opened a new text message thread and stared at the blinking cursor for a long time.

Just keep it simple. Direct.

Hey, she wrote, and pressed send. *Are you at work?*

Though Piper knew visiting Scarlett at work was a bad idea. How many times had Scarlett said she resented their friends popping into the shop and seeing her in her apron like that? More than once, she'd complained about the low-key rage she felt whenever it happened.

The chat bubble appeared on Piper's phone, and her heart skipped a beat.

not today. y?

Piper thought of the first time Scarlett had kissed her. It had been at the Wild Cat. They'd been leaning against the far wall with a group of their friends, drinking and talking about a whole lot of nothing, when a very drunk Scarlett leaned over and kissed Piper on the ear.

Before Piper had recovered from the shivering sensation of Scarlett's lips on that tender bit of flesh, Scarlett had whispered, "Come home with me."

And Piper had. That night and the three nights that followed. They'd barely slept, but Piper didn't care. She'd been doing everything she could not to go home in those days, home to her drug addict mother passed out on the living room couch with track marks on her arm. Home to her mother's asshole boyfriends who made lewd comments or came on to her.

On the nights that Piper didn't have an invitation to some girl's bed, she'd crashed with Henry and his boyfriends.

What she had now with Dani was so much better. A safe home that she actually looked forward to at the end of a long day. How could she explain to Scarlett how much that meant to her? How much Dani meant to her?

Wanted to talk, Piper wrote. *When are you free?*

The chat box appeared and disappeared several times.

Finally, she replied, *this is the first time you text in months and you wanna talk?*

It was true that Piper had ignored her texts once Dani had become her official girlfriend. She'd thought that was the respectful thing to do. It seemed rude to keep talking to someone she'd slept with before, especially if that girl wasn't very nice to said girlfriend. But now Piper wondered if cutting Scarlett off without much of an explanation had been a mistake.

fine, i'll talk to you on one condition, Scarlett replied.

What condition? Piper wrote back.

i'll tell you when i see you.

With that reply Piper remembered why Scarlett hadn't been her favorite out of all the local girls she'd slept with.

Scarlett was fickle. Scarlett could be cruel. But worst of all, Scarlett liked to play games.

When Piper made no response, Scarlett sent, *where and when?*

Piper hadn't thought this far ahead. On the one hand, she'd wanted it to be somewhere with people so that Scarlett wouldn't try anything that would get Piper into trouble. On the other hand, if Scarlett decided to cause a very loud, very public scene—which she'd done in the past—then that would be equally embarrassing and might reflect badly on either Melandra's shop or King's agency.

I'll come to you, Piper wrote. *Just tell me where you'll be.*

18

Lou had almost been asleep when her compass snagged, seizing her attention. She breathed in, exploring the emotion trembling through the connection. Not fear. Not anger or danger. It was something like desire, though free from the hot, sexual tension that sometimes ran through her when Konstantine longed for her.

And she was with Konstantine now. He slept beside her, his eyes closed, dark lashes resting on his cheeks.

She let the darkness overtake her, melting her from his bed to a parked car on the other side of the world.

Instantly she regretted it. She didn't have her mirrored shades or her leather jacket. More importantly, she hadn't brought her gun. She was sitting just as she was, in black sweatpants and one of Konstantine's shirts, in the passenger seat of a car.

It was parked outside La Casa del Diablo and its driver was still in his seat.

He turned, not seeming all that surprised to find Lou suddenly beside him.

"I was just thinking about you," he said. "I wanted to see you again and you're here. How funny."

The car smelled of fried fish. Lou supposed his uniform was likely soaked in kitchen grease.

"Are you starting or ending your shift?" she asked. It was as good a place as any to begin a conversation.

"Just finished," he said.

"Heading home?"

"I was—I was trying to decide," he said.

Then his eyes fell on her exposed shoulder. They widened, exposing more of their whites. "What the hell bit you?"

She looked down at the jagged scar encircling her shoulder. It had warped with age. When Jabbers sank her teeth into Lou, she'd been ten years old. It wasn't only that the scar had faded as the years had gone by but also that it had stretched as her body had grown, matured.

"What do you think bit me?" she asked him.

"Not a wolf," he said. "I know what a wolf bite looks like. A panther, maybe? A cougar?"

"No," she said simply.

"Come on, tell me." The same playfulness had returned. "I'm dying to know."

"You wouldn't believe me even if I told you," she said, and thankfully he let it drop. He returned his gaze to the steering wheel, then to the restaurant's glowing sign burning in front of them.

"What do you do to control it?" he asked.

There was something so innocent about the question, so —hopeful? Lou searched his face.

"To control what?" she asked.

"The thing that bit you. It lives in you now. It has to. They become a part of you forever once they taste you, and they live in you and make you a monster too."

Lou searched his eyes for insanity. For any gleam of

psychosis. But he seemed lucid, in control of himself and firmly connected to reality.

The car was dark enough that she could slip if he reached for her, if he so much as twitched a muscle in her direction.

But he didn't.

He remained on his side of the car, his eyes wide and expectant, and again she had the feeling she was looking at a child. A child trapped in this strange, lanky figure of a man.

"She's not inside me," Lou said simply. "But I can visit her when I want. We're friends now."

She wondered if her explanation sounded as bizarre to him as it did to her.

He was frowning.

"She has to be inside you. If she bit you like that, then she's a part of you. And you're a part of her."

Lou tried to imagine a part of ten-year-old Louie inside Jabbers, somehow affecting or controlling the beast's behavior. It was true that Jabbers did not act like the rest of her kind. Of course, Lou'd had only one other run-in with—whatever the hell they were—and it had been all ferocity and murderous intention.

"How did you do it?" he asked her. And now he looked ready to cry. "Did you give her what she wants?"

Lou thought of the bodies she'd hauled onto the shores of La Loon. Hundreds and hundreds of corpses. Jabbers seemed as equally pleased to see her when Lou didn't have a corpse in tow as when she did.

"She doesn't expect anything from me," Lou said. *At least, I don't think she does.*

"Nothing I do makes it happy," he said darkly. "It's only calm if I—"

He never finished.

Lou asked, "Is that why you hunt families?"

"That's what the beast wants. *Him.* Always him." The boyish tone fell away and something darker took its place.

Him.

"Him who?" she dared to ask, even though the energy in the car was rapidly changing. His curiosity and boyish charm were gone. Something else was rising up to replace it.

She just wasn't sure yet what it was.

Will I meet the other one tonight? she asked herself. *This so-called beast living inside him.*

"The sins of the father shall be visited upon the son," he whispered to the steering wheel. For a moment it was as if he'd forgotten Lou was there at all.

Then he stopped, staring out at nothing for a full minute.

Lou's compass didn't move. There was no warning cry.

So Lou waited. She felt like she was so close to understanding what was happening here.

"Alan?" she asked after several minutes.

When he looked at her, the boy was gone.

"They deserve it," he said, eyes dark.

Lou's fingers twitched toward a gun that wasn't there. *Shit.* "What about the children? Do the children deserve to die?"

"It's a mercy. You don't know what it's like to have a father like that. They're better off dead."

"A mercy," Lou repeated. She'd remained in control of herself until that moment. But now her anger was rising.

When he turned toward her, his eyes were cold and something was happening with his jaw. Was he grinding his teeth? Was that what the horrible cracking sound was? He seemed to realize he was doing it the same time she did.

Lou's compass pulled, urging her to move.

But she was fixed in her seat, fascinated by the strangeness of the moment.

She watched as panic consumed him. His hands fumbled

frantically with the console between them, ripping it open and rummaging inside.

He pulled out something that looked like it had come from a BDSM shop. It was all leather and metal buckles.

He shoved the mouth guard between his lips and fastened it around his head with shaking hands. It was some sort of muzzle that immobilized Rathers's jaw.

He began growling even as his hands yanked furiously on the straps to ensure they were as tight as they could be. His cheeks bulged around the leather.

Her compass spun with renewed urgency. Suddenly, this car felt like a very, *very* dangerous place to be.

Rathers growled around the leather bit in his mouth, his eyes full of terror.

Lou took this as her cue to leave.

She fell through the dark of the car and reemerged on the flat of her back, returning to her place in Konstantine's bed as if she'd never left at all.

The only difference was the pounding of her heart and the burning image of him biting down hard on the leather guard between his teeth as his eyes pleaded—no, *begged*—for Lou to run.

"What is it?" Konstantine asked, stirring.

Her movement must have woken him.

"*Amore mio?*"

"Nothing," she said over the thunderous pulse in her ears. "Go back to sleep."

THE KILLER SHOVED ALL THE BOTTLES OFF HIS BATHROOM sink. When that did nothing to quiet the fury within him, he kicked his shower door, forcing it to rattle on its hinges. He landed a second kick, but it did not shatter the glass. He succeeded only in falling back against the wall, where he balled up his towel and hurled it to the floor.

He stormed through his apartment, went to his bedroom. He threw back the covers on his bed, looking for his journal. He found it on the floor, half covered by a wayward pillow.

He began scribbling and didn't stop.

I blew it

I fucked up

I could've made it good

Could've made it right but now it'll never be

She won't come back

She won't want to see me after that

It almost happened right there in the car

It was never this bad

I used to have more warning than that. I'd get feelings, you know, and I had time but tonight there'd been no warning

No warning at all

The beast tells me that I can't be her friend

The beast tells me I can't have anything I want because we have a mission. We have a purpose

If she knows, she'll stop me

I don't believe it. I think she's like me. She knows about beasts

I think she knows how to conquer beasts and that's what scares the one in me

I just want her to come back

I want to talk to her more

I want to explain everything

Everything.

Tamara Jones's office was in the business district, high up in one of the glistening skyscrapers so at odds with the older architecture of the city. The Quarter was full of old creole cottages and the Garden District had its mansions. Sure, some of the other neighborhoods had typical suburban housing, but these skyscrapers—they belonged somewhere else. At least, that's what King thought every time he saw them.

"Just a quick chat," he reminded himself as he slipped his hands into his pockets to hide his nervousness and stepped into the chilly lobby.

A receptionist with an especially bright smile greeted him, and when he mentioned his appointment with Jones, he was directed to the forty-fourth floor of the building.

King took the elevator. Usually he tried to do the stairs, anything to keep his joints from going fully arthritic on him, but forty-four floors was out of his range.

He was surprised to find himself in a second waiting room five minutes later. This one had a group of pretty young women, all of them Black, with thick binders and satchels on their laps. Their postures were perfect and their smiles bright.

They were called into Jones's office before he was, and it was nearly thirty minutes past his appointment before the girls left, excited and bright-eyed. Then he was called.

When he entered the well-lit office, Jones was there, extending her hand toward him. "Mr. King."

"Ms. Jones," he said, returning her firm handshake.

"I hate to ask, Mr. King, but it's been back-to-back meetings for me today. Would you forgive me if I left you here alone for a few minutes and visited the ladies' room?"

That would be perfect, actually.

He'd love a chance to look around without her gaze on him.

"It's no problem at all," King said, releasing her hand. "Take your time."

She thanked him and pointed at the leather sofa resting against one wall. "Make yourself comfortable and I'll be right back. I'll send Deidra in to get your drink order."

Before he could object to a drink she was out of the room, her heels snagging on the carpet ever so slightly with each step.

King had crossed to the bookcase beside the sofa when Deidra appeared. She was an older woman, certainly past retirement age, with thick bifocals and a smile King suspected was fake. Her cheeks were too soft, and the lips sagged the way they usually did around false teeth.

"Would you like coffee or tea, Mr. King?" she asked in a raspy tone.

"A black coffee would be great," he told her.

She shuffled from the room again and returned with a ceramic cup full of coffee balanced on a saucer. "One black coffee for the gentleman."

"Thank you so much, Ms. Deidra," he said, and because

he was a man that rarely let an opportunity pass him by, he asked, "Do you like working here?"

"Oh yes," she said.

He took a calculated sip of his coffee. "This is delicious. I couldn't persuade you to come work at my office?"

"Not a chance."

He laughed.

"Is it the pay or the benefits?" he asked, keeping his tone light and tinged with humor.

They were making jokes, after all.

"You could offer me a hundred times the pay and I wouldn't leave Tamara," the woman said. "That woman saved my life."

"A good reason to stay loyal," King said, tipping the coffee at her.

Deidra spared him a small smile before she shut the office door on him, and that smile gave King the distinct impression that Deidra hadn't been fooled by his questions. Either she was an especially perceptive woman or King was getting rusty with his charm.

With his remaining minutes of freedom, King circled the office, looking at the bookcases and desktop for any clues as to the woman's character or interests. But he knew that unless he could steal her computer and make off with it, there was little he was going to find here in this immaculate room with its expansive view of downtown.

It seemed Jones was too smart to leave any evidence out in the open for a detective like King to find. All he saw was what she wanted him to see. The plaques and awards for her years of service. Pictures of her arms around young women in school uniforms or business-casual attire. A few photos of her family, including a handsome Denzel Washington doppelgänger for a husband and a couple of sweet-faced, if nerdy, kids.

Books on everything from leadership to law to the history of New Orleans.

Without anything to help him along, King turned his attention to practicing the interview questions he'd prepared in his head.

The office door opened a heartbeat after King took a seat on the leather sofa. He'd only just crossed one leg over the other when Tamara shut the door behind her.

"Mr. King, thank you so much for waiting," she said. "You mentioned when you phoned in for the appointment that you wanted to talk about our fundraiser."

"I do," he said, returning the coffee to its saucer. "I have a friend who wants to join your association, and she's been very worried she won't be accepted as a full member if she doesn't raise enough."

Ms. Jones took a seat on the sofa beside him, keeping a polite distance between them. She rested her manicured nails on her knees.

"Forgive me for asking outright, but I assume your friend is a Black woman," she said. "And a business owner."

"Yes, she is," King said.

"Those are the only qualifications for joining, so I'd say she has little to worry about."

"She mentioned something about tiers?" King pressed.

"Those are for recognition only," Tamara insisted. "A higher tier proves only that a member has offered a great deal of service to the organization, either through time or money."

She tilted her head slightly on *money*, as if this were an acknowledgment of the truth in his inquiry.

"But the benefits are equally accessible to all members. If the association has the power and resources to help a woman in need, we will. She doesn't even need to be a member of the organization to be paid that respect. We look out for one another. Being a business owner is a real difficulty. It's even more challenging for those who are offered fewer resources than most. Though I applaud your friend for seeking membership. As a member, we'll get to know her better, and therefore, will know how to better help her if she is one of us."

One of us.

Those words struck him in the chest, and for the first time, he was able to recognize the jealousy that Dick had suggested might be there.

But that's ridiculous, he told himself. *I'm not losing Mel because she joins a club or starts hanging out with other people. Nor am I losing Beth because she wants grandchildren.*

Yet here he was in an office, drinking a good cup of coffee, because—what?

What was he afraid of?

"For the sake of time, Mr. King, may I be direct and ask you what your concerns are?" Tamara asked. Her nails were resting lightly on her pencil skirt as she regarded him with golden eyes.

They were kind eyes. A bit hawkish, King noted, but warm. He supposed she would have to be a bit of a hawk to run an organization like this. He couldn't fault her for that.

And he prided himself on being mostly right about people. The only time he'd *really* gotten it wrong was with Chaz Brasso, his longtime partner who tried to kill him.

Then again, he'd always known Brasso was a bastard. The only part he'd underestimated was how far he was willing to go for money.

"I care a lot about Mel," King admitted finally. "Doing well in this fundraiser matters a lot to her, and I want to help her if I can."

The woman's eyes softened, and King felt even more convinced that his assessment was correct. There might be problems in the association, but if there were, they weren't worth digging up for the chance to justify his jealousy.

"I admire your loyalty," she said with a smile. Then she blinked. "Wait, did you say Mel? As in Melandra Durand?"

"Yes, that's the one."

Jones put a hand on her chest. "Are you *that* Mr. King? The detective?"

King almost laughed. "Yes. Given the way you say it, I wonder what you've heard. Nothing bad, I hope."

She laughed. "On the contrary. You know, the whole reason I reached out to Melandra and invited her to join us was because I was *so* impressed by how she handled that attempted suicide down by the market. When was that? January? February?"

"January," he said.

She was talking about Zoey Peterson. The girl had almost shot herself, blaming herself for her boyfriend's death though all parties agreed it was the fault of the drunk driver who struck him.

King thought it best to leave out that the gun she'd gotten had been stolen from Mel—or that it would have been Mel's bullet that would've punched a hole in that girl's chest. It was also probably best to leave out that Mel had been so interested in saving the girl because of ominous dreams she'd been having about her before they'd even met.

Mel would *kill* him if he mentioned either.

"She was amazing," King said instead. "Mel's very good in situations like that, when pressure is high. She cares a lot about people."

No need to add on that he'd seen Mel act well under pressure because they'd been kidnapped and almost *murdered* together.

More than once.

"Yes, her reputation precedes her," Jones said kindly, but

there was a curiosity in her eyes now. King wondered if he was going to mess this up if he kept talking. When he didn't offer anything more, she said, "You're saying she's worried about the tiers?"

King was grateful that the attention was shifting back toward the fundraiser and off of their lives. "She might resent me telling you this, but she wants very badly to impress you. Or maybe it's not about impressing you so much as—"

"She wants to belong," Jones said.

"Yeah." King turned his coffee cup on its saucer. "Yeah, I think that's right."

Jones nodded. "I understand. Well, between you and me, she can't go wrong. I'm as determined to bring her into the fold as she is to join us. Probably more so. I personally believe that good-hearted people like her are the best asset we have in this city. If Katrina taught me anything—and Lord, it has taught me a lot—it's that when things get rough, it's the community that matters. So I won't pass up the opportunity to recruit her if I can."

Another pang of jealousy shot through King, but instead of indulging it, he threw back the rest of his coffee.

"*But*," Jones said, pointing a finger at the ceiling, "if she's *really* worried, I'd be happy to send you back with some tips and perhaps a phone number or two. I've done this enough to know the best practices for hosting a fundraiser. Would you like that?"

King returned his empty coffee cup to its saucer. "Yes. Yes, I would."

ALL THROUGHOUT THE DINNER, KONSTANTINE HAD BEEN nervous. It seemed that the leather bag at his feet had a vortex of its own. He felt its weight pulling at him through every course, and even the delicious wine they'd ordered hadn't been enough to release the tension between his shoulder blades. When the waiter brought him a fourth glass of wine, Lou arched a brow. She'd stopped after one.

"You wanting to get drunk tonight?" she asked with a mischievous smile. "I'm going to need your consent to whatever happens *before* you get too drunk to give it."

A nervous laugh escaped him. "I will need more than four glasses of wine to get drunk, *amore mio*."

I'll need at least six.

Because he was already buzzed. He could feel the heat in his cheeks and the tips of his ears. And the world had slowed down around him and grown heavy.

The thought of what she might do to him after they finished their dinner made his stomach and groin tighten. His arousal stirred. But then he thought of the folder he wanted to give her, and his arousal was replaced again with fear.

"You're cute when your cheeks are red," she told him over the rim of her own glass. "How is she?"

Konstantine's mind sputtered. His confusion must've shown.

"Gabriella," Lou added. "Have you figured out her deep dark secret yet?"

His stomach turned. "No. I haven't, but I'm getting close."

Lou looked out over the piazza, where the crowds gathered around the fountain. The clocktower was lit from within, serving as a beacon against the encroaching night. A peal of children's laughter rippled past them, and Konstantine caught the whiff of cigarette smoke.

Now or never, he thought. *Before I lose my nerve.*

He reached down and pulled the folder out of the bag, and placed it beside her emptied plate with its smear of blood from her steak.

"What's this?" she asked.

He licked his lips. "I compiled a list of properties around Florence."

Lou's face was unreadable. The playfulness he'd seen moments before was gone.

But it was too late to turn back now. Konstantine had no choice but to go on. "I'm open to the idea of purchasing a property anywhere in the world, if there is somewhere you'd rather be. I only chose Florence because it's convenient. But given your gift, we could make a home anywhere."

Say something, his mind begged.

Please. Say something.

She didn't. She opened the folder and flipped the first page. Then another. And another.

Konstantine was on the verge of pleading for a response when the waiter brought the bill, and he was able to distract himself with the business of paying.

"Why are they so expensive?" she asked at last.

"Location. All but one is here in the city center," he replied. It was his rehearsed answer. In truth, he just wanted to give her something beautiful and he had the means to do so, so why not?

As soon as he paid the bill, Lou closed the folder and stood. Konstantine followed her, downing the last of his wine for courage and grabbing his bag off the patio at his feet.

She waited until a patch of shadows overtook them before she pulled him through the dark.

His bedroom formed around them. Octavia let out a small meow of hello upon their arrival and blinked her large golden eyes at them lazily.

As soon as she released him, she turned away as if she were going to leave.

"Wait," he said. "If I've upset you—"

"I need to take care of something," she told him, but her eyes were gone again, hidden behind her mirrored shades, and she was so still that he couldn't gain an ounce of insight from her body language. She turned back toward him. "I'll be back. Thank you for dinner."

Then she was gone.

And Konstantine sank to the side of the bed and exhaled the tension from his body.

"She took the folder, at least," he told the British Blue, who stretched her soft paws toward him.

Octavia meowed again.

"Yes," he said. "All we can do now is wait."

Lou stepped from the linen closet and threw the folder onto her bed. She paced by it once, twice. She looked at it lying there on the top of her comforter accusingly, as if it had any right to be there. One of the listings had slipped an inch out of its sleeve, and Lou could see a hint of blue.

She thought it might have been the one with the shimmering pool.

"A fucking folder," she muttered to herself. *I thought everyone found their apartments online these days.*

She rotated her shoulders as if gearing up to hit someone. Only she wasn't sure who.

There was no one in her apartment but herself.

Calm down, she told herself. *It's just another folder with some papers inside. Nothing more. You see them all the time. Dani just handed you one the other night.*

But it felt like more as she flipped the latch on the side of her kitchen island and revealed the stairs leading down into the dark.

She took them one at a time, carefully. At the bottom of the stairs, she found the string overhead and pulled it until light flooded the space.

It was her arsenal.

Guns were organized in old shoe boxes, and knives by color and size. There were her bulletproof vests and Kevlar sleeves, her grenades, smoke bombs, and even a flamethrower.

She remembered building this place. Before it, she'd used a storage unit. For a hundred dollars a month, she'd kept all her guns in the Omaha unit, which stayed permanently locked from the inside.

That was because she hadn't had an apartment of her own. In the early years of her hunting, when she ate, slept, and breathed revenge for Angelo Martinelli, the bastard who shot her father in the face, she'd been a vagrant.

She never slept in the same place for long. She'd begun by sleeping in vacant vacation homes while their owners were away for the season. But she'd found it difficult to relax with photographs of other happy families looking back at her. Mostly she'd stuck to warehouses or half-formed buildings or construction projects where she would be out of the way and unfindable by anyone, except, of course, for her aunt Lucy.

There was no hiding from one who also had a gift for slipping through the shadows.

And it had been Lucy who had begged her to get a place of her own. A place she could call home.

Lou held out for a long time.

But there had been something about this apartment. About the gorgeous view of the river. She'd said yes to the view more than to the apartment itself, but Lucy hadn't cared what her motive was.

She'd just wanted her niece to have a place to settle down.

Was that why Lou was so bothered by Konstantine's offer to move in together?

Was she so in love with this view that she couldn't give it up?

She didn't think that was it. After all, there was always the roof.

The roof.

Lou slipped from her apartment to the roof of her building. The wind tore at her hair, and it was nearly thirty degrees cooler than it had been inside, partially because of the torrent rolling off the water but also because she was stories above the street below.

Still, she stepped away from the shadows and walked to the edge of the roof, looking out over the river.

Apart from the assault on her hair, she had to admit this view was even prettier than the one from her apartment. The fresh air and the light on the water both held an extra dimension that she couldn't experience when behind glass.

She could come here anytime she wanted. She could have this view and—

It's not about the view or the apartment, she thought. Or at least, it's not *just* the apartment or view.

There was something else going on here. And when she felt herself move toward it, that indescribable feeling within her, her insides hardened against it. Cold washed through her.

A distance spawned. A pulling back.

She turned away from the sky and went back through the darkness.

Howe, she thought. *I want to hunt Howe.*

No, you want to run. You want a distraction, a voice countered. It was her father's. As stern and no-bullshit as ever.

She ignored it.

After fitting twin Berettas into her holsters and one knife into her forearm sheath and another for her boot, Lou let the darkness overtake her again.

When the world reshaped itself, she was wedged between two stacks of cardboard boxes. She stepped out into a storage room, noting the bottles of liquor along the shelves and the familiar names of brands she'd come to know.

She pushed open the door on her left and stepped out into the liquor store.

She spotted Howe immediately. He was behind the counter, smacking a piece of gum between his weaselly lips. As his jaw worked, she caught glimpses of his teeth, and they only served to emphasize the rodent-like quality of his features.

Lou took a bottle of vodka off the shelf and approached the register.

He made the mistake of trying to meet her eyes. He flinched away from his reflection in her mirrored glasses.

"Will this be all for you, sweetheart?" he asked in a thick East Coast accent. She wondered if maybe she was in Boston or Rhode Island.

"Unless you have something interesting in the back," she said, and nodded toward the storage room door.

His eyebrows flicked, betraying his surprise.

"I don't know," he said cautiously. He was appraising her with a different sort of gaze now. Part arousal, part suspicion. "What are you looking for?"

"Something that goes down easy," she said. *Like you will.*

He snorted. "Then let's see, shall we?"

Howe pushed himself off the wooden stool and tugged at his sagging jeans, trying to get them to sit better on his hips. He was either wearing someone else's pants or he'd recently lost a lot of weight, she realized. Didn't matter either way. All his hard work was about to be for nothing.

He stepped into the dim storage room and she went in after him.

Before he could even fully turn around, her hands were on him, pulling him from one side of the world to another.

He stumbled when their feet met the forest floor. Lou

released him, watched his hands go out to brace himself on the evergreen in front of him.

"Whoa," he said. "What the fuck?"

He pulled his hands away and inspected the sap covering his palms.

Lou breathed deeply. She'd always loved that smell. It reminded her of Christmas.

"What's happening?" he asked

"For you?" she said. "Nothing."

His eyes doubled in size as she reached into her leather jacket and pulled out one of the Berettas. Howe hardly looked like a two-gun job.

"Whoa, hey," he said again. "Now what's a nice girl like you doing with something like that?"

A nice girl like her? Lou almost burst out laughing with the absurdity of it.

She hadn't been a nice girl in a *very* long time. And she was absolutely certain that no one, surely, ever looked at her and thought, *Now there's a nice girl.*

That's why she was smiling when she pulled the trigger and blew Howe's brains out across the trunk of the tree.

20

P iper had just finished ringing up her last customer, putting the receipt and a flyer for the fundraiser into a paper bag, when Scarlett strode into the shop. Immediately, Piper knew she was in trouble. Not just because Scarlett had done up her makeup and hair—signaling that they both had very different intentions for their meeting— but also because Scarlett was wearing the shirt that Piper had given her for her birthday not long after they first slept together. And her pants were so tight that Piper's eyes had started tracing her curves before she fully realized what she was doing.

Pull yourself together, she scolded herself, forcing her gaze north and fixating somewhere in the neutral territory of Scarlett's cheek.

But she was too late. Scarlett was already smiling, clearly aware that her outfit had made the impression she'd wanted.

This was why Piper had wanted to visit Scarlett, not have her here. But Scarlett had refused. She'd insisted they meet at Mel's shop or not at all. What was Piper supposed to say to that?

"Hey, P," she said, leaning her full weight against the counter. "You wanted to see me?"

Seeing Scarlett's fingers on the glass sobered Piper more than anything.

I just cleaned that, man.

Scarlett saw the stack of flyers on the countertop and took one, bringing it up to her face for closer inspection. "You're throwing a party?"

"Yeah, for the shop," she said. "It's pretty important to Mel."

Dani and I will be there. Please don't come, please don't come, please don't—

Scarlett took half the flyers off the top of the stack and said, "Do you want me to hand these out for you? It'll be like that Halloween party we threw together. Wasn't that fun?"

Scarlett was looking up at her through her long dark lashes.

It *had* been fun, but Piper found her voice was stuck in her throat. She knew what she wanted to say to Scarlett, what she *should* say, and yet she was clamming up.

Scarlett misinterpreted her silence and took one coquettish step toward her, then another. She stopped within arm's reach.

When she spoke, her voice was low, coaxing. "Did you call me here to help with the party or did you just want to get me into the storage closet again?"

Piper realized why she'd been avoiding Scarlett all this time.

Piper was *terrible* at confrontation, and even worse at sharing how she felt if she knew it was going to hurt someone. And there was no pretty way to say what she needed to say to Scarlett.

"No, no." Piper took a step back, holding the broom out in front of her like a shield. "No to the closet."

Anger flashed through Scarlett's eyes, and she turned away.

"I guess she wanted you to talk to me," Scarlett said, keeping her back to Piper as she pretended to read a candle on the shelf. "I make *one* comment and she comes crying to you like a little bitch, is that it?"

There was no need to ask who *she* was.

"One comment? What did you say?" Piper was surprised by her own anger rising. "Have you really been giving her a hard time when I'm not around?"

Scarlett seemed to realize her mistake. "Just tell me what you want."

"No, you answer me first. What did you do?" Piper asked. "Be honest."

Because while Scarlett admitted to saying *one comment*, she'd also told Piper that she'd only made out with Heather *one time*, when in fact they'd been screwing around behind Piper's back for months.

Scarlett had a gift for understatement.

"What did you do? What did you say?" Piper asked. She could feel the heat in her face.

"Ask her," Scarlett said. "If you're so close, get her to tell you."

"She wouldn't tell me even if I asked." This was true, but Piper hadn't meant to say it aloud.

Scarlett's pout morphed into something more hopeful. She took another step closer to Piper. "Not so close then."

Piper took a deep breath against her pounding heart. *I can do this. I can do this for Dani because I love her.*

Mel's cards had been clear that if Piper didn't deal with this situation, she would regret it.

"Scarlett, listen. I don't know what you've been saying to Dani or doing to her. I don't know how bad it's gotten because she's too stubborn and independent to ever come crying to me about anything—"

Piper rubbed her brow.

"But I love her, okay?"

Scarlett started as if she'd been struck. "Don't say that."

"I mean it, I love her. And I want to be with her and I'm asking you, please, *please*—" Piper clasped her hands so Scarlett wouldn't see them shake. "Stop trying to ruin this for me."

Scarlett's jaw worked furiously for a full minute before she said, "I suppose this is the part where you tell me if I really care about you, I'll leave her alone."

Piper said nothing.

When she finally met Piper's gaze, she had tears in the corners of her eyes. "Is it so wrong that I want you? That you're the only person who's ever mattered to me?"

Fuck.

Don't fall for it, she told herself. *She's using tears because she knows you're a sucker for women who cry. Don't you dare fall for it.*

"Is that what you were thinking when you shoved your tongue down Heather Bitmore's mouth?"

Scarlett threw up her hands. "You kissed her first! You kissed a lot of people!"

Because I was depressed. Because I hated myself. Is that what you want me to say?

Piper rubbed her forehead with her fist. "Look. It's not just that we're no good for each other. What I've got with Dani—"

"Stop talking about her!" Scarlett screamed. "I came here to talk about *us*. I don't give two shits about her."

Piper fought to hold on to what was left of her calm. "Fine. It's not about her anyway. It's about *me* trying to get through to *you* that we're over. Forever. Whatever you think is going to happen. *Isn't.* And if you don't accept that, if you keep trying to ruin my life, I'll get a restraining order if I have to."

Scarlett scoffed. "That's crazy."

"Yeah, it is." Piper snorted. "But I'll do it if that's what it takes to get you to back off."

Scarlett turned away. When she met Piper's gaze again, her face had changed. It was softer now.

"You really want me to back off?" she asked.

"Yes." It was best to just be clear, as clear as she possibly could be.

Scarlett's lip trembled. "You want me to just give up hope that I'll ever get you back?"

Piper tried looking at Scarlett's ear in order to avoid the feelings of guilt her pitifulness was bringing up in her. "Yes. That's what I want."

"I'll give you what you want if you give me what I want," Scarlett replied, a coldness returning to her voice.

"No, I told you—"

"One kiss," Scarlett said, taking a step toward her, then another. "One kiss and then I'll know it's really over and I'll leave you alone. Both of you."

"That is the *worst* idea," Piper said, throwing her hands up. "I don't know how that is going to do anything for anybody."

"Aren't you the one who told me you could tell a lot about a person from one kiss?" she said, looking up at Piper through her tear-stained lashes.

She had.

That's why Piper had kissed Lou, wasn't it? Piper had thought she was in love with her at first, but one kiss told her that *no*, actually, whatever she was feeling for Lou wasn't romantic. And all of that was before she'd met and fallen in love with Dani anyway. It's not like she'd go around kissing everyone *now*, just to figure out how she felt.

"Okay, fine. It's true I said that but—" Piper began, but Scarlett's mouth was on hers before she could finish.

Her lips were as soft as they ever were, but the eagerness was all wrong. It was overwhelming and sticky. Domineering and repulsive in its desperation.

Piper grabbed Scarlett's arms and pushed her back, holding her at arm's length. "Stop it. I told you this isn't happening."

Scarlett wrenched her arms away. She no longer looked pitiful.

She looked *pissed*.

"Fuck you, Piper. Fuck you both. I swear to God, you're going to regret this."

She stormed out of the shop without so much as a backward glance.

As she passed the counter, the flyers for the masquerade slipped off the glass and fell to the floor in a miniature tornado.

Piper couldn't find it in herself to care. All she could think was, *How am I going to tell Dani about that kiss?*

DANI SAW THE KISS. TWENTY MINUTES *BEFORE* SHE SAW Scarlett lean forward and kiss Piper, she'd received a text from a blocked number telling her to hurry to Melandra's Fortunes and Fixes, that something was going to happen to Piper.

She'd suspected Scarlett was behind it even before she'd arrived at the shop, though she was only about ninety percent sure that this was typical lesbian drama and not, say, one of her fears come to life. That somehow Dmitri Petrov's goons had found her and wanted revenge for their murdered boss and were going to take it out on Piper, and all because Dani had the audacity to survive their boss's torture rather than die as expected.

Dani's suspicion, however, moved to full certainty when she arrived outside the shop and saw Scarlett and Piper through the large glass windows. Piper didn't seem to see her, her eyes remained fixed on Scarlett as if she were some wild animal to tame.

But when Scarlett turned away, she'd seen Dani. Dani was sure the second she'd seen the little smile tugging at Scarlett's lips.

That's when she'd kissed Piper. And Piper had just stood there and taken it. And as difficult as it had been to see Scarlett trying to shove her tongue down Piper's throat, it had been worse the moment Piper reached up and took Scarlett by the arms.

That's when Dani looked away.

Her heart wobbled, her stomach knotting. She felt sick.

She was going to have a panic attack right there on the stupid street in front of all those stupid people.

She was still trying to catch her breath when the shop door flew open and Scarlett stormed out with tears in her eyes.

The look she gave Dani wasn't friendly. It wasn't even triumphant.

It was furious.

And it was so soon after the kiss that at least Dani could rest assured that Piper had put a stop to it—whatever *it* was.

Yet—

She leaned her full weight against the brick wall of the building. She pinched her eyes shut and tried to remember what her therapist had told her about moving through panic attacks. The only problem was, it was harder to actually move through them in the moment.

She put her hand on her heart and felt it rabbit-kicking against her palm.

She'd begun to shake when a leather-clad arm wrapped around her, enveloping her in darkness.

Then she was nowhere. The night was complete.

"Breathe," Lou said, easing her down onto a sofa.

It was her sofa. They were in the apartment Dani shared with Piper.

"Not here," she begged. Piper could come home. Piper could see her like this, and she'd have to explain what she saw and why she had reacted this way—which Dani herself wasn't entirely sure of—and she couldn't.

She *couldn't*.

"Not here," she pleaded again. "Piper can't—"

Lou was already pulling her through the dark again. When Dani opened her eyes once more, Lou was easing her down onto a different sofa. It was purple suede and soft, and the light coming through the big windows was cheerful.

It had been a moment since Lou had brought Dani to her apartment, but nothing had changed. There was the same Picasso print, *Girl with the Mandolin*. There was the same mattress against the windows, the sheets and pillows rumpled. The same brick façade running along one wall to the front door, past the open kitchen and island with its stone countertops.

"Breathe," Lou said again.

And Dani was trying. She focused on the glass coffee table in front of her. On it was a manila folder opened to reveal a property fact sheet. If Dani was reading it right, it was for an Italian villa somewhere.

Lou seemed to notice that Dani was staring at the folder, so she closed it and took it away, out of sight, leaving Dani with only the glass itself to focus on, and the way the light danced prismatic across its surface.

Slowly, the tightness in Dani's chest relaxed. Her breathing evened out. The sensation that her throat was closing disappeared and it was possible to draw enough air into her lungs again.

The pounding in her temples subsided but left in its wake a horrible headache.

"I could use some aspirin," Dani squeaked out.

And as Lou disappeared out of Dani's field of vision, she realized that dark smudge beside her had been Lou all along. Close, ready. But not intrusive.

Lou placed a glass of water in her hand as well as two little blue pills. Dani threw them back, doing her best to keep her throat relaxed, which was harder to do when panic consumed her.

She followed with the water.

"Do you need anything else?" Lou asked once Dani sat the empty water glass on the table.

"Need? No. Want? *Yes*." She pressed her fingers into her temples, knowing it was too late to be embarrassed by her reaction to Piper and Scarlett's kiss. "I *want* her to crawl in a hole and die."

"Would 'her' be Scarlett?" Lou ventured. "Has she done something else?"

She told Lou everything, starting from the moment she got the text at work and how she'd hurried to the shop just in case Piper really did need help, only to find Scarlett's trap.

"But it must not have worked as well as she thought it would because she didn't leave happy," Dani finished, thinking again of how Scarlett had pushed past her.

When she turned to look at Lou, she found her face placid, unreadable. If she was perturbed by Dani's reactions, it didn't show. This was just another thing that needed to be dealt with.

"I envy how calm you are when shit happens. Some of the smallest, stupidest things set me off," Dani said.

But there was a flick of Lou's eyebrow. What was that? Disbelief?

"You don't think you're calm?" she asked.

"I get upset," Lou said without elaboration. "Often."

A tight laugh escaped Dani's throat. "It doesn't show."

Lou took Dani's water glass to the kitchen, refilled it, and returned it to the coffee table.

"What do you want to do about Scarlett?" she asked.

Dani fell back against the sofa with a huff. "What can I do? If I attack her, I'll go to jail. If I dig up her dirty laundry and publish it somewhere, she'll know it was me, and it will likely just escalate the situation. At least Piper knows how devious she is now, and she stopped the kiss. If Scarlett was really going to get what she wanted, she wouldn't have stormed out of the shop in a huff. If I really had to worry about Piper, they'd be in the storage closet right now."

"She does like that closet," Lou conceded. "Are you going to tell her that you saw the kiss?"

"I don't know," Dani said. "I have no idea what the best course of action is here. Ugh, god, this is awful. Can we talk about something else?"

"There's always Alan Rathers," Lou said with a smile.

"I actually learned more about him," Dani said. "I was interviewing one of his high school teachers when Scarlett sent me that text."

Dani took a sip of water and tried to relax her shoulders. She appreciated that Lou never rushed her or made her feel like she had to hurry up or do something to put Lou at ease. This pocket of steadfastness was one of her best traits, in Dani's opinion.

Once she felt calmer, she went on. "He's twenty-eight years old, an only child. I haven't found his mother's cause of death yet, but his father died when Rathers was just eighteen. His teacher thought Rathers's father died of alcohol poisoning, though he didn't sound sure. I want to look into his parents' deaths more. The father *did* have three DUIs and two drunk and disorderly charges, so it's probably safe to assume he *was* an alcoholic. There was also a record of an attack on Rathers when he was a kid. By a wolf."

"A wolf," Lou repeated.

Dani rotated her shoulders and stretched her neck from side to side. "He was in the hospital for a week afterward and they had to do reconstructive surgery on his jaw. Honestly, the whole thing reminded me of my finger."

Dani waved her finger at Lou, the one that Petrov had severed from her hand while torturing her. He'd intended to keep it as a trophy.

"But what was really interesting was what his high school guidance counselor wrote about him. He'd given Rathers several evaluations and thought he needed serious medical care. His theory was that Rathers's father had taken him out to the desert on *purpose* and had left him there to be eaten by wolves."

"Rathers told him that?" Lou asked.

"It's not clear if Rathers said that explicitly or if it was the counselor's theory. The counselor went so far as to do a home visit, thinking he might be able to uncover some abuse and get Rathers removed from the home. But when they went to his house, Rathers's mother stood up for her husband."

Lou crossed her arms. "Was she abusing him too?"

"The counselor thought so. The police had been called to the house at least twice over domestic violence concerns. Neighbors reported hearing his father shouting in the middle of the night and the sounds of glass breaking."

"It's a leap," Lou said after several beats of consideration. "From an alcoholic father to cannibalism."

"But he eats the fathers' hearts, right? What if they're not just fathers but also alcoholics? Is it possible he developed a fetish of some kind after the wolf attack?" Dani bit her lip.

"I spoke to him," Lou said.

Dani arched her brows. "When?"

Lou recounted slipping into Rathers's car. His strange monologue insisting that once something took a bite out of a person, they remained a part of that person forever.

"He kept asking me how I control the beast inside me."

Dani's eyes slid to Lou's shoulders, but she couldn't see the scar under the leather jacket. She'd seen it before in the gym, though, while she'd worked out with her and Piper.

Piper.

Her stomach dropped.

"Then it got really *weird*," Lou said.

Dani tried to focus on what Lou was saying. "Weirder than insisting you have an animal inside you?"

"He put on a muzzle," Lou said. "He started to restrain himself as if he were an actual dog. I watched too many horror movies as a kid. I thought he was going to transform in front of me."

Lou looked ready to burst out laughing.

"*Did* he start to turn into a wolf?" Dani asked cautiously. Because while she was a realist and had refused to believe in things like werewolves, it was hard not to relax some of her views after meeting someone like Lou. What she did in the darkness and in water was incredible. It made Dani wonder what else might be possible.

"No. He didn't sprout a single extra hair, from what I could tell," she said. "But the look in his eyes was different."

"You know," Dani said, "this is familiar. I've read about something like this. God, what was his name?"

Dani pinched her eyes shut. Then it came to her.

"Stumpp! There was a German farmer named Stumpp

from the fifteen hundreds who killed and ate people because he thought he was a werewolf. At least, I think he ate them. I'm not one hundred percent sure on that part. Did Rathers say anything else?"

"I left when he pulled out the muzzle," Lou said, and the deadpan seriousness of her delivery made Dani laugh.

"You look better," Lou said. "Your color is coming back."

Dani snorted halfheartedly. "Nothing like a cannibal to take your mind off your girlfriend's psycho ex."

21

Alan drove by their house twice. Both times, the child was sitting in the front yard on a blanket. An arrangement of plastic toys was spread before him. He picked up a truck and threw it down. The mother fussed with the hat on his head, positioning it to better protect his face from the sun. It was a nice house. Two stories, a brick façade on its front facing the street. Cheap vinyl siding everywhere else.

Always gotta put your best face forward, he thought bitterly.

His childhood home had been like that too.

Only it had never been *his* home. Not really. His father had made that perfectly clear.

When he passed their address for the third time, the mother looked up, a question in her eyes.

He stopped the car on the street, right in the middle of the road, and rolled down the window.

"I'm sorry to bother you," he called out, forcing his smile into his voice. "But I seem to be lost. My friend lives on Shadowmoss. Is that close to here?"

The woman's face relaxed but not as much as he would have wanted. "It's back that way."

She pointed in the opposite direction of where his car was headed. "You have to veer right at the curve rather than follow the road on through. You might not have noticed that the name of the road is different for that little part."

He had noticed. He'd driven through this neighborhood at least twenty times in the past week, at all hours of the day and night. How else would he have known there was a Shadowmoss Road in this subdivision to begin with?

He looked over his shoulder in the direction she'd pointed. "My bad! I should pay better attention to where I'm going, huh?"

Her friendly smile wilted at its edges, and he wondered if she would recognize him from La Casa del Diablo. She'd seemed pretty occupied by the baby, but he had to be careful. He wasn't wearing his work uniform, at least.

"Thanks for your help," he said, and pressed on the gas, pulling out of her line of sight.

At the end of the street, he looked in the rearview mirror.

She was gathering her son up from the blanket and carrying him into the house. When she turned toward the door, she glanced his way again, the frown on her face hardening.

Tonight, he thought as he turned on his blinker and eased his car out into the flow of traffic.

It had better be tonight.

LOU SUGGESTED THAT DANI CALL INTO WORK FOR THE afternoon, and it seemed she needed little encouragement. However, Lou didn't want to sit in her apartment with the real estate folder staring back at her. It had been bad enough that Dani had kept insisting that it was embarrassing for *her* to fall apart in front of Lou and how Lou must never struggle with strong emotions.

Tell that to the guy whose brains I blew out, she thought. And for what reason? All because Konstantine had given her a folder with some property listings in it?

I also get upset, she wanted to tell her. *I just hide it better.*

But Lou hadn't known how to tell her that without making it sound like an accusation or bragging.

Once Dani's tears dried up and her breath was steady again, Lou offered to take her to Boise. Maybe there they could search the library archives for obituaries or news stories that would give a more accurate account of what had happened to Rathers's parents.

Lou kept seeing his eyes wide with fear as he forced the leather bit between his teeth and sealed his mouth shut.

The Boise Public Library looked a little like Lou's old high school in Oak Park. A boxy brick building with bright, cheerful displays stacked in the windows in order to encourage patrons to come inside.

As soon as Lou stepped through the front door, a nostalgic feeling overtook her.

She remembered this smell. Instantly, she was back in St. Louis with her father. Six years old, holding his hand as he led her to the circulation desk and helped her get her very first library card.

He'd not been a reader, her father. But he'd loved that *she* loved books and encouraged that love whenever he could.

"She said it's downstairs," Dani said, crossing back to Lou from the large circulation desk.

"What is?" Lou asked, snapping out of her thoughts.

"The archives. There's even microfilm of the news stories from before the internet. I *love* microfilm."

"Nerd," Lou said.

The librarian behind the desk gave Lou a wary look.

She wondered if the woman knew Lou was packing. She didn't think so. Lou had perfected the art of concealment.

Maybe it was the leather jacket and the mirrored shades. It didn't matter. Lou had accepted long ago that some people just didn't like the look of her, and there was little she could do about it.

The library's basement wasn't as well lit as the main floor and lobby. Probably because there were no windows, only the flickering overhead lights.

"My god, it looks like a horror movie waiting to happen down here," Dani said.

Lou snorted. "You read my mind."

Though she couldn't remember which movie she was thinking of. There had been an occult researcher and an unsolved mystery. And the killer had been a ghost. Lou remembered that part because she'd spent the better part of the night wondering how she would handle a killer ghost herself. When neither guns nor Jabbers could help her and even the possibility that her slipping wouldn't provide her with escape—she didn't like it.

Lou was back to running through the scenarios of such an encounter while Dani lost herself in the microfilms.

Every few seconds the machine clicked and whirled as Lou stretched out on the scratchy loveseat that looked like it belonged in a 1970s office, with its tweed fabric and stiff wooden arms.

Over two hours had passed before Dani's head snapped up. "I think I've got something."

Lou rose and came to where Dani sat.

"Just look in here," Dani said.

Lou didn't bother to tell her she knew how to use microfilm. Or that she had, in fact, spent months in a library basement just like this one, looking at the stories about her own parents' murders.

As she pressed her eye to the view finder, a bold headline came into focus.

Husband Beats Wife to Death. Attempts to Murder Son.

There were headshots of all three of them, the mother, the father, and Rathers—the cannibal.

Though he wasn't a cannibal yet. He was a fourteen-year-old boy.

A fourth photo, of the three of them together, looked like it had been taken in a studio. There was the vague textured background and the posing, the father's hand on his son's shoulder. Not a single genuine smile in sight.

Lou blinked, and for a second she felt like she saw her face—twelve-year-old Louie—looking back at her instead of Rathers.

A memory surfaced, one she hadn't replayed in a long time.

The white flash of a gun going off in her parents' bedroom. The sound of a wine glass breaking. The back gate flying open as Angelo Martinelli stepped into view, his gun raised and pointed at them. Her father lifting her and throwing her into the pool, counting on her ability to slip through water to save his daughter's life.

Lou's heart had been broken when her father died. When she'd lost the only family and home she'd ever known, it had left a wound in her that never fully healed, or so Lucy had told her. Her aunt claimed that was why Lou had felt compelled to hunt down everyone who'd betrayed him.

Had it been different for Rathers? When his home had never been safe, his parents never loving, had it felt more like liberation the moment they were gone?

Or was he still looking for ways to fill a hole inside him? Was it the same hole that Lou knew all too well herself?

I could be him, she thought. *I could have lost myself in the darkness.*

"So Rathers's father didn't die of alcohol poisoning—that was a lie. It says he hanged himself to avoid going to prison for killing his wife, but what if it was Rathers? It wouldn't be the first time a killer's first murder was mistaken for an accident."

Lou pushed herself away from the machine. "No, it wouldn't be."

KING WAS BEGINNING TO FEEL GOOD ABOUT HIMSELF again. With the help of three coffees, he'd spent the morning catching up on the casework he'd neglected. He'd made progress on everything that he *could* make progress on and reported to everyone he *could* report to. There was a pending interview that a witness had yet to agree to and the DA office hadn't been able to get back to him yet with the details on their end, but King didn't take that personally. Beth was one of the busiest people he'd ever met. If she had to deprioritize one of their hand-offs for some reason, he was sure it was for a good reason.

By the time 4:30 rolled around, he was starting to think about what he wanted for dinner. He'd finally decided he wanted gumbo and maybe some fried chicken from the chicken shack up the road when the bell rang and Piper strode in.

"Hey," he said. "How's the shop?"

She hesitated. And if King wasn't mistaken, she also flicked her eyebrows.

"It's fine," she squeezed out, along with a tight smile. But her words didn't match her body language.

"Mel okay?" he pressed. Because it wasn't beneath Piper to lie to protect Mel. She'd done it before.

"She's fine," she said. This, at least, rang true.

Not Mel, then.

It was close enough to the end of the day that he was about to close down his computer and head out, but the storage closet door opened and Lou walked out with Dani behind her.

"Look who's here," King said, leaning back in his seat. "It's a regular party."

Only it wasn't a party. Or at least, King hadn't been to a party where the tension was this high in a long time. It had happened once when Brasso had run into two of his girl-friends at the same time, but King couldn't be sure what was playing out here.

"Hey," Dani said with a cold bite in her voice that King was ninety percent sure wasn't directed at him.

"Hey," Piper returned, and the tips of her ears were turning red. "Where have you guys been?"

"Boise. We were working on the cannibal case," Lou said.

Lou, at least, didn't look any different. Then again, her sunglasses were down, covering her eyes, so maybe she was hiding something too. It was moments like this that he wished he had Lady with him. The Belgian Malinois's need for belly rubs would adequately diffuse this situation.

Whatever this situation was.

"Tell me about the cannibal," King said, very aware that Piper was standing between him and the door and neither Dani nor Piper appeared to be getting any closer to each other.

"We know his name, where he works, and some of his backstory," Dani said. She was using her reporter voice, but he didn't think it was for his benefit. They'd worked together too much for her to fall back on formalities for his sake.

Every few seconds, one would cast a furtive glance at the other.

I feel like I'm in a regency romance, he thought, one in which glance choreography was the only means for a couple to communicate.

"Do we have a motive?" he asked.

"Maybe," Lou said, and proceeded to give him a lengthy explanation of what they'd learned about Rathers and his past. It was quite the speech for Lou. "He might be targeting alcoholic fathers who still live with their families. His father was an abusive drunk, so he might be playing out some revenge fantasy."

King accepted this assessment. Lou would know about revenge fantasies.

"What do you think our next move should be?" Dani asked.

"If you tell a courtroom what you just told me, they'll go for the insanity plea. A beast made him do it? Drunk and abusive father, murdered mother. Even if his father didn't leave him in the desert, he did try to kill him the same night he killed his wife. The cannibalism is wild enough to put most people off, but his past might garner more sympathy than we want."

Piper threw up her hands. "Just because someone murders your parents doesn't mean you can go around killing people. Plenty of people lose family, and they don't become psycho killers."

Dani and King looked at Lou at the same time.

Piper's cheeks went crimson. "I mean, sometimes it's okay. It's not like you eat people."

Lou snorted.

King tried to steer the conversation back to work. "If they manage to get the insanity plea, they'll lock him up, but I don't know if that's punishment enough." He looked to Lou. "Would you take him from an asylum?"

"If I did, they'd think he'd escaped and was on the loose,"

Lou said, her eyes still hidden and her hands resting in her pockets.

"Then the police would waste resources hunting for a dead man instead of protecting the living," Dani added.

"So we don't want the insanity plea, but we also want to make sure they know the families were avenged. It's a tricky one."

"Do you have someone in the Boise area who can break this open?"

"No," Dani said. "My nearest contact is in Vegas."

"Who's in Vegas?" Piper asked.

"An ex," Dani said. "You know all about exes, don't you?"

Oh shit.

King stood up. "I think the three of you can finish this without me. Let me know what you decide and if you need any help. I'll see if I've got a contact in Boise, or if there's a tip line we can use. Lou, you've got one ear to the ground, right? If he tries to make a move?"

"I do," Lou said.

He gave her a nod. "Then I'll leave you to it."

Whatever was going on, King knew one thing. He was too old.

"See you all tomorrow," he said, gathering up his things and pushing in his chair. "Lock up behind me, will you?"

22

When Lou appeared in the corner of his office, Konstantine had already resolved to not mention moving in together again. If she wanted to live with him, she would tell him.

I will prove to her it doesn't matter to me either way, he thought. *I am a calm and sensible man.*

He smiled for her. "There you are. I want your help with something."

She stilled. "Do I need more ammo than what I have on me now?"

"Hopefully we will need no ammo at all, *amore mio.*" He rose and gathered the papers on his desk into a neat pile. Then he put a large book on top of it to keep them down.

"Where do you want to go?" she asked, crossing the room and stopping just short of him.

"I want to see into that house, the one Gabriella goes to with the medicine," he said. He quickly filled her in on what he'd learned from Isadora. "I want to see her situation with my own eyes."

"Most houses have closets and bathrooms," she said wryly. "But we might be limited to what we can learn by hiding. You can't always see or hear much from a closet."

She leaned her weight against his desk. If she was agitated by his earlier proposal, she was hiding it well. Of course, Louie Thorne always hid it well. She made him look like the emotional one.

It wasn't like I asked you to marry me, he thought.

Yes, but only because she already said she'd refuse, a second voice countered.

Aloud, he said, "It won't hurt to try. Are you free now?"

She stepped forward and slid her arms around his waist. Her lips were on the curve of his collarbone, her breath soft on his neck. He wondered if they should postpone this mission long enough to make love to her on this desk. They'd done it before, so he didn't need to wonder if it was strong enough to hold them.

No.

Stefano had texted him ten minutes ago and said the girl was in the house now. If Konstantine wasted so much as an hour on his own pursuits, he might lose track of her again.

Besides, there was always later tonight.

"Stop breathing on my neck," he said finally. "Or we won't leave this office."

Lou kissed his throat. "Are you sure you want to go now?"

He pulled back and looked into her eyes. "Are you distracting me so that Gabriella can keep her secret?"

"No," Lou said, and as if to prove it, she chose that moment to pull him through the shadows. It was as if the walls had all rushed in on him from every side. Now they were less than a foot from his face, no matter which way he turned. Plaster pressed into his back, and the door in front of him was open the smallest crack.

A small closet. Very small. Barely enough room for the two of them.

Lou had been right. He could see nothing except for the light seeping in around the door.

He heard the slur of Italian. The hatefulness and cursing that spewed from an old man's raspy voice. That voice broken only by the occasional punctuation of a girl's soft replies.

Lou moved first, her hand going toward the handle.

Konstantine wasn't sure how much of it she understood. She'd picked up some Italian before they'd ever met in her quest to find and kill his brother Angelo. She'd learned more since knowing him, though she'd never spoken more than a word or two with him.

Lou's hand hesitated on the handle, his laid on top of hers. It was hard for him to see her in the darkness. The sliver of light from the doorframe cut a line across her right cheek.

Konstantine kept listening, his eyes on her lit cheek. But he heard no master plans. No familiar names or dangers. He heard only an old man hurling abuse at a little girl.

Konstantine leaned close to Lou's ear and whispered, "Take me to the front door."

She looked like she might refuse him, but his hand squeezed hers and the closet fell away.

The smell of damp stone and the flowers of early evening sprang up around him as he lifted his fist and rapped once on the door. Hard.

"What if they don't answer?" Lou asked beside him. She turned and looked up and down the street, her hands in her pockets.

"Then we'll go back through the closet. But this would be better," he said.

He lifted his fist to pound on the door for a second, third, and fourth time. On the fifth, the door swung open and there was Gabriella, her face pinched in fury.

She'd clearly been ready to tell off whoever had dared disturb them.

Only, when she saw Konstantine and then Lou, she went to slam the door in his face.

Lou was faster. She had her hand braced against the door, forcing it open before Gabriella could get it shut.

"*Che mi vuoi fare?*" Gabriella asked.

"*Parla con lui,*" he replied.

She tried to push harder against the door, but Lou's arm didn't even flex. The door remained immobile.

"Don't be scared," Lou told her in English.

When she only looked back at them, Konstantine said it again in Italian.

Then the girl was running up the stairs away from them, to the green door at the top of the landing.

Lou entered the apartment first, and then Konstantine. They followed the sound of the old man's voice and the low hum of a television to a living room.

Whatever he might have had in his youth, the old man had lost it now. He was short, compressed, with a large belly that rested on his knees. His shirt had sweat stains and his skin sagged, sallow. The hair on his head—if he could call it hair—was only a few gray wisps. His dark eyes were bright but menacing and his mouth hung slightly ajar. A breathing tube ran beneath his nose and across his upper lip.

Konstantine noted the closet on the other side of the room and realized where they'd been.

"*Che cazzo vuoi?*" the old man said, looking from Konstantine to Lou.

"I want to make you an offer," Konstantine said. It wasn't until that moment that he was sure of what he would do. "*Gabriella è tua nipote?*"

"So what if she is my granddaughter?" he asked.

"I work for a prestigious boarding school in Milan. L'Istituto Milano. *Poichè Gabriella ha mostrato del talento, le vorrei offrire un posto nell'istituto.*"

"He's lying!" Gabriella cried. "*Non è vero niente!*"

"I don't care if he wants to sell you to a brothel!" the old man snapped at her. "Shut up."

Gabriella pressed her lips shut, but her glare remained fixed on Konstantine.

"She has talent. *Talento*," the old man said, and laughed bitterly. "I don't believe you. Don't you know what she is?"

Konstantine said nothing. He knew that whether he spoke or didn't speak, the old man would say his piece.

"She's been with me for ten years, ever since her whore of a mother dropped her off on my doorstep. My wife wanted her, so fine. *E va bene!* We keep her. But my wife has been dead for three years and I can't stand the sight of her. Every day she looks more and more like her whore of a mother. She comes and goes all hours of the day and night. She brings home money. How? From where does she get the money? No. I know where. I know what she is. The daughter of a whore. I knew where Greta was all those years. I knew when she turned up here, with a child but no man."

He nodded at Konstantine.

"Maybe you're her father, for all I know. If you are, then you owe me money."

"I'm not her father," Konstantine said. "But I will give you money if you allow us to take her to the school. And once she's enrolled, you will never see her again."

"Please, Nonno." Gabriella threw herself on her knees before the old man. It was hard to understand her pleading through the tears.

As weak as the old man was, he still had the strength to shove her away. "Get off me. I told you, *non mi importa se è un magnaccia!* I'd rather have the money than have you."

Konstantine's guts hardened to stone. He was suddenly very glad he didn't have a pistol on him at that moment. The old man might be a sick, cold-hearted bastard, but it was clear that—for whatever reason—Gabriella still loved him.

"How much?" he asked. "*Quanto mi vuoi dare?*"

"How much do you want?" Konstantine asked, unfeeling.

"At least twenty thousand euros," he said.

"That is quite a lot of money."

"I am sure she will earn it back," the old man said. "At your *school*."

"Fifteen," Konstantine countered. It wasn't that he couldn't pay the money. Konstantine had other reasons for keeping up this charade.

"Done. And this *school* in Milan, it is paid for, is it?" the old man asked. "Books, tuition? I won't be receiving any *bills* from you?"

"No," Konstantine said. "You will never hear from us again."

"Can I get that in writing?" he asked.

"Yes. But I want any papers you have for the child. Her records, her medical—"

The old man hissed. "I don't have anything like that! I told you. Her whore of a mother dropped her here and then left. She didn't even leave a stitch of clothing for her except for what was on her back."

Gabriella had begun to cry.

"Get your things," Konstantine said. "Whatever you want to bring with you, go and get it."

She disappeared from sight.

"I will come back tonight with the money and the written agreement," Konstantine said. "You'll be here."

The old man gestured at himself. "Do I look like I get around much to you?"

Konstantine said nothing. He caught sight of the pills on the side table.

"Are you sure you will be all right without her?" Konstantine asked.

The man followed his gaze and snorted. "With one less mouth to feed and fifteen thousand euros? Somehow I'll manage."

Gabriella appeared with a small backpack on her shoulders. Her eyes were red and her cheeks were wet.

"Is that everything?" Konstantine asked her.

She nodded, but Konstantine found it hard to believe that all the needs of a thirteen-year-old girl could be found in one small backpack.

"If there's something else, I'll get it when I come back with the money," Konstantine told the old man.

Before he could acknowledge this, Gabriella threw her arms around the old man's neck and whispered something too low for Konstantine to hear.

For a moment, it looked like the old man would soften. But he only pushed Gabriella away.

"*Go on*," he said. "With any luck, I'll be dead before you are old enough to turn up with a baby of your own."

Downstairs, Konstantine placed one hand on the door but didn't open it. To Lou, he said, "Is it dark enough here?"

She replied by pulling them from the apartment's stairwell into his office at the church.

With a little gasp, Gabriella moved away from them. She turned and regarded Lou with fear, her hands covering her mouth.

"Have Matteo and the other boys told you about La Strega?" Konstantine asked her.

Still covering her mouth, she gave a furious little nod.

"Then listen closely. You will live here from now on. You

are never to go back to that house or to pick up his medication. Do you understand?"

She uncovered her mouth, but her eyes remained the size of espresso saucers. "*Sì.*"

"You will sleep in the dorms again, in the same bed I gave you before. I might find you a room of your own soon, but for now, it will have to do. You already know the mealtimes. You *will* go to school, and you will stay there for the *entire* day. If you try to sneak out and wander around the city again, La Strega will come and get you and you will be punished. You are never to go to that apartment again. Do you understand?"

"*Sì,*" she said, but she seemed less happy about these instructions.

He nodded to her backpack. "Is that really all you have? No clothes? No toys? No books?"

"I hid some of my things here," she told him, not meeting his eyes.

Konstantine laughed. "Of course you did. Get them out of hiding and put them above your bed, in the cabinets, properly. I will ask Matilda to look at your clothes and see if you need anything, so don't be upset when she asks to see your stuff."

"*Sì.*"

"That's all for now. Go find Matteo and eat something," he said, dismissing her.

She ran from the room with her backpack slapping against her back. She only cast one last look over at Lou as she went. Lou winked at her.

Once they were alone, Lou asked, "He would have sold her to anyone, wouldn't he?"

"*Sì,*" Konstantine said. "He did not care."

"And the things he said..." Lou began.

"Be glad your Italian is not any better than it is, *amore*

mio," he said, his own anger rising again. He pulled out his phone and began to compose a message.

"Who are you texting?" she asked, leaning her weight against his desk.

"Stefano. I have a job for him."

Stefano appeared in the doorway, an unlit cigarette in one hand and a lighter in the other, a moment later. "Boss?"

Konstantine wrote an address on a sheet of paper and slid it across his desk to him. Stefano lifted it, read the address.

"This is the house you had me watch earlier," he said in English, clearly for Lou's benefit.

"I want you to go to the address with fifteen thousand in a briefcase. When an old man on oxygen answers, I want you to show him the money and tell him I sent you to collect the girl's things. Once you are in the apartment, you will send him on vacation."

Stefano's brows lifted. "And the money?"

"Take it to our bank and ask Stella to open an account in the name of Gabriella Luna Barone."

"Like Matteo's account?" Stefano asked.

"Yes, exactly," Konstantine said. He took a seat behind his desk. "Search the apartment for any important papers and photographs. I want everything and anything important that might belong to Gabriella."

"I'll take Fausto, Filippe, Luca. Maybe Rosario."

Konstantine waved his hand. "Take whoever you want. I only ask that you be discreet and clean up after yourself. I'll buy the apartment tomorrow and sell it next week. Contact Sofia and tell her."

"I hope that's not the apartment you want us to live in," Lou said.

Konstantine laughed, surprised by her joke. "No. I want to give you something far grander."

Lou said nothing to this. Her silence filled him with dread and tension.

"Have you—" he began.

She cut him off. "It's a shame."

"A shame?" he asked.

She pushed her fingers into Konstantine's hair, and relief washed through him. "That I won't be the one to kill him."

23

As Dani closed the apartment door behind them, Piper's heart was pounding. She didn't want to do this. She did *not* want to tell Dani that Scarlett had kissed her. She'd seen Dani get mad before, mostly at her mother, but even secondhand, it was a terrifying experience. Piper wasn't sure she could handle being on the receiving end of that fury.

It's best to rip the bandage off, she told herself. *The longer the wait, the more I'll drive myself nuts.*

"I should—" Dani began.

"Scarlett kissed me," Piper blurted.

Dani blinked at her.

Once the words were out, Piper couldn't stop herself. "I know you didn't want me to see her, but I knew something was going on and—"

"Wait," Dani tried to interject. "I—"

"And Mel was like, 'This will end badly if you don't handle it,' and that freaked me out, so I just—"

"Piper—"

"—because you're like the *best* thing that's ever happened to me and if anything—"

"*Piper!*" Dani grabbed both sides of her face and smushed her cheeks together until Piper's lips puckered like a fish's.

It was impossible to speak when her face was in this shape, so Piper had no choice but to shut up.

Dani took a deep breath. "I know she kissed you. I saw it."

She released Piper's face.

"Wait, what?"

"She texted me, or maybe one of her friends did. I don't know. It was a blocked number. But whoever texted me did so *before* she went to the shop. I'm sure it was because they knew what she was going to do and wanted me to see it."

"That devious little—" Piper began, but she wasn't sure how to end the sentence without using a really mean word.

"Honestly, I'm more upset about the SUV."

Piper took a step back and pointed at her. "I knew it! I *knew* she did something to the SUV. You lied about the belt thingy or whatever you said because you know I don't know anything about cars."

Dani didn't seem to hear her. She rubbed her forehead. "Or maybe *The Herald*'s window was the worst. I'm just glad no one at work saw it. God, that would've been so embarrassing."

"Wait, *what*? She came to your work?"

Dani went to the sofa and collapsed against it. Piper's heart sank. This wasn't the fiery, passionate Dani she knew and loved. This Dani looked exhausted, the bags under her eyes pronounced.

Look at her. This is all because of me. This is my fault.

"Please tell me what's happened," Piper said, taking a seat beside her. "I want to know how bad it was for you. Scarlett wouldn't tell me."

Dani snorted. "I'm surprised she didn't want to brag about the lengths she'd go to to get you back."

Piper took her hands. "You're scaring me. You know I'll just imagine the worst, most horrible things I can think of unless you tell me what really happened."

Dani searched her face before sighing. "Fine. All right."

Dani told Piper about the months of shoulder checks and snide comments on the Quarter's streets when Dani had the misfortune of crossing Scarlett's path. She told her about the spilled drink at the Wild Cat, the extensive damage to the SUV, and the soap marker insults on the window at work. She told her everything, and Piper listened.

Piper had no choice but to listen, even though each new confession weighed heavier and heavier on her heart.

It was worse than I thought. Piper's stomach turned. *So much worse than I thought.*

Dani ended with her attempt to meet Scarlett at work and resolve the problem like an adult.

Piper grimaced. "Was the car thing before or after you went to the praline shop?"

"I honestly don't know. After, I think. Why does it matter?"

Dani's lips flattened with irritation.

Piper squeezed her hands. "It doesn't. She should have never done any of that. It's just that I know she's really sensitive about people seeing her at work. It's like a complex. That's no reason for her to take it out on you. I'm the one who stopped talking to her and I'm the one who wants to be with you. You probably don't want to be with me anymore, but—"

Dani pulled her hands away. "Are you kidding me?"

There was the fiery, passionate woman that Piper knew.

"I'm not worth all this trouble," Piper admitted.

Now it was Dani who was squeezing her hands. "If you

think I'm going to give up on us because of some second-rate bullying—*no*." She shook her head. "No way. My mother couldn't get us to break up and she's *way* scarier than Scarlett."

"You're right about that." Piper rubbed her thumbs across Dani's knuckles. It felt so good to be connected again, with all the secrets and avoidance removed between them.

"I'm just tired," Dani said with a little frown. "But that doesn't mean I'm giving up. I just don't have a good solution that doesn't involve asking Lou to make her disappear."

Piper fell back against the sofa cushions, lost in thought. Slowly, the lines on her face smoothed out.

"What are you thinking?" Dani asked. "I don't know what that look on your face means."

Piper rubbed her neck. "I'm just relieved. I thought you didn't like me anymore. I even got a tutor for Spanish 'cause I thought it was one less thing I could burden you with."

"You got a Spanish tutor? From where?"

"This guy at the gym has a sister who wants to be a teacher. So I'm going to meet with her twice a week for lessons." Piper pointed at her. "See! Don't act like you aren't glad."

Dani spared her a crooked smile. "It's not that I don't want you to learn Spanish. I think it's wonderful that you're learning it, and I can't wait to speak it with you. *Someday.* It's just a lot harder teaching someone than I thought it would be."

"I'll keep my appointment with the person who *wants* to be a teacher, then," Piper said. "What about your car?"

"I'm supposed to pick it up Friday."

They adjusted themselves on the sofa, stretching long so they could face one another.

"I feel like I should pay for it. How much was the damage?"

"I don't need your money." Dani nuzzled close, putting her face in Piper's neck. "I need to solve the problem of Scarlett."

This was probably not the right time to tell Dani that Scarlett had declared war when she'd stormed out of Mel's shop, promising to make Piper regret rejecting her. It would only be a matter of time before Scarlett formed some new, horrible plan of attack.

For a long time, they only lay there in the growing darkness, the light outside their window turning from the soft orange of late afternoon to the purple of twilight.

Dani reached up and pulled the blanket off the back of the sofa and covered them both with it.

She'd almost dozed off in their soft, warm cocoon when an idea sprang fully formed into Piper's mind. She gasped, excited.

"What?" Dani asked. "What is it?"

"You know, Scarlett is *really* superstitious. Like, she screams bloody murder in haunted houses and can't watch scary movies without peeing herself. She'll have nightmares for days. And cemeteries scare her more than anything."

"I hope you're not going to ask me to dress up like a ghost and jump out from behind a tombstone or something," Dani said. "Because I'd like to hold on to the last of my dignity, if it's all the same to you."

"No, not you," Piper said, adjusting the blanket over Dani's shoulder. "But who do we know that can be *pretty* spooky when she wants to be?"

LOU'S COMPASS WASN'T WRONG. IT WAS STRANGE THAT *HE* would call for her, but she knew better than to doubt what she felt. She pushed away from her lunch plate—a salad with grilled chicken, pineapple, and creamy dressing—and stepped into her converted linen closet.

When she pushed the door open again, she was back in the apartment she'd seen earlier that day. Only now the old man, Gabriella's abuser, was sitting on his sofa, his eyes open and unseeing. A single bullet hole had been punched out of the center of his forehead.

Stefano was standing over him, a pistol in one hand, a half-exploded throw pillow in the other. Feathers were still raining down from the air, a few clinging to his solid black suit and leather gloves.

"If you wanted to have a slumber party or a pillow fight you could've just sent an invitation," Lou told him, unable to hide her amusement.

He turned and looked at her. "It actually works. The way Matteo described it."

She wasn't sure what he meant.

He added, "If I ask you to come in my mind, you come."

Matteo has more self-restraint than I've given him credit for then, Lou thought. Because the boy was one of her biggest fans. If he knew how to reach her so easily but had yet to use this knowledge, then he was showing her a great deal of respect.

She'd have to pay him a visit soon.

"What do you want?" she asked. "I was in the middle of lunch."

"Oh, you eat?" he teased. "I thought you only fed on the souls of bad men."

"Maybe I do," she said.

He snorted, then quickly hid his amusement as if it were something to be ashamed of.

He wears his disdain like a badge of honor. He never wants to be too pleased with the world.

"The others will be here in a minute. Before they arrive, I wanted your help with the body."

"Doesn't Konstantine have his own methods for getting rid of bodies?" Lou was certain he did, as he'd never asked Lou for her help before.

"Your way is easier than dragging his fat ass down all those stairs and throwing him into a trunk, isn't it?"

Lou admitted that it was.

"Then I ask you to please help me," he said. "And in the future, I will do something for you."

"Like what? I won't need your help with any bodies."

"Whatever you ask," he said. Then he quickly added, "Within reason."

It amused her that he didn't want to give her too much leverage.

But the fact was Lou wanted to take the old man to La Loon. She hadn't understood all of the insults he'd hurled at the girl, but she knew a bastard when she saw one. If she couldn't be the one to put a bullet in his head, she'd love to watch Jabbers rip his guts out.

If satisfying her own desires also got a favor from Stefano, so be it.

"I'll do it," she said. She hauled the body from the sofa as if he weighed little more than a child.

Stefano's brows rose. "You're very strong."

She couldn't hide her smile. "Remember that."

A rough knock came at the door downstairs. He turned toward the sound.

When he turned back, she was gone.

24

Rathers was hiding in the trunk of his car. He'd parked on the neighborhood's quiet, tree-lined street in the early evening. Then, pretending to climb into the back to get something, he'd lowered the backseat and crawled into the trunk, before replacing the seat to its original position. This way, should anyone pass by or look in, like a police officer, they would see no one at all. With any luck, they would assume he was a guest at any one of these houses.

This was not the first time he'd used the trunk in this way. He was comfortable in the confined space, even if it was a little cramped for his height.

Through the crack created by the trunk's lid, he watched the last of the afternoon light melt away. Then even the darkest blue became black.

Still he waited. Time passed.

He didn't dare to consider leaving the trunk until the air had grown uncomfortably cool and he hadn't heard so much as the squeak of a tire in hours.

He checked his clock. It was after eleven.

He pressed the button on the back of the seat and lowered it once more. He peeked out of the windows slowly, looking up and down the street for any eyes that might catch sight of him.

There were none. The street was dark. A few empty cars sat parked along the curving road or safely in their driveways.

He scanned the walkways and shadows for a second time, but saw no one.

Not even her.

Most of the families had already called it a night and had gone to bed, their windows dark.

The house he wanted had one light still on in an upstairs window. Through it, he could see the father at a desk, in front of a computer, looking at the screen in front of him, his brow pinched in concentration.

Rathers watched him work, looking away only to check on the street and other houses as necessary.

After eleven, the mother came to the door and said something. Rathers could see her in a plaid bathrobe, her hair pulled up on top of her head. No makeup.

Whatever the father's reply was, she hadn't like it. She turned away, red-cheeked, and disappeared from Rathers's sight until a light flicked on at the other end of the house.

It was only on for a few seconds before it went out again.

The waiting went on.

After midnight, a pack of raccoons scurried past his car in the direction of a solitary trash can left on the side of the street.

He ignored them. Let them enjoy their hunt. He had his own.

It was after one when the office light finally clicked off.

Rathers's breath hitched but he didn't move.

Several seconds later, another light clicked on and there was the momentary flash of a tiled wall before the curtain was drawn. The father took his time in the bathroom, and twenty minutes later, he pulled back the curtain, revealing his wet hair.

He turned off the light.

The last light to turn on in the house that night was the bedroom light.

Rathers saw the husband walk into the room shirtless, his face hard, and the light clicked off again.

Rathers checked the clock one last time.

It was after two in the morning when he finally opened the car door. He stepped out with a black case in one hand, leaving his other free.

Touching the muzzle fixed across his face for good luck, he shut the car door behind him with only the faintest of clicks. Then he was crossing the moonlit road and strolling up the front walkway as if he had an appointment at this house, with this family.

But he didn't knock or ring the bell. Instead, he turned left, tracing the perimeter until he found the back patio.

The back door was unlocked.

When he pushed it open, somewhere in the house, a robotic voice chimed, "Back door."

He stepped into the dim kitchen, noting the way the light fell across the clean countertops and table. Noted the cheerful prints of flowers and fruit on the wall. The closed cabinets that gleamed with moonlight.

He stood there in the kitchen and listened to the silence of the house, the swell and fall of it.

He took four steps before the kitchen opened on a formal dining room. Around it were six carved chairs and a bright red table runner.

It was perfect.

Somewhere in the house, a bed creaked. He listened to cautious steps on the floor above. Someone was coming.

It didn't matter.

They were ready to begin.

LOU STOOD ON THE SHORES OF HER NOVA SCOTIAN LAKE, her hair dripping wet. She'd only just bent down to collect her leather jacket off the rock where she'd placed it to keep it dry when her compass snagged.

One hand grabbed her jacket. The other went to her gun.

But the threat wasn't here. Nor was it a familiar energy radiating toward her down the line. No one was calling her.

This was an alarm bell.

Lou had wanted to take a shower after throwing Stefano's kill on the shores of La Loon, but it would have to wait. Something was happening.

She pulled on her leather jacket and adjusted her pistols, one for each hand.

The cold was just beginning to dry the water droplets along her skin and nip at the back of her neck as she stepped from the shadows beneath a large evergreen. Its Christmas fragrance followed her through the dark as she moved thousands of miles to the west.

When her feet were on solid ground again, she was in a living room. The furniture sat in shades of gray as moonlight fell through the open curtains. A child was crying. The loud, desperate wails of pain. A woman was also screaming, but it was muffled, as if something might be in her mouth or covering it.

Someone was also humming a tune, a haunting lullaby, and this music, more than the screaming, chilled Lou's spine.

The guns warmed in Lou's hands as she took one step, then another, across the carpeted floor. Then the living room ended, and she was at the threshold of the dining room.

Her heart sputtered in her chest.

A man was sitting at the table with his head down as if asleep.

Or maybe he was dead.

Blood coated the side of his skull from a considerable blow.

The screaming baby was in the center of the table. It had been wrapped tightly in some kind of rope and laid on a serving platter in the middle of a red table runner.

Beside the table, Alan Rathers had the child's mother on the ground, pinning her arms with his knees.

He had sewn one of her eyes shut with a bent needle and coarse black twine. Now he was working on the other. He was the one humming.

Lou would have been able to approach Rathers from behind and yank him off the woman if she hadn't rolled her half-sewn eye toward Lou at that moment.

Rathers looked up then, the spell cast by his preoccupation with his work broken. He wore his muzzle, the leather straps tight across his face.

Lou was so fascinated by the device she didn't see him pick up the knife. It was a large, angled blade, certainly made for a chef. It wasn't something a fighter would use.

He slid it across the woman's throat before Lou fired a bullet into his side, knocking him off of her. Lou dropped down beside the woman, trying to compress the wound with her free hand, but it was no use. The blood was pumping too fast and Lou would have to put her gun down in order to apply proper pressure.

She couldn't.

Rathers threw himself at Lou, knocking her onto the flat of her back.

He snarled and snapped around the muzzle, saliva escaping its edges and wetting her face.

She kicked him hard and he fell back, rocking the table and the baby on top of it.

The man who'd been resting his busted head on one end slumped from the chair and collapsed to the floor.

Before Lou could get to her feet, he was on her again. There was no humanity in Rathers's eyes. No recognition of her.

She felt as if she had a cougar, or a wild cat of some kind, trying to claw her eyes out. Lou tried to raise and point her gun at his head, but he slammed her wrist against the ground. Pain shot up her arm. Her wrist burned. She was forced to release her hold on the gun.

Then he had the knife in his hand again. He went for her throat, but she blocked this with her forearm, feeling the ice-hot fire of the blade cutting across her skin. She hissed and rocked her hips, managing to throw him off her.

He fell to the ground beside the burbling woman.

Lou bent to get her gun, and for a third time Rathers collided with her, this time throwing her against the dining room wall and pinning her there.

What the fuck is he on? Meth? Bath salts? What?

Lou tried to raise her gun hand to shoot him, but she couldn't get it high enough.

She rotated the gun in her hand and pulled the trigger blindly, shooting upward.

She didn't succeed in blowing the top off his skull, which was what she'd hoped for. Instead, she struck only the light that had kept the dining room in full illumination. The bulb and fixture exploded. Glass rained down on them and the baby screamed louder, its voice growing hoarse from the effort.

Despite the unnerving sound of the child screaming, Lou had what she needed.

It was finally dark enough.

Lou faded through the black. No doubt to Rathers it looked as if she'd simply vanished through the wall, only to reappear on the other side of the dining room table.

She didn't like it. This was a terrible position. She didn't want the baby between them.

He seemed to acknowledge the source of the wailing almost as soon as she did. They dove for the baby at the same time, but Lou was quicker.

She had the child in her arms and was gone before his knife buried itself in the table.

WHEN LOU APPEARED OUTSIDE THE EMERGENCY ROOM doors with the screaming, hog-tied toddler, the two nurses who'd been smoking in the shadows cried out.

"Take him," Lou said. "Make sure he's okay."

The nurses looked at Lou's wet hair, the blood pouring from one arm and drying along her hands, and then at the gun she held.

"Take *him*," she said again.

One of the nurses threw her cigarette down on the pavement and reached out for the child.

"Thank you," Lou said, and this seemed to scare them just as much as the baby.

"What the hell did you do to him?" the other nurse asked.

"It wasn't me," she said. And that's all the explanation they would get, because Lou was already stepping through the dark again.

She reappeared in the house, gun up and at the ready.

The dining room was quiet, perfectly still. The man was collapsed at her feet, glass glittering all around him. She kept her eyes and head up even as she bent to check his pulse.

It was erratic, but it was there.

Next, she checked the woman. Nothing. The halo of

blood around her head told Lou all she needed to know. There would be no saving her.

Lou stepped out of the dining room into the kitchen, her gun still up.

No Rathers.

He wasn't in the living room either.

A screech of tires sounded from the street outside, and she crossed to the curtain, pulling back the drapes in time to see a car tear up the street, driving way too fast for the hour.

Lou considered going after him. Considered melting through the dark once more and into the passenger seat of Rathers's car. She could pull the trigger and blow his brains out right then and there.

But the man with the erratic heartbeat might not have that long. And the child she'd just dropped off at the hospital was going to be an orphan if she didn't at least *try* to save him.

Lou holstered her gun and lifted the father off the carpeted floor, glass falling from the folds in his clothes.

There was no nurse to accept him when she appeared for the second time. Lou supposed they'd both gone inside with the baby.

No matter.

Lou had enough strength left to carry him through the doors of the emergency room herself.

25

R athers hobbled about his room. Back and forth, back and forth. He growled and tore at his hair. He caught sight of himself in the vanity mirror, saw the blood smeared along his face and his wide eyes.

I told you, I told you, I told you, the beast was chanting.

You can't trust her. She's not like us. She's not your friend. She's not—

His hip ached from where her bullet had grazed him. He could pull apart the tear in his pants and see the cut and scorched skin beneath. Blood soaked his clothes and the flesh looked tattered, but he would not die.

She shot me. She fucking shot me.

He pulled a lamp off its side table and hurled it across the room. It shattered against the wall.

He felt like his skin was sloughing off his body. He hadn't been able to complete the ritual. He hadn't been able to feed the beast or sate its hunger, and now the beast was awake, furious, and ravenous.

Its power and energy coursed through him but had no

outlet. Nowhere to go. So it churned and twisted inside him, unbearable.

He pulled his journal from the drawer and spread it on the vanity's tabletop with shaking hands.

Furiously, his pen scraped across the paper, blood smearing over the page as he wrote.

I have to find her. I have to speak to her. She doesn't understand she doesn't. And I saw—

He broke off, his trembling hand hovering above the open page.

He could hear the wolves howling. He could hear his own screams burning his small throat. He saw his father's taillights disappearing into the night as he called after him.

He hit his head again and again and again, trying to free himself from the memory and from that endless howling.

Why had she come? Why had it all gone wrong?

He'd lost the moment she turned off the lights, he realized.

When the lights had still been on, he'd been alone with his beast and the mother. He'd sung her the lullaby that she'd sung him as a child, before she became useless.

Bad mother, bad mother, bad mother, he scrawled across the page.

He'd sung the lullaby and it had worked. It had calmed the beast and himself and he had almost been ready to set her at the table and begin the preparation of the sacred meal.

Then everything changed.

Then she was there.

Why did she come? She didn't have to. She had no reason. It wasn't her family.

It was mine. It was mine!

Why did she have to, why did she—

He wiped the sweat from his brow.

He'd held his own against her. Or rather, the beast had.

Alan hadn't wanted the beast to hurt her. He'd tried to stop it, tried to hold it back, but he'd been so surprised at seeing her, so surprised to find his private moment interrupted.

She should've never stopped me. I would never. I wouldn't —Why I—

Then before he knew it, that beast was awake and in control. It had taken over his body the way it only ever did when Alan dared to remove the muzzle.

She had no right. That was my family. That was my—

He should've known the danger of letting her shoot out the light. He had been fine until he'd lost the light. Once the dining room had been given over to the darkness, the tide had turned against him.

Her beast must be one of darkness, he thought.

Slowly, his panicked scrawl evened out. The letters grew larger, looped more, and the hand that held the pen began to relax.

You know what to do, the beast wrote. *You don't have to be afraid of her. You know what to do with animals like her.*

He did.

He laid the pen down in the crease of the open journal and went to his dresser.

He opened the middle drawer and pulled out the row of sweaters hiding a box in the back.

He put the box on the bed, pushing open the lid to reveal a gun.

The gun itself wasn't so special, he knew that.

It was what else was in the box.

That's what would stop her.

That's what could bring down a beast.

Still he was angry. He was furious. He thought they had understood one another. He thought she was like him.

It hurt to be wrong.

He grabbed the remaining lamp off the second side table

and dashed it against the wall, tears staining the corners of his eyes.

The lamp shattered and a pair of fists beat on the wall in response.

"Quiet down in there or I'm gonna call the cops. Some of us have to fucking work in the morning, asshole!"

The killer checked the clock and saw that he still had a couple of hours before sunrise. Plenty of time to hunt a beast.

Rathers rose from the bed and slipped the gun into the waistband of his pants.

His gaze fell on the muzzle but shifted away almost as quickly.

There was no point in pretending now. No point in holding back when he needed to be a beast in order to destroy a beast.

He reached up behind his head and unfastened the strap. Relief washed through him as the leather fell away, as his jaw softened. Free.

He tossed it to the bed, forgotten.

He stepped into the corridor outside of his apartment and padded barefoot down the hallway to his neighbor's door. Blood from his wounded side dripped onto the carpet as he walked, leaving a trail in its fibers.

He knocked on the door once. Twice. Three times.

With a huff, his neighbor threw it open. She was young like him, her hair falling in braids over each shoulder, her glasses falling down her nose. She pushed them up.

"What the hell is wrong with you? Do you know what time it—"

He grabbed her by the throat and pushed her backwards into the apartment. He kicked the door shut behind him.

Before she could recover, before she could cry out, he sank his teeth into her throat.

· · ·

LOU STAYED AT THE HOSPITAL LONG ENOUGH TO CONFIRM that the child and its father would make it. It had taken over an hour before someone was willing to speak to her, and even then she'd overstayed her welcome. The blood on her, the visible holster, her guns. It had drawn the attention of the hospital security.

Lou recited the lies King had taught her, a vague script for situations like this when she couldn't help but be seen but also didn't want to reveal anything to the authorities. Just enough to give the impression that she was on the right side of the law, perhaps an undercover agent or cop, and that they need not look too closely at her.

This only bought her time, of course. Time for Lou to disappear into the shadows again. Time for Konstantine to scrub the videos and remove any trace of her existence.

It had worked.

She'd been allowed to stay in the waiting room until the nurses informed her that while the father had a brain bleed, he would recover. And that the child had broken his arm and there were rope burns on his skin where he'd struggled against the bindings, but otherwise, he would survive.

She'd only just thanked them for their time when the alarm bell went off inside her again.

Without thinking, Lou stepped from the hospital's shadow into an apartment with a gruesome sight.

Rathers was kneeling over a girl their age, his mouth bloodied from nose to chin. She was already dead, her mess of a throat emptying itself on her floral rug.

Lou had only a second to take this in before Rathers raised his gun and the bullet slammed into Lou.

She stumbled back, her head connecting with the wall. The room blurred and her arm where the bullet struck was on fire. He fired again and the plaster beside her head exploded, raining white dust down on her shoulder. Lucky for her, he was a terrible shot.

"You should've stuck with your knives," she said, and melted through the darkness.

When she reappeared, she grabbed the back of his hair and pulled.

Then the apartment was gone and they were left only to the night.

But she hadn't taken him to one of her lakes. Neither Alaska nor Nova Scotia.

I better not regret this, she thought. She wanted to keep him alive for the little boy she'd taken to the hospital tonight. When he was old enough to understand what happened to his mother, she wanted him to know who was responsible. She didn't want him to have a hole in his heart the way Rathers had.

The way she had.

Yet she'd be lying to herself if she said she didn't want to tear out Rathers's throat on the spot.

Once he regained his balance, his gun hand swung out, firing two more shots. They missed her.

Lou moved through the darkness, working the shadows of the empty park around them, staying just beyond his reach and out of his sight.

As she moved, she pulled a blade from each of her hidden sheaths.

"You like blades," she told him.

He whirled at the sound of her voice.

She thrust the blade into his gut before he could fully turn to face her. He fired a shot as he cried out, kicking earth and grass up into the air.

She punched another hole in his gut with her opposite hand before pushing him off the blade.

He stumbled, falling to his knees.

She was fairly certain she hadn't hit any vital organs. But she wanted to do enough damage to slow him down.

Growling his fury, he pushed himself off the ground. Lou sliced his arms four times in quick succession. When he opened his mouth in a snarl, she drew the blade across his lip.

The flesh split, blood blooming.

Lou took this moment to grab the back of his neck and pull him through the dark again.

When the dining room of the night's earlier horrors reformed around them, Lou shoved him hard.

He fell onto his hands and knees in the living room. From where Lou stood, she could see the pale foot of the dead woman resting on the carpet. The red polish of her toenails made the foot look even paler.

Rathers was bleeding all over the floor. Still, he staggered to his feet again and charged her. Lou sidestepped him and thrust her blade into the muscle running along the spine. He cried out, arching his back. Lou twisted the knife in her fist, feeling the warm blood wash over her hands.

She was about to deliver a second blow with her other hand, but it didn't move.

In fact, that side of her body was on fire, alternating between numbness and searing pain.

Maybe his shitty shot had nicked something important.

Rathers collapsed.

He was laughing from the flat of his back on the carpet. Blood spread around his torso as he tried to push himself up but failed.

"I know what you are," he said. "I was prepared."

I was prepared.

The edge of Lou's vision darkened.

Never a good sign.

She knew it wasn't the bullet's placement. She'd been shot

enough times to know where she could take damage and where she couldn't.

Had he dipped it in something? Was she poisoned?

She'd wanted to stay until Rathers was unconscious. Her plan was to pin him to the crime scene until the police and an ambulance could arrive.

Then they would know exactly who was responsible for all of this.

Forget about him, her mind warned. *Worry about you.*

Lou took an uneasy step back, then another.

"Don't," Rathers said. His eyes were soft blue again, his eyebrows rounding in fear. "Don't leave me here."

Lou couldn't shake the feeling that he wasn't speaking to her. He was begging someone else not to leave him. There was a distance in his gaze as if he were looking at something far, far away.

It didn't matter.

If Lou wanted to see sunrise herself, she had to go.

KING STEPPED FROM THE SHOWER AND TOOK THE TOWEL off the hook. He dried himself, considering what he wanted to wear as he rubbed most of the moisture out of his hair. He decided on black slacks and a polo t-shirt. A braided leather belt to match his leather shoes. He dressed without fanfare, having moved on to the consideration as to whether or not he would go to Café du Monde for a coffee or just make some when he got to the office.

He had time to get a coffee and maybe even a breakfast muffuletta from the café around the corner. But he also wanted to get to the office early today and recover the last of the ground he'd lost on casework when he'd been distracted by Mel's fundraiser. There were a few things for the fundraiser, too, that he hoped to scratch off his list before noon.

His phone pinged with a text. He lifted the screen close to his face and read the small script.

It was from Beth. *Morning, handsome.*

He smiled, considering what his response would be as he fetched a Q-tip from the bathroom closet to clean the dampness from his ears.

He'd only just decided on his compliment when Lou staggered into view.

He swore.

Her arm was soaked in blood. She looked pale and sickly. He dropped the Q-tip and took hold of her before she could fall.

Hissing, she wrenched her left arm away from him.

"Sorry, sorry." He released her, holding his hands up in surrender. "What happened? Are you okay?"

He felt like an idiot as soon as he said it. Of course she wasn't okay. Look at her.

"Are you going to make it?" he asked instead.

Lou pressed something into his hand, sweat standing out on her brow. "Call it in. He's there now. He's hurt but he might try to run. Tell them to search the house and the neighborhood, too, if they can't find him in the house. He'll be on foot."

She'd given him a driver's license. A pretty woman with sad eyes looked back at him.

"That's the address," Lou said. "The killer is there now. He's hurt like me. Call it in."

"Hold on a minute. Are you okay?" Catching the cannibal would be great, but Lou was the one bleeding all over his floor. Again.

She didn't answer him. Instead, she disappeared.

"Okay," he said to the dark bedroom. "I guess you'll take care of yourself and I'll take care of this bastard."

He went to his dresser drawer and dug around until he could find the burner phone he kept there. It was about time to replace it, but one more call would be all right.

He called the Boise police department, not knowing which one might be closest to the house in question and unsure if it really mattered at this point. Given the high-profile nature of the case, they would have federal, state, and local agents working it.

King just needed to get the ball rolling.

"911, what's your emergency?"

"Oh my god! Oh my god!" King cried. His voice broke on the second *god*. He pulled his mouth away from the receiver and cleared his throat.

I'm getting a little rusty at this.

"Sir, can you please tell me where you are calling from and what's your emergency?"

"I was walking my dog on Heatherhills and I saw a fight through the window. There was a man attacking them. They're screaming. There's blood! A lot of blood."

"Sir, please calm down and give me the address of your location."

King pretended to look for an address, and after the appropriate pause, he read the license. "61171 Heatherhills Lane. Please hurry. Please! He's going to kill them!"

King hung up before the woman could ask any questions that he wouldn't have the answers for anyway, considering that he wasn't actually in Boise, walking a dog—his or any other.

This wasn't the first time he'd had to call in a fake tip on Lou's order, and yet he hadn't been pleased with his performance.

You'd think I'd be a pro by now, he thought.

He pinched his nose in disappointment.

Hopefully it was enough to get an officer out to the house, at least, and get Rathers into custody. Once they had him, hopefully they'd have enough to keep him.

Seeing Lou hurt had forced all the important questions from King's mind. He should've asked more. What kind of state was the house in? Would they make the connection that he was the cannibal killer they were looking for? Was there any evidence left behind? Anything that could lead back to her? Had anyone survived who could testify to what happened?

With a swipe of his thumb, he smeared fresh blood across the plastic surface of the woman's driver's license.

"She'll be okay," he told the empty room. "She'll be okay."

26

L ou went to Isadora. It wasn't a hard choice. She hated hospitals and she'd already walked into those garish bright lights twice tonight. Perhaps it was also because she trusted the woman. Not necessarily because she was in Konstantine's employ but also because there was something in the old woman's manner that Lou liked.

She was steady. She was certain. She had the lovely, no-bullshit manner of someone who had seen it all and took whatever she saw at face value.

As soon as Lou appeared in her clinic, bleeding from her upper arm, she knew she'd made the right choice.

Isadora took off her glasses and arched a brow. "The hell is this?"

"I've been shot," Lou said.

"*Sì*, I can see that," Isadora replied, her accent melodic. Its rise and fall wasn't helping Lou to stay conscious as the darkness pressed harder against the corners of her vision.

Lou stumbled and hands took hold of her.

The instructions the doctor barked next were completely in Italian, so Lou didn't know what they were saying.

In English, she said, "I forbid you to die on my table, do you hear me?"

Lou tried to laugh but didn't think she managed it.

"If you die here, do you know what hell you will bring me? He will never forgive me."

Lou didn't need to ask her who "he" was. Konstantine.

"I will have to cut your coat," Isadora said. "Yes, I know. A shame. But you can keep your coat or your arm, and I get to decide which it is."

Lou was in no state to argue. The pain in her arm was pulsing now. It felt as if someone were stabbing her with each heartbeat.

"Don't grit those pretty teeth or they'll crack," Isadora said. Then she hissed. "What the hell were you shot with?"

"Something was wrong with the bullet," Lou ground out, doing her best to relax her jaw, slow her breathing. She wouldn't be of use to anyone if she went into shock from the pain.

"There we go," Isadora said. "Good drugs, yes? They will help."

They were helping. Lou was finally able to relax enough to realize she was on a table now. With the jacket cut away, she could see that her injury looked bad. Blood had covered most of her arm from the bicep down and had dried dark. But where the bullet went in looked worse. The skin looked burned. Blackened.

"This is a chemical burn," Isadora said. Her eyes were made larger by the magnifying lens she wore as she bent over Lou to inspect the damage.

More shouting in Italian and hands appeared from nowhere. Solutions were splashed on Lou's arm though she heard this rather than felt it. The drugs that Isadora had given her had numbed her limb completely.

Lou watched as Isadora inserted a metal clamp into her arm and dug around for the bullet.

After a moment, she pulled it out and frowned. "Is this —Wait."

Isadora disappeared from her line of sight, but it didn't matter. Sleep overtook Lou then, and she was pulled down into the waiting darkness.

When she woke, Konstantine was there. He was on the phone with someone, one leg crossed over the other, gesturing with his free hand as he spoke.

Then he caught her eye and ended the call.

"*Amore mio*," he whispered, bending over her. "How do you feel?"

"Like I got shot," she said. Her mouth was sticky, and it was hard to speak. "How long was I asleep?"

"Six hours," he said.

"Did they get him?"

"They did. I just spoke to King. He says it is all over the news."

"I want to see," she said, trying to sit up.

"Please don't do that. Lie down. I'll find it on my phone, hold on."

Lou heard the click of Isadora's heels before she saw the woman.

"Good evening," she called out. "Would you like to know what he shot you with?"

"Yes," Lou said.

"A silver bullet."

Lou only blinked at her. Then she said, "A silver bullet."

Konstantine's disbelief outmatched hers. He stopped searching his phone for the news long enough to frown at Isadora. "A silver bullet? *Come per i lupi mannari?*"

Isadora laughed. "*Sì.* I don't know who you were fighting, but he obviously thought you were a monster."

A monster.

"The bullet felt different," Lou admitted. "When he shot me, it felt like something was wrong."

"You lost a lot of blood and the bullet was crudely made. It's possible he struck a nerve or two," Isadora reassured her. "But you are no *lupo mannaro*. See for yourself."

She held the bullet out to Lou, and she took it with a shaking hand. It was poorly shaped, and certainly homemade. It probably did Rathers no favors when it came to his aim. Lou had thought he was simply a lousy shot, but maybe that had only been partially true. Even a steady hand might have a hard time getting this bullet to land where it wanted.

"Can I keep this?" Lou asked.

Isadora laughed and held up both hands. "It's yours. If you care to know, I also cleaned and patched up the cuts on your arm. Two were deep enough for stitches, but I suspect they aren't as exciting as a silver bullet."

"Thank you," Lou told her.

Isadora dipped her head in response. "*Prego.*"

Konstantine found the news reel he wanted and turned his phone so Lou could watch the video play across his screen.

Rathers's mugshot was on one side of the screen with his name printed beneath, while the other side depicted the view of him being dragged into the Boise County Jail wearing a bulletproof vest. The officers had their hands on the back of his head, keeping it down so he couldn't make eye contact with the crowd.

Then he disappeared through the jail's glass doors and out of sight.

"I already took care of the hospital footage," he told her.

"Do they know he's the one they're looking for?" she asked. "Or do they just think he killed the woman?"

"When they found him with the body, they got a warrant

for his apartment. They found the knives he used in the other killings and the body of the neighbor. They have enough to convict, I believe."

It was a fair assessment, but Konstantine wasn't King. He knew more about breaking laws than enforcing them.

"May I make a suggestion?" Isadora said. "As your doctor?"

Lou turned to look at her. "Yes."

"Go to your special place. You know which one I mean," she said.

La Loon. Isadora knew about it because she'd been one of the few to see Lou's blood results. She knew how each visit gave Lou a certain dose of microbes that seemed to speed up her healing.

"I've done all I can for you," Isadora said. "But if you can do something for *yourself* and you will heal even faster..." She shrugged. "Why not?"

"It's good advice," Lou said, and began sitting up. "I'll go now."

"*Amore mio,*" Konstantine said, but Lou silenced him with a kiss.

"I'll see you tonight."

WHEN LOU PULLED HERSELF ONTO THE SHORE OF LA LOON, arms shaking and soaked, the familiar monstrous landscape greeted her. A sky the color of a dark bruise. Twin moons coated in a faint yellow haze. The distant mountains framing the lake's edge, their pale peaks reflected back in the calm patina of the blood-red waters.

"Jabbers?" Lou called, but there was no answer. Jabbers was not there.

She remained in the shallows, dipping her wounds beneath the surface of the water and searching the shore. But the twilight remained still. A light breeze rustled the black foliage gathered at the water's edge and something moved in the waters, disturbing the smooth surface.

"Jabbers?" Lou called again.

Lou was not going to go search for her. The last time she'd gotten worried about Jabbers and had gone looking for her, she'd almost gotten eaten.

Jabbers was probably fine. She would be here the next time Lou pulled herself to shore, or so she told herself.

She lay in the warm water, irritated about her lost jacket and the lingering vision of the mother's slit throat, the blood pooling like a halo around her head.

When Lou closed her eyes, she could still hear the baby screaming.

And for some reason, as she reviewed the details of the encounter, Lou realized what she wanted was to go home to Konstantine.

She wanted to go home to him at the end of a night like this one.

Home.

The feeling grew stronger and stronger until she was certain it wasn't just his small courtyard apartment over-looking the Arno River that she longed for.

It wasn't even his perfect mattress or the way she woke to the smell of coffee in the mornings, or him singing Italian in the shower.

Somehow, when she hadn't been looking, when she hadn't been paying attention, Konstantine had become *home*.

Her refuge, waiting for her at the end of each hunt.

The nexus of her comfort and ease, a centering presence in her life.

She held on to this thought as she waded out into the lake again and disappeared beneath its red waters.

27

L ou found Stefano in bed with a woman. She slept even though he sat up almost immediately, pointing the gun in Lou's direction with decent accuracy.

He swore when he saw her. "What is it? Is it Konstantine?"

His irritation folded into concern.

"No," Lou said.

And the sound of her voice was enough to rouse the naked sleeping woman.

"*Che sta succedendo?*" The woman sat up. "*È tua moglie?*"

"I told you I don't have a wife." To Lou, he said, "You can't be here."

Lou realized she was dripping on the floor and wondered why she'd felt the urgent need to come. "I've caught you at a bad time."

He waved his hand. "Just tell me what you want."

"Were you serious about repaying that favor?" Lou asked.

"*Sì*," he said. "But is this an emergency? Did you have to find me right *now?*"

Then he seemed to notice her wet hair, the lack of coat

and sunglasses, the wounds and stitches in her arm.

His irritated expression softened. "Are you all right?"

"*Non mi hai pagato pure per questo.* Good night to both of you," the woman said, and rolled over, disappearing under the covers again.

Lou understood enough Italian to realize this woman was a prostitute. Lou's timing had been even worse than she'd thought. She hadn't simply woken Stefano late at night in his bedroom.

Stefano clicked on the lamp. "Can you find me again in twenty minutes?"

"Okay." She didn't know what else to say. It was clear that he was naked and the covers lying across his lap were the only thing keeping their mutual dignity intact. He couldn't get up and come with her. That was out of the question. "See you in twenty minutes."

It was enough time for her to go back to the apartment and grab the manila folder.

She spent the remaining minutes looking through the folder one last time, but the same property caught her attention.

Holding the facts sheet in hand, she wandered the property. First outside, then inside, turning on the lights in each empty room.

Her heart knocked wildly in her chest.

She liked the layout. She liked the security measures the previous owner had installed.

It was a beautiful place.

She was still standing in the moonlit living room of the vacant apartment, taking the place in, when she felt a tug in her navel and knew that Stefano was ready for her.

Lou found him on a quiet Florentine street.

It was still dark. Stefano's thumb struck a lighter, briefly illuminating his face.

Then only the cherry of his cigarette burned in the dark. "Well? What did you want?"

She handed him the folded property listing. "I want you to buy this."

Stefano flicked his lighter again before opening the sheet. He looked it over by the light cast by the flame, and when he saw the price, he whistled.

"This is extortion," he said, and slapped the page as if it offended him. He took the cigarette from his mouth. "And I have never bought a woman an apartment in my life."

"It's for me and Konstantine," she said. "He asked me to pick a place for the two of us, and I want this one. I haven't told him yet."

Stefano's brows went up. "You want to surprise him. You're a romantic?"

"Do you think he won't like it?" she asked.

"Oh, he'll love it," he said, taking another drag of his cigarette. "Because he *is* a romantic."

"Then buy it and don't tell him," Lou said.

Stefano snorted. "He will ask where the money has gone."

"He trusts you."

"I suppose you also want help furnishing it?"

"No," she said. "I just need you to buy it."

He folded up the listing and slipped it into his pocket. "Don't you want to see it first?"

"I already have," she said.

He waved his hand. "Of course."

He took another drag on his cigarette before dropping it to the street and grinding it out with a boot.

"I will do this for you on one condition," Stefano said. "Please don't visit me so late again, unless it is an emergency."

She'd already embarrassed herself once tonight—there was no point in holding back now. "I didn't know you were with someone."

He waved his hand again, looking especially Italian at that moment. "You don't know where you're going before you go?"

"Sometimes I get an impression of what's happening on the other end, or I can feel it out, but—"

His face pinched in confusion. "The other end?"

She made a motion with her hand to suggest the distance between herself and her targets.

"Ah, okay. *Sì.*"

"But I don't *know* everything before I go," she said. "I can sense danger or the time of a place but not, you know."

He considered this, exhaling gray smoke into the early-morning air. "In that case, maybe you can just text me next time."

KONSTANTINE DEVOTED THE MORNING TO SORTING THE paperwork acquired from Gabriella's apartment. It wasn't much, but that in and of itself was a problem. There was no proper paperwork for the girl, no list of vaccinations or medical care. He had a few school records, but all were older than three years, which made him wonder if the grandfather had stopped sending her to school when his wife died. Perhaps that was why she didn't like it, if she was behind. He would need to do an assessment and provide a tutor if necessary.

Isadora could give the girl a physical and make sure she was up to date on her immunizations, and he knew someone at the central records office that could redo her birth papers. These were hassles, but not travesties.

When he'd finished sorting it all and had gained a clearer sense of what needed to be done, he called for Gabriella. Five minutes later, she and Matteo ran into his office with big smiles.

When he saw Matteo, he waved him away. "You can wait for her outside, please."

"*Sì!*" He spun around and closed the door behind him.

Her happiness evaporated almost instantly.

"You're not in trouble. *Vieni*," he said.

Slowly, she approached his desk.

He pointed to the pile of photographs. "Are there any that you would like to keep?"

"Did my grandfather say I could have those?"

Konstantine wasn't going to tell her that he was dead. When she was older, she might seek him out, but by then it wouldn't be hard for her to believe he'd died of old age. Konstantine would support this belief by saying the money in her account was what she'd received upon his death.

"*Sì*, they are yours," he told her.

Slowly, she sorted through the pile with her small hands. When the tears began to well up, he said nothing. Once she was finished, she had a small stack of six or seven photographs in her grip. Three or four were of her mother, the rest of her and her grandmother, with the exception of one of her grandparents together.

As she held her little stack, she began to cry in earnest.

"Come here," he said, waving her over. "*Vieni*. What's wrong?"

He took her gently by the shoulders.

She did not answer him.

"*Stammi a sentire*," he said. "I don't know what happened with your mother. I can't imagine what choices she made or how that caused your circumstances, but you are safe here with us, Gabriella. *Qui sei al sicuro*."

Or at least she was as safe as anywhere else in a world where children died of disease, starvation, or war every day.

"You will stay here with us until you are an adult, then you can go wherever you like and do whatever you want. You will have a bit of money and you will have your freedom, and I will always support you." He pressed her chin up gently, forcing her to look at him. "Do you hear me?"

She nodded, but her lip continued to tremble.

"How is your new room?" he asked. Just that morning he'd had Matilda convert one of the storage rooms beside the kitchen into a warm bedroom suitable for a young girl.

Gabriella sniffed. "I like it. You can smell the breakfast in the morning."

He smiled. "Good. Listen, later today I'm going to take you to a doctor I know just to make sure you are healthy, and I may come to your school tomorrow and ask to speak to your teachers. Is that all right?"

"I don't mind doctors," she said.

"But you don't like school," he said. It wasn't really a question. "Can you tell me why?"

"It's boring."

He stifled a laugh. "Then I will ask someone I know to come and speak with you. Maybe you will learn better with a private teacher. Or we can try another school."

"I like going with Matteo," she told him. "He's my friend."

"Yes, he is a good boy," Konstantine agreed.

"Why do I need school? Did you go to school?"

"Yes," he said. "And if you want to be a free woman, you must have options. Do you understand?"

She nodded.

"Then go have lunch, and I will come find you later for the doctor. Don't go far."

She ran from the office, and Konstantine called out for Matteo.

He poked his head into the room. "*Sì?*"

"Send me Stefano if you see him."

It was fifteen minutes before Stefano appeared in his doorway, his hands hidden in the pockets of his Armani suit.

Konstantine tried to read him, search him for any signs of tension or fear.

There were none. If anything, he seemed less tense than he had yesterday.

"Close the door," he said.

Stefano did as he was told.

"May I ask," Konstantine began, "where the *six point seven million* dollars you took out of my account went yesterday? Did you buy something for a woman, perhaps?"

Stefano's lip twitched. "Not for my woman, no."

"Maybe you have children I don't know of? Maybe you're in trouble?"

"No," he replied. "There's no trouble."

"Are you paying off a bribe for me? Did someone threaten us?"

"No," Stefano said.

"Then what's happened?"

"I can't tell you," Stefano said.

"You can't tell me." Konstantine fell back against his seat. "That is a lot of money for something *you can't tell me*. Are—"

"Don't ask me any more questions," Stefano said. "I can't tell you."

"Am I in danger?"

Stefano shook his head, a ghost of a smile crossing his lips. "No, I don't think so."

"Your humor confuses me. Do I get a hint?"

Stefano pulled a cigarette from his pocket. "No. You will know soon enough."

Lou found Konstantine at home that night. He was sitting at his desk, an empty espresso cup beside his computer. He looked up when she appeared in his living room.

"How do you feel?" he asked her.

"Fine," she said. "How do you feel?"

"Puzzled," Konstantine said.

Then he proceeded to tell her about the conversation he'd had with Stefano earlier that day.

"All day I've been replaying his words in my mind. I triple-checked our accounts. I looked for any suspicious purchases, but whatever he's done, he took the money and paid cash for it. It's *very* suspicious."

"Don't you trust him?" Lou asked, leaning one hip against the desk.

"With my life," he said. "But it's a lot of money to disappear without an explanation."

"Do you need the money back?"

"No, we can spend that a hundred times over," he said. "But that isn't the point."

"He must have his reasons." Lou was doing her best to appear casual, normal, despite the wild knocking of her heart.

Konstantine rubbed his brow. "He said I would know soon enough. But I don't like surprises. It was so hard for me to focus today while I took Gabriella around to her appointments."

"How is she?" Lou asked, glad for an excuse to steer the conversation away from the money.

"Healthy, but she has a reading disability. It is why she struggles in school. I have a good tutor for her now who says she's very smart. She will catch up."

He reached for her, and she came to him, letting him pull her close. "I missed you today."

She kissed his forehead. "You don't miss me every day?"

"Of course I do, but—" It looked as if Konstantine wanted to say more, but if he did, he decided to let it go for now. "Before I forget, this is for *your* friend."

"I love how you put the emphasis on 'your.' Melandra has a name," Lou said.

"I have told you. I cannot forgive her for shooting you."

"Even though it was an accident?"

"*Sì*, even though it was an accident." He trailed his fingers down Lou's arm, looking at the bullet hole as he did. "You healed. Good. When is the fundraiser?"

"Tomorrow night."

"Will you be with me tonight then?" he asked. "I have a gift for you. But I will only give it to you if you stay."

Lou opened her hands expectantly and he pulled a bag from the floor.

"Armani?" she asked, reading the brand aloud.

He shrugged. "I know you don't care about these things—"

Says the man who loves his clothes almost as much as he loves his cat.

"—but I saw it in the window this morning and thought of you," he finished.

Lou opened the bag, pushing aside the tissue paper, and pulled out the leather jacket.

It was nice. *Too nice*, considering what she would put it through. Mostly she found her leather jackets well worn from thrift stores. This one didn't even have a scuff on it, let alone a stray thread or patch of gray. The one before last had had a duct-taped sleeve.

"Why spend so much money on something I'm going to destroy?" she asked him.

"You deserve nice things."

Holding the jacket loosely in one fist, she ran the fingers of her free hand through his hair, pulling his head back until his face was angled up toward hers.

"I have nice things," she said. And kissed him.

28

It had been a long time since Robert King had been in a suit. But he wore it better than he'd hoped. He'd shaved, slicked his gray hair to one side, and even splashed a bit of cologne on his neck beneath the collar.

He was standing in his bedroom, admiring his ensemble, when he felt the familiar *pop* between his ears.

He turned and found Lou there, her eyes dark and her face as unreadable as always.

He arched a brow. "Nice jacket. Is it new?"

It had to be new. Her old one was beat to shit and looked like a homeless person had given it a ten-year tour of the world's back alleys and dumpsters.

"Yeah, thanks."

"Have you seen the news?" he asked, turning back toward the mirror.

"I haven't had time."

"I guess not. You left a lot of blood on my carpet," he said. Then, before she could accuse him of complaining, he added, "But you look good. Glad you're all right."

He made the final adjustments to his tie and then went to

the living room, grabbing the remote off the coffee table and turning on the television. He flipped through his usual news channel options before finding what he was looking for.

For several minutes they stood side by side and watched the TV without comment.

"They're going for the insanity plea," King said. "Something about a journal that was full of the rantings of a troubled man. His defense is putting a lot of weight on his troubled childhood. There was also something in the journal about the wolf attack being planned. Sounds like his father was trying to kill him and make it look like an accident."

Lou said nothing, but King wondered if he'd upset her. Her eyes gave nothing away, but he thought he'd seen a momentary flex of her knuckles.

He asked, "If the insanity plea sticks, what will you do?"

His eyes slid toward Lucy's urn on the coffee table.

How am I doing, Lucy? he wondered. *Is this what you wanted for her?*

You're doing just fine, Robert.

His throat tightened.

"I could leave his body in his cell," Lou said.

"If you go that route, don't shoot him," King said. "Someone will have to answer for that if you do."

"I wouldn't shoot him," she said.

A rough knock came at the door, and King called out, "Coming!"

He opened his front door and Lady bounded into the kitchen, tail wagging.

"I don't think it was you who knocked," he told her, giving her a scratch behind the ears.

Mel swept into King's kitchen behind the dog. An air of panic radiated from her. "It's five minutes before showtime and no one is here. Not even Piper and Dani."

She began pacing his tiled floor, wringing her hands.

"This is going to be a disaster. I know it. I just know it."

"No one shows up for these things on time," King assured her. "All you need to do is make sure the decorations are how you want them, that you've got the food ready, the drinks ready, the door is unlocked, and—"

The door to the shop dinged.

King stepped out onto the landing for a view of the shop below. It was Piper and Dani, their hair and face done up in glitter, their clothes sharp. Each was carrying a party platter of meat, cheese, and veggies.

When Piper saw him, she nodded toward the door behind her. "Can you come help me carry in the rest of this?"

"Sure. Let me put on my shoes."

"I don't know why you should bother. *No one* is coming. It's gonna be the five of us eating deli slices until midnight."

King slipped on his shoes and then laid a hand on each of Mel's shoulders.

"I'm going to need you to stay positive," he told her. "That's all you've got to do. The girls and I will handle the rest. Isn't that right?"

He looked to Lou, who was standing in the kitchen now, her face unreadable, her hands hidden in the pockets of her jacket.

When she caught King's eyes, she replied, "That's right."

The bell dinged again, and this time it was Henry with three other drag queens. They wore sequined masquerade masks with elaborate feather headdresses. Their outfits glittered and their nails shone.

"Hello!" Henry called up with a wave. "Sorry we're early. We just wanted to see if you need any help setting up."

"I need help," Piper said, clearly giving up on King. "My punch stuff is gonna melt if we don't get it into the fridge."

"Oh, it's so spooky in here," one of the drag queens said, pressing her lacquered nails to her sequined chest. "I love it."

"Me too," the other agreed.

"Give them something to do," King said, urging Mel toward the stairway. "Focus on what needs to be done and you'll feel better until the guests arrive."

She took a deep breath.

"Okay, ladies," she said, descending the stairs. "You're both tall, so you can help me with this banner."

With Mel sorted, King turned back to Lou. She was still standing in the kitchen.

"Do you have a mask?" he asked. "Are you ready for this?"

"Piper has one for me," she said.

He gave his bowtie one final tug. "Then shall we go down?"

MELANDRA'S NERVES DID START TO EVEN OUT AS PEOPLE arrived. The panic that kept her limbs heavy and mind buzzing lessened once she counted her first one hundred guests. Mel had no idea who most of these people were. Considering that Piper, Dani, and the drag queens carried the conversations, she suspected that they were their friends from that bar up the street, the one on Bourbon. Mel knew Piper visited it a few nights a week.

She hadn't expected for most of the bar to end up here at her shop, yet she had no complaints. At fifty dollars a head, Mel was more than a little grateful to run a popup gay bar for a few hours.

It helped a great deal that she had a job to preoccupy her. She wasn't expected to simply walk around the room and make painful small talk with everyone or stand in the corner awkwardly.

She thanked everyone for coming, of course. But otherwise, she could focus on making sure that everyone got their crystal bag with *Melandra's Fortunes and Fixes* printed on the purple velvet exterior. And she could offer quick palm readings and fortunes as she went.

Piper was also doing a great job of working the room, covering the sections that Mel missed and then pointing out new groups that came in. Dani had her own box of crystals, walking around behind them and making sure both Dani and Piper stayed well stocked.

"Ms. Durand," a voice called, and Mel turned to find Beth Miller, the DA, walking toward her.

She extended a check in Mel's direction by way of hello.

Mel took the check and noted the thousand-dollar amount printed clearly in the total box.

"This is too much!" she cried.

The DA's smile only widened. "No, ma'am, it isn't. I give quite a bit of my money to the association, and I've got two nieces in Jones's leadership program. It don't bother me a bit that some of it will make its way there by your hand."

With a gentle squeeze on her arm, she slipped away into the crowd before Mel could make a fuss about the check.

"I suppose I should give you this too," a voice said. This time, Mel found Lou wearing a skull mask, looking like a spirit from Día de los Muertos.

The dark surrounding her eyes made them look more golden. They almost glowed ghostly as they peered out at her.

My Lord, she really is Death incarnate, Mel thought, her eyes tracing the colorful swirls and red starburst of flowers painted along the white surface.

"Where'd you get that mask?" she asked, opening her hand to accept the check Lou offered.

"Piper wanted me to wear it. The contacts too."

That explained the ghostly eyes then.

"They're something," Mel admitted.

"Is that enough?" Lou asked.

"Oh, I'm sure—" Mel looked down to check the amount

and cried out. Several patrons who'd been drinking Piper's punch turned toward her before looking politely away.

She hissed at Lou under her breath, "Ten thousand dollars! You can't be giving me ten thousand dollars! It's too much!"

Lou's skull grin stared back at her. "It's from Konstantine. I gave my money to Piper."

Mel touched her chest. "Can he spare this?"

"He spends his money on worse things."

"Wait." She leaned in close to Lou and whispered, "Is this drug money?"

"If you don't want it, I'll take it back," Lou said.

Mel snatched the check away. Realizing what she'd done, she gave Lou a sheepish grin. "Even if it came from bad places, it's going to do something good," she said, and put the two checks safely out of sight.

Mel looked up again and caught King's eye across the room, then Piper's and Dani's in the opposite corner. One by one, she noticed all the people crowding her shop, laughing, smiling, joking. Henry and another drag queen working the door, accepting funds, slipping them into one of the blue bank bags that Mel had given them to collect the money.

Then she noticed the others waiting outside to be let in. The line was so long it snaked past her windows and out of sight.

So many people had come. So many more than she'd expected.

Not only were they having a great time, happy to spend a night here in her little shop, she also couldn't count on both hands how many compliments she'd received about her store since the night began.

A wave of gratitude washed over her.

"Thank you," she whispered. She turned back to Lou. "Tell Konstantine I said thank you very much."

Mel wasn't sure that she'd heard her.

Lou's head had turned ever so slightly in the direction of the door, her eyes fixed on the girl with black curls who was calling Piper's name.

"Excuse me," Lou said. "I have to take care of something."

LOU HAD SEEN SCARLETT COME TO THE DOOR EVEN BEFORE Piper had whirled toward Lou, giving her the hand signal.

Lou excused herself from the conversation with Mel and cut a path through the crowd toward the door where Scarlett was arguing with Henry.

"You can't come in here," he was telling her.

"Piper *invited* me," Scarlett said. She was trying to look around the massive drag queen into the shop and catch sight of Piper, no doubt hoping that the other would confirm her invitation.

Henry wasn't having it. He forced Scarlett from the shop amidst her cursing.

Lou stepped behind the purple curtain into the little nook that had been roped off for the event and used the darkness collected there to take her to the street outside.

Scarlett had her hand in the air, flashing her middle finger at Henry and the other drag queen guarding the door.

"You fuckers," she grumbled.

The people on the street waiting to get in snickered with amusement. King, Beth, and a few of the older crowd were less amused. They scowled through the glass at her.

Lou wasn't worried about Scarlett causing a scene. She wouldn't let it come to that.

Lou waited in the shadows until she got her cue from Piper. It came a minute later, when Piper appeared on the street.

She pushed her way past the crowd blocking the door and out to Scarlett.

"You call me over here, insist that you need to tell me something really important, and then you don't even—"

Piper interrupted Scarlett's rant with a handful of glitter to the face.

"What the hell, Piper! What did you do?" The girl coughed and spat the glitter out onto the street, trying to clear it from her eyes and face. "What was in that? Was that incense or something? What's that smell?"

But Piper didn't answer. She was pointing frantically at Scarlett, motioning for Lou to take her.

Lou came forward.

"I'm sorry, Scarlett," Piper intoned. "But with all your threats and everything, I couldn't take any chances."

Lou found Piper's tone a tad *dramatic*, but this wasn't her show.

"You've left me with no choice. I had to be *sure*. I did the only thing I knew would work. I asked for divine intervention."

"Divine intervention?" Scarlett tried to squint through the glitter stuck to her eyelashes. "What the hell are you talking about?"

That was Lou's cue. She wrapped one hand around Scarlett and pulled her through the shadows outside the shop, just beyond the halo of light thrown onto the street by Melandra's Fortunes and Fixes. If anyone saw anything, they wouldn't be sure what they'd seen.

When the world reformed around them, they were in a deep dark wood. Lou released her, giving her a moment to wipe her eyes and see the new scenery for herself.

Scarlett used her shirt to clear her vision. Then she gasped. "What the fuck?"

She turned in a circle until she saw Lou.

She took a step back. "W-what are you?"

Lou rushed toward her. She was trying to make her movements as unpredictable and phantom-like as possible. Piper had insisted the more she seemed like a spirit, the more terrified Scarlett would be.

Scarlett screamed when Lou grabbed ahold of her again.

Lou tried not to laugh as she took Scarlett to her Alaskan lake. The night was cold. Something howled in the distance.

Scarlett reached for the nearest tree as if it could steady her in this ever-shifting world, but Lou took her again, this time to the top of the Empire State Building.

"Please stop," Scarlett begged. "Why are you doing this? What do you want?"

Lou pushed her over the side, holding her pinned against the ledge, upside down.

Scarlett screamed, twisting beneath Lou's hands as she tried to see the city hundreds of feet below.

"Are you going to leave them alone?" Lou asked at last. She spoke lower than usual, hoping that Scarlett would not recognize her voice. She couldn't remember if she'd even spoken to the girl when they'd met all those years ago, but it was better to be safe.

Piper had been very clear that Lou was to sound scary if she could.

"Don't drop me! Please don't drop me!" Scarlett had tears in her eyes as she clawed at Lou's arm.

"Will you leave them alone?" she asked again.

"Who? *Who?*"

"Piper and Daniella. If you don't leave them alone, I have to kill you."

Lou pushed her over the edge a little farther, and Scarlett screamed as if someone was sticking her hand into boiling water. "Okay, okay, okay! Stop pushing me! Just stop pushing me, please! Get me down from here."

Lou pulled her through the dark one more time and wasn't surprised that Scarlett was screaming bloody murder when they resurfaced again. Hadn't King once described her slipping as a drop-kicked feeling? Surely she thought Lou had let go and she was falling off the top of the building.

But she wasn't.

They were in the Siberian shipping container that Lou hadn't visited in a long time.

Lou struck a match to illuminate the space.

"I could leave you here forever," Lou said, again keeping her voice low. "Would you like this as your grave?"

"*No.* No, please don't do that." Scarlett's breath came in heavy, desperate pants. "*Please.*"

"Then give me your word," Lou said. "Tell me you won't bother them again."

"I won't," she said, pressing against the rusted walls as if looking for a door. "I promise."

Lou extinguished the match.

For a long time she stayed here, perfectly still, careful not to move, knowing her boots would make a sound against the container's rough floor and give her away.

She heard Scarlett's hands on the walls again, beating against the metal siding.

She'd begun to cry.

"I promised!" she screamed. "I *promised*! Please! Please don't leave me here! I swear to God I won't even look at them, okay? I won't even look at them!"

Lou reached out and grabbed her, eliciting one last screech from the girl.

Piper had been very clear as to where their last stop should be. Lou was allowed to take Scarlett where she wanted, wherever she thought would be the most disorienting and terrifying, as long as Lou dropped her off here when she was ready to let her go.

Here. In the cemetery.

Lou didn't understand the significance of the place to the girl, but one look at Scarlett told her that it had been a wise choice. She looked at the grave, then at Lou's skull face, then back at the grave again.

"I'll be watching you. If you break your promise, I'll be back," Lou said. "And we can spend the rest of eternity here."

Lou tapped her nails against the tombstone.

"Together."

Scarlett took one last look at Lou, then turned and ran for the cemetery gates as if the hounds of Hell were snapping at her heels.

29

It was late when Lou appeared in Rathers's room at the asylum. He was on the floor, his face hidden in the corner. The room was padded, and they'd removed all the furniture except for a slim mattress that rested against the opposite wall.

A single window, high on the wall, showcased a sliver of night sky. The moon was nearly full, and its line shone on the hunched figure.

His arms were bound behind his back by the straitjacket, and seeing him wrapped like that roused an unexpected pang of sympathy in her.

She'd been trapped like that once, by Nico, Konstantine's rival.

"You stabbed me in the kidney and in the spleen," he said.

"You cut me first," she said. "Do you want me to leave?"

"No. I hoped you would come," he said. "And finish the job."

She stared down at him, and a terrible realization solidified in her.

I could be him.

Had only one or two things gone differently, she could be here where he was.

If Lucy hadn't come for her.

If King hadn't shown faith in her.

If she'd never met Piper, Dani, or Mel.

If Konstantine hadn't done any of the million things he'd done for her.

When she didn't answer him, Rathers leaned forward until half of his face filled with moonlight. The one visible eye was wet and full of torment. The other half of his face remained dark.

"Please," he said, his lips gleaming. "Please kill me."

"Why did you shoot me with a silver bullet?" she asked.

"It told me to. It told me you weren't my friend. You're not my friend, are you?" There was a strange hope in his voice.

"No," Lou said.

"Then kill me," he begged. "Do you still have the bullet? It's a special bullet. Shoot me with it."

"I don't have it," she lied. There was a weight pressing down on her shoulders. It felt as if the gravity in the room had changed.

She got the sudden urge to look behind her, but she refrained. There was no one in this late-night cell but the two of them.

Take him, a little voice said. *Take him and let King and his methods be damned.*

But it wasn't King she worried about. It was the motherless child that would grow up trying to understand what had happened to his family on the night one man entered their home and changed everything.

Lou understood that child because she had been him. Once.

A lifetime ago.

"Do you want to see my beast?" Lou asked. "Would you like to know what she looks like?"

The one visible eye widened. "Can she kill me?"

"Easily," Lou said.

"Yes. Yes, I want to meet her." Rathers struggled to get to his feet. "Please."

He searched her face, her body. He was clearly looking for a sign, awaiting her transformation.

"I told you, she's not inside me like yours is you."

He recoiled, his brow pinching in suspicion.

"I'll take you to her," she said, and placed one hand on Rathers's arm.

The moonlit cell disappeared, and in its place formed the Alaskan night. The insects singing to the night sky fell silent.

A distant owl's hooting caught her ear.

It must be pretty far away, she thought.

Rathers was looking out over the water, his straitjacket shining with collected moonlight.

"We have to go into the water," she told him. "That's how I cross over."

"All right," he said, and she realized he was barefoot.

His pale feet sank into the mud at the lake's edge.

She led him out into the water. The moon's reflection rippled, disintegrated into scattered starlight, but Lou kept her hand on his arm, guiding him toward the center of its cool waters.

"Aren't you scared I'll drown you?" she asked. Because he seemed disturbingly calm.

"I want to die."

"Take a deep breath," she told him. "We will have to wait under water until it warms. Then it will turn red and I will help pull you to the surface."

"Okay."

She had her own moment of concern when she dipped

beneath the surface and wondered if *he* might try to kill *her*. He could climb on top of her, force her to the bottom of the lake with his weight. And there was a moment in his eyes when it looked like he'd considered the same thing.

I have to mind those teeth, she thought as she pulled him under the surface.

Then they were in the cold dark together. His eyes were open, searching.

The waters began to shift from midnight gray to red. Lou tugged hard on the straitjacket, but the canvas was filling with water, resisting.

She still managed to get him into the shallows.

I can't take him back with that on, she thought. *He'll sink to the bottom of Blood Lake and that'll be the end of it.*

Lou wasn't sure if Jabbers would be there or not. There was a possibility she would still be gone, and if that happened, Lou planned to lie. She was going to point out one of the strange orca-like reptiles that hunted the lake and say that was her beast.

But she didn't have to lie. Jabbers was there, her great yellow eyes open and solemn.

As soon as Rathers saw her, he stumbled, his foot slipping in the shallows.

"My god, oh my fucking god, oh my—"

Lou couldn't understand the rest of the words pouring from his lips. He was babbling. His wet hair clung to his face, his eyes showing far too much of the whites.

"This is her?" he asked. "This is her?"

Lou couldn't answer because she'd seen Jabbers's nostrils flare, the shiver in the muscles contracting along her back. And she knew that when the plates rose like that, she was preparing to attack.

Lou put herself between them, placing both of her empty hands on the beast's head.

"You can't," she said. "Not this one."

That sharp intelligence focused on Lou.

"I can't explain," she said. "But *no*."

Jabbers pressed her head into Lou's stomach, and the force of it knocked her back a couple of steps. But if Jabbers was frustrated, at least she didn't tear Rathers apart or take a bite out of Lou.

Rathers fell to his knees before her. He looked into the eyes of Lou's beast and the beast looked back. The clicking in her throat was the closest thing to a growl Lou had heard from her.

"I see you in her eyes," Rathers said. "And I saw her in your eyes. I didn't know what I saw because she's—she's not like anything I could've imagined, but I know now. *I know*."

He began to laugh. He began to laugh as if he never intended to stop laughing.

That's when Lou placed a hand on either side of his neck and twisted it hard to the right, feeling the vertebrae crack in her grip.

Rathers collapsed to the shore, dead.

Jabbers regarded her reproachfully. If Lou could voice such a look, she would have said that Jabbers thought, *What a waste*.

"There's a child and—" Lou cut herself off. "I have to take him back. There's a child."

Jabbers chuffed and pivoted away from her.

Lou would have assumed this was her frustration if the beast hadn't turned back and looked at her after putting twenty feet between them.

"You want me to follow you?" Lou asked. And now, in profile, she could see that Jabbers's stomach was smaller.

Had she had her babies?

"I have to take him back," Lou said. She couldn't chance leaving Rathers on the shore while she hiked into the wilderness after Jabbers. If she came back and his body was damaged or gone—her caution would have been for nothing.

"I'll be back," she promised, stripping him of the straitjacket. "I promise I'll be back."

She grabbed one of Rathers's bare ankles and dragged him into the shallows. Jabbers only turned away, sauntering from the shore with the sleekness of a panther.

"When I come back, I'll bring you something. I promise," she called out, before disappearing into the water again.

30

Mel must have opened her purse and looked at the check hidden inside no less than forty times as she rode the streetcar from the Quarter into the business district. From there it was only a short walk to Tamara Jones's office.

As she entered the shiny building, she caught sight of herself in the glass door.

She was relieved to see that she did not look like a fortune teller today. She'd decided on simple black slacks and a loose blouse. Her hair was natural, with a scarf cutting across the top of her head to help give it shape.

And she still wore her bangles. Mel never went without her bangles.

But by all other accounts, she looked as calm and professional as a woman could with over *thirty thousand dollars* in her purse.

If I don't stop looking in my purse, someone is going to rob me, she thought.

She peeked at the check one last time to convince herself that it was still safe and secure in the folds of her wallet before zipping her purse tight and holding it against her chest like a beloved child.

To the receptionist's credit, she didn't raise her brows at Mel, though her eyes did stray to the purse once.

"Can I help you?" she asked, her smile neutral.

"I'm looking for Tamara Jones," Mel said with convincing calm. "Is she in today?"

The girl pointed at the elevators and gave the directions, which Mel thanked her for. But the elevator ride was the longest of Mel's life.

By the time she actually reached the seats outside Tamara Jones's door, Mel felt as if she were on the edge of a breakdown.

The office door opened and Tamara Jones stepped out with a red coffee cup in one hand. The cup matched her freshly painted nails.

"Why, Ms. Durand. What a lovely surprise. Come in." She stepped aside, inviting Mel into her office.

It was as impressive as Mel knew it would be. With its abundance of sunlight and sturdy furniture, this office was nearly twice the size of her whole apartment.

"You know, we have the meeting in two days," Tamara said, taking a seat on the sofa and motioning for Melandra to do the same.

Mel perched on its edge. "I know, but I don't feel safe with this kind of money on me, so I wanted to hand it over to you right away. I got the bank to make it into a single check. I didn't think you wanted me to hand you all those bills."

"A handful of crumpled bills spends just as well as a pristine check." Tamara's smile was bright. "How did the fundraiser go? Was Mr. King of any help to you?"

This gave Mel pause. "Mr. King? Well, yes. He was there."

"And did he call Bennett Weiss and Abigail Hoyt like I told him?"

Mel frowned. She wasn't sure she had been introduced to anyone with those names. By the time they'd finally closed the doors it was just past three in the morning. At that hour, Mel had met, and forgotten, what seemed like all of Piper's friends from the Quarter and everyone from the DA office and local precinct. There had even been Zeke and his crew from across the street. Turned out he'd been passing out Piper's flyers almost from the beginning.

"The turnout was far more than I'd expected," Mel admitted.

"Good on him. You know, when he came by to ask for my help, I wasn't sure he was going to take my advice. I'm glad he did."

Mel clutched her purse a little harder. "King came here? To see you?"

"He did," she said. "He was very sincere in his wish to help you. And I thought, why not? The DA has spoken highly of him and his work, so I took a chance. Looks like it worked out well for you. It's a good friend you've got there."

Mel's heart ached. "Yes, he is. A very good friend."

At last Tamara opened her hand. "All right then. Let's see how you did."

Mel reached into her purse and produced the check. She handed it over, trying not to let the paper shake between her fingers and betray her emotion.

Tamara looked at the check once. Then again.

Mel's heart raced. "I know it doesn't meet the full goal of a hundred thousand dollars, but I'm hoping it will still help."

She refrained from fidgeting, but the urge to move her purse around on her lap was strong.

"This is a check for thirty-five thousand dollars, Ms. Durand," Tamara said.

"I know. I really tried to do more, but—"

"More? *More!*" Tamara held up a hand. "I'm going to stop you right there."

Mel's heart began knocking against the base of her throat.

"Are you telling me that you—*you*, a relatively new business owner who has never so much as run a lemonade stand let alone hosted an official fundraiser—raised thirty-five *thousand* dollars all on her own?"

"Not on my own," Mel interjected. "Mr. King helped, as well as some of our friends."

Tamara barked a laugh. "Good friends! Honey—and forgive my informality, but *honey*. Do you understand what you've done?"

Mel suspected by the look she was receiving that she did not, in fact, understand what she'd done.

"Perhaps not," she said.

"It's true that when we have our big drives in late June and November we've brought in millions. In the fall because it's the holidays and everyone's looking to spend and in June because the new fiscal year is around the corner and everyone wants to balance those books and get as many *tax-deductible donations* as they can. But for a random first-quarter sweep, I'd expected you to turn up with no more than a few grand. I would've been impressed with five thousand, to be honest."

Five thousand dollars.

Mel blinked. "But you said a hundred thousand."

"A hundred thousand for *everyone in that room*," Tamara said with a pointed look.

"Oh." Mel touched her throat. "Oh, I see."

A look passed over Tamara's face then, her eyes softening.

"Melandra," she said softly. "May I call you Melandra?"

"Yes." Of course she could. This woman could call her *dirt*.

"May I share an honest assessment with you?" Tamara

asked, her voice remaining low and cautious, as if they weren't the only two people in this room.

Something in Mel hardened. "Yes. I can handle it."

"I'm sure you can, but the fact you're bracing yourself as if my tongue is a serpent won't do. I'm trying to pay you a compliment. It seems to me that you've been on your own for a long time. Maybe a *very* long time. Perhaps the world hasn't paid you much kindness. Or it's made you feel like more than a few things were your fault."

It was like the terrible dreams in which Mel found herself naked in the grocery store and everyone was looking at her.

"You could say that," she said, trying to feign indifference despite how hard Tamara's words had struck home.

"It won't be like that anymore." Tamara took her hand and squeezed. "We look out for our own here. We do this work together. Nobody, not a single one of us, is expected to go it alone. I'm sorry I didn't reach out to you before. I admit I have a terrible bias toward locals, but you're one of us now, you hear me? You're not alone anymore."

Mel didn't trust herself to speak. Her throat was too tight with unshed tears. She simply nodded.

Tamara squeezed her hands again.

"And you better come to the meeting Tuesday. I've got about two dozen women I want you to meet who I think you'll like very much. And at the last meeting of every month, Estelle brings her chocolate cupcakes and they are *divine*. So tell me you'll be there."

"I'll be there," Melandra said.

Tamara released her, giving her hand a friendly pat.

When the meeting ended and Melandra found herself on the busy street again, she kept replaying Jones's words in her head.

You're one of us now. You're not alone anymore.

King's face sprang to mind the way he'd looked in his

masquerade mask and handsome suit. Piper with her abundance of glitter and even Lou wearing her painted skull. So many people had showed up for Mel when she'd needed them.

Not one person had let her down.

I was never alone, she thought. *I was never, ever alone.*

KING COULD FEEL SUMMER COMING. THE HUMIDITY HAD seemed to double in the past week, clinging to his skin and pooling at the back of his neck. But as much as the weather annoyed him, it only held his attention at a distance.

He was focused on the news, and the breaking story that two stony-faced anchors delivered with all the zest of coma patients, a sharp contrast to the content.

"Alan Rathers, also known as the Hammersmith Cannibal, was found dead at the Idaho State Sanitarium this morning. Authorities say the cause of death was a broken neck, believed to be caused by suicide. Despite being placed on suicide watch, the young man managed to use his straitjacket to suspend himself from some water piping in a nearby utilities closet. Rathers's drenched body was discovered by the janitor when he opened the door, searching for the source of the leak.

The camera panned to the second news anchor, who was no more lively than the first.

"An active investigation is in effect, and authorities are examining the events of last night to determine how Rathers escaped his room and whether foul play has led to the young man's death."

The screen shifted to a reporter on the street with his microphone pointed at his interviewee.

"Do you believe Alan Rathers hung himself because he felt remorse for what he did?" the reporter asked.

"Nah, I think someone killed 'im," a stout man with a red hat and blue bomber jacket said. "I think somebody was real mad at 'im for what he did to those families, to those little babies, and they killed him for it."

A second interviewee appeared on the screen. An older woman with curly hair cropped close to her head.

"Do you believe justice was served in this case?" the reporter asked, and extended his microphone toward her.

"Of course. He's dead, isn't he?"

King took another drink of the tea he held. He had no doubt that Lou was responsible for the broken neck. And he was certain that she'd returned him to the asylum for the sake of the families. What King was less sure about was why she'd killed him.

Had she done it to complete her hunt? To gain a sense of resolution? Had she felt it was her duty to ensure justice be delivered to the families, and she didn't want to risk Rathers succeeding in his insanity plea?

Normally, King would say yes.

But he'd seen something in Lou the last time he'd spoken to her. There had been a *look*—as rare as *looks* were on Louie Thorne's face—and if he hadn't known better, he would have called it sympathetic.

Lou had felt sorry for him. He was almost sure of it.

He couldn't help but wonder if she'd killed Rathers not out of a sense of justice but to put him out of his misery.

His eyes slid to Lucy's urn on the coffee table. "I don't know how you did it all those years, Luce. She's harder to read than small print at the bottom of a contract."

A rough knock sounded at his door. He placed his tea on the table and rose.

When he opened it, Mel stood there. Her face soft, eyes bright. Lady sat on her haunches beside her, her tail gently thwapping the floor.

Before King could reach out and give the dog a welcoming scratch behind the ears, Mel wrapped her arms around him and squeezed.

He laughed out of surprise. "What's this now? You okay?"

His surprise folded into concern. Mel had never hugged him before. Maybe she'd felt compelled to now because something was wrong.

"Hey, seriously. Are you okay?" he asked.

"I'm fine," she said, pulling back. "It's only a hug. Ain't anybody hugged you before?"

Sure. But never you.

The only person that could surprise him more with a hug would be Lou herself.

King rubbed the back of his head. "All right, but what's it for?"

"I wanted to thank you for all of your help with the fundraiser. Without you, it wouldn't have gone so well."

He shrugged this off. "You would've done just fine without me. Piper and Dani really packed the place. Did your meeting with Jones go well? Are you an official member of the association now?"

"Oh yes." She rattled off names and dates for upcoming meeting and brunches. Her plans to find another helper in the shop, how Jones had offered to send over girls for her to interview and solve her long-standing staffing issues.

"There is even a ladies' poker night every other Thursday," she said, still beaming.

The dog's tail began wagging again at the word *ladies*.

Mel didn't notice. She went on, and King fought to keep a smile on his face as he leaned against the doorframe and listened.

He was happy for her.

Or rather, he was determined to *be* happy for her. He'd always thought Mel was too much of a recluse. He could hardly get upset now that she was venturing out into the world.

When she finished, she searched his face expectantly. King forced his smile to widen.

"It sounds like a lot of fun," he said. "I'm glad it worked out for you."

"Me too," she said, and gave his arm a little squeeze.

But try as he might, sadness washed over him, and he could tell by the way she flinched that she saw it. Lady must have sensed it too, because she pushed her cold nose into the palm of King's hand. Her tail stopped wagging.

"Don't worry about Wednesday," King said.

She frowned. "Why would I be worried about Wednesday?"

"I'm just saying if you're too busy just now, with your new duties and friends, I'll understand."

Mel cocked her head. "Understand what?"

"I'll understand why you can't make it for lasagna night. For—" He stopped short of saying *for our night*. "For the lasagna."

She placed a hand on her hip. "Mr. King. I don't recall saying anything about canceling our Wednesday nights. In fact, I just told Ms. Jones that I'm not free on Wednesdays and she said that's fine. Did you think because I joined some club I was going to forget all about you?"

Yes. "No."

She pursed her lips. "I'll have you know that Wednesday is my favorite night of the week, Mr. King. I don't think a couple of brunches or even a poker game is going to change that."

His heart lifted and the muscles in his back relaxed. He wasn't sure why he had needed her to say it.

"All right then. It's my turn to make the lasagna anyway."

"It sure is," she said, twisting the bangles on her wrist.

"And do it like you did last time with the fresh pesto. I loved that."

"Okay. I will. It only takes about five extra minutes."

She nodded as if it was settled. He thought she would leave then, but she turned back at the last second.

"You keep Lady tonight," she told him. "I think you need the company."

King laughed. "It's possible."

"*Allez*," Mel said, encouraging the dog to go to King.

She did, with a contented swish of her tail.

"You have a good night," Mel told them.

"You too," he said, watching as she crossed the hall to her own apartment and closed the door behind her.

When he turned back, he found Lady sitting in the middle of the kitchen floor, her ears erect.

Hopefully, her tail began to thump the floor again.

King stooped to give her a good scratch.

"We'll be all right," he told her. "We'll be just fine."

31

Dani and Piper spent their morning picking up Dani's car from the repair shop. Piper stood in the lot with the invoice in hand, walking around it twice.

"They did a great job," she declared. "I don't see a scratch on it."

Dani laughed. "You'd be more impressed if you'd seen what it looked like before."

Piper frowned. "I wish you would've taken pictures."

"It was a memory I didn't need." Dani pressed the fob and unlocked the doors.

Piper climbed into the passenger seat and buckled herself in. "Looks like they detailed the inside too. Nice."

"They should have, for what I paid." She turned the key in the ignition. "We headed straight home or do you want to grab coffees and breakfast somewhere?"

They decided to eat at the new vegan soul food restaurant in Mid-City for brunch. And once their bellies were full of potato salad, red beans and fried cauliflower, okra gumbo, cornbread dressing, collard greens, candied sweet potatoes, and even a bit of bread pudding, they waddled back to the car with plans to waste the afternoon on a long nap.

Dani drove them back to the Quarter, and Piper had almost been asleep when she spotted a familiar head of dark curls.

"Slow down, slow down!" Piper waved her hand frantically.

Dani hit the brakes. "What? What is it?"

"Scarlett."

Dani swore. "I wish you wouldn't do that. I thought I was about to hit something."

"Sorry, but slow down." Piper mashed the button on her door that rolled down the window.

"What are you going to do?" Dani frowned from the driver's seat. "Don't yell out the window at people. It's rude."

Piper sputtered her lips. "*Please*. She's done so much worse. *Hey!* Hey, Scarlett!"

Scarlett, who'd been strolling up the sidewalk with a green apron slung over one shoulder and a cigarette burning in her opposite hand, turned at the sound of Piper's voice.

To Dani it looked like she was about to smile, about to wave a hello. But her hand froze mid-motion once she saw who it was.

Scarlett whirled away from them and began hurrying up the street.

"Wait, come back!" Piper called, unable to repress her laughter. "I just wanted to see how you were. I felt like I was really rude the other night and—Why are you running?"

Now Scarlett was sprinting, trying to escape Dani's creeping SUV as if it might actually be the devil's own carriage come to retrieve her.

They'd almost caught up to her when Scarlett bolted down a side street onto the pedestrian thoroughfare too narrow for Dani's SUV to follow.

Once she was gone, they burst out laughing.

"Guess she didn't want to talk to us," Dani said, easing back into traffic.

"I'd say our plan worked," Piper said with a grin. "I told you Lou would scare the shit out of her."

"Honestly, I feel a little bad about it."

Piper snorted. "You're too nice. She messed with you and got what she deserved."

"I happen to believe in karma, so how do you know that I didn't deserve all the horrible things she did? Maybe I did something terrible in my last life."

"I don't believe that." Piper took her hand. "You're just as kind and beautiful and sexy in this life as you have been in all the others."

Dani's expression was soft. "Are you sure?"

"I'm sure," she said, and turned Dani's hand so that she could brush kisses across her knuckles. "I've never been more sure of anything."

JABBERS HAD SHOWN LITTLE INTEREST IN THE CUTTHROAT pimp that Lou had thrown on the shores of La Loon as a peace offering. The beast had simply sauntered away as soon as Lou pulled herself out of the water.

At first, Lou thought she was getting the cold shoulder. A silent rebuke for not letting her kill Rathers. But Jabbers turned back to her before she'd gotten too far away, clearly waiting for Lou to catch up.

"Your boyfriend better not be around," Lou said, squeezing the water from her hair. "I have no interest in getting eaten."

This earned her a chuff from the beast's snout but no sharp look.

Lou fell into step behind her and remarked how large she

looked from this angle. Was it possible that she was *still* growing? Even after all this time? Lou didn't see how that could be.

They'd walked several miles, Lou's soaked socks rubbing calluses on her feet, before Jabbers stopped.

They weren't at the cliff where Jabbers had made her nest. Lou had thought that perhaps that was where they were headed, back to Jabbers's lair, where Jabbers would show her —*what* exactly?

A baby monster?

But instead of heading toward the base of that mountain, Jabbers turned left and made for the cliff face that ran along the edge of the field. This vertical wall of stone rose so high that Lou couldn't see the top, lost in a haze of cloud cover.

"If you expect me to climb that, it won't happen," Lou said. "Unless you're going to sprout wings and carry me on your back."

Jabbers didn't try to climb the rock wall. She was nudging a stone aside with her massive head to reveal a dark hole set in the side of the cliff.

"You want me to go in there?" Lou asked. In response, Jabbers entered the pitch black, leaving Lou behind.

Lou took her phone out of its waterproof case and turned on its flashlight. She shone it into the darkness and found that there was a stone tunnel, roughly carved, curving out of sight.

Lou followed the beast into the bowels of the mountain.

The tunnel seemed to travel down at a gradient, going back the way they came. Given the rough shape of the walls and ceiling, Lou thought it had been water that had carved the stone.

There was something about the shape of the rocks that made her think of the Grand Canyon.

She felt like she walked forever, her light barely casting a halo of illumination before her.

The darkness was too complete to give up much ground.

And yet it was getting lighter. A soft blue-green glow sparked in her vision up ahead and every step seemed to make it bigger and bigger, until it was so bright that Lou turned off her phone and returned it to its case in order to save the battery.

The tunnel broke open to reveal a lagoon. The light had come from shallow waters that pooled along the stone floor before dropping away to deeper depths.

She wondered if this waterway led to Blood Lake, or connected somehow.

She'd only just knelt down to touch the water when Jabbers made a sound behind her. Lou turned.

In a niche in the wall, not four feet from the water's edge, Jabbers stood beside six smooth stones.

No. Not stones. *Eggs.*

Lou crossed to them and placed a hand on the surface of the closest one. It was warm compared to the cool temperature of the underwater cavern. And she felt something *move*, coiling and sliding under the press of her hand.

Six eggs.

Six baby monsters.

Lou reached out her other hand and placed it on the large black head resting against her.

"Congratulations. I'm sure you'll be a great mom."

32

L ou stood at her apartment window and took in her view of the Mississippi River for the last time.

The only thing left behind was the bare mattress on the floor. She would drop that off at a dumpster after dark. Her sofa, her medical kit, clothes, paintings, and books— everything she'd decided to keep—had all been moved to the new place. She'd even brought her two coffee mugs and four water glasses along.

Her armory had also been packed up and moved. Every gun, every knife, every flash bomb and piece of Kevlar. Her beloved flamethrower. Her father's bulletproof vest.

It hadn't been difficult for her to pack up alone, and she suspected her form of moving was far easier than what most people endured. She'd only needed enough shadow to shift her furniture and boxes from one place to another. It had required little labor to position her possessions as she'd liked.

But it was strange to be standing here now, in this hollowed space, looking at the last of the sunlight sparking along the water.

She took in the scene. The pinks and oranges skittering

along the surface. The white waves rippling and the wind tearing at the flags waving behind boats that, from this distance, seemed like children's toys.

She'd stayed in St. Louis because this was where her parents had been buried. This was where she'd been born and where they'd died.

But now she knew, as she regarded the last of the light, these reasons had only been excuses.

Why stay just because their bodies were nearby? With her abilities, her power, why should the distance matter to her?

Even if she made her home in Florence, she could reach the Bellefontaine Cemetery in just as many steps.

No.

Distance wasn't the reason she'd hidden herself here in this high tower.

There had been other reasons as to why she hadn't been ready.

And one by one, Konstantine had stripped those reasons away.

Are you proud of me, Lucy? she thought. *I'll finally have the home you always wanted for me.*

Lucy did not answer, but that was okay.

Lou kept her eyes on the water, silently saying her good-byes to the light.

This last look at the horizon was the most beautiful thing she had seen in a long time.

KONSTANTINE'S SHOULDERS AND NECK ACHED. HE'D ONLY just decided to return home for the night when Stefano knocked on his office door.

Konstantine looked up from his computer. "Yes?"

Stefano came into the room and handed him an envelope without comment.

Konstantine took it but frowned. "What is it?"

"Open it." And with that, Stefano left and closed the door behind him.

Konstantine opened the envelope and found three things inside. A set of two keys on an iron ring. An electronic keycard, like what he'd often used when staying in hotels, and a piece of paper with an address written on it.

He turned the paper over and back again, but there was nothing more.

It was only the address printed in Stefano's careful script.

The envelope itself was empty of anything else.

Unable to contain his curiosity, Konstantine packed up for the night, slipping the keycard and metal keys into his bag along with his papers and laptop.

After turning off the lights, he followed the winding corridors of the church across the courtyard, past the kitchen, and out into the cathedral. He heard the children under the table behind the statue of the Virgin Mary, their hushed voices exchanging the collected secrets and stories from the day.

Konstantine smiled when he caught Gabriella's excited tone among them.

Then he was out of the church and in the early-evening air.

He recognized the address as not far from his own apartment. It was only four hundred meters upstream from the section of the Arno River he considered his own, so he didn't have to change his route in order to reach it.

He passed the same piazzas and same shops. He waved his good evenings to the same familiar faces.

Then he was there, standing outside a brick wall almost twice his height and an imposing iron gate. It was impossible to see through either to gain a glimpse of what lay on the other side.

He checked the address again and confirmed that this was it.

This was where he was meant to be.

He removed the iron keys from his bag and the keycard from his pocket and discovered immediately that the keys were for the gate.

They twisted easily in the well-oiled lock, and the massive door swung open with a satisfying creak.

Once it closed behind him, locking automatically, he was in a small private garden, looking up at a two-story villa. The cream-colored façade had several large windows set into its face and the large wooden door was framed by an arched overhang and matching pillars. There was something familiar about it.

Beside the door was an electronic pad for the keycard. Konstantine pressed his plastic key to it and the red light flashed green. The door clicked, and he pushed it open to find a cool entryway and yet two more doors.

Above each hung a camera.

A lot of security in this place, he thought. *Whatever Stefano is planning—*

The keycard also unlocked one of the two doors, and Konstantine found himself at the base of a staircase.

"Hello?" he called up. "*C'è nessuno? Sono nel posto giusto?*"

"I'm up here," a voice called back.

His heart sped up, and by the time he'd reached the top of the stairs, it was practically choking him.

But his ears had not deceived him. He'd heard correctly.

It was Louie.

He found her in the living room at the top of the stairs. She wore a loose black shirt and tight black pants that hugged her curves. Her hair was pulled up off her neck, exposing her slender, very kissable throat.

He put his bag on the floor. "What's going on here? Is this a party? My birthday isn't until November."

"I know when your birthday is," she said.

"Then what's going on? What is this place?"

"You don't recognize it?" she asked. "I guess there was only the one picture, and it was pretty small and grainy."

He looked around, trying to get a sense of what game this was, when his eyes snagged on the purple sofa.

On the glass coffee table.

"Your furniture is here," he said, wiping his sweating palms against the front of his pants.

"Yes, it is," she said with the hint of a mischievous grin. "You're very observant."

He clasped the back of his neck. "Did this villa happen to cost six point seven million dollars?"

Her grin widened. "Thereabout."

He grabbed her then. "Did you buy this villa for us? Is this *our* villa?"

"Technically, *you* bought it. Well, Stefano took the money and paid for it. I picked it out, but you wanted it. So I'd say it was a group effort."

He placed a hand on either side of her neck. "You will live with me? This is *our* villa?"

He hugged her so hard that her feet came off the floor in his embrace.

Ours, his mind chanted. *Ours. Ours. Together. Ours together—*

Lou was saying something into his hair.

He released her. "What did you say?

"I *said*, I brought my sofa, but I want to keep your bed. I love that bed."

"I love you in that bed," he said, his reply automatic.

She laughed. "And I wanted to keep the river view, so both the living room and the bedroom above face the Arno. We can see it from the rooftop patio too. Maybe we should put some chairs up there."

He didn't care about the roof. His heart was soaring. *She said yes, she said yes, she said—*

He kissed her. She kissed him back, her eagerness matched his own.

The pleasure he found in this moment made it easy to forgive Stefano for his secrecy. Though he would ask for an answer to that mystery later, why she'd gone to him rather than speak to Konstantine directly.

The back of Konstantine's knees hit the side of her sofa —*Our sofa*—and he fell back, Lou landing softly on top of him.

Finally, he broke off the kissing, their mouths red and swollen, their breath strained. He couldn't take not knowing any longer.

"*Perché?*" he asked her. "Why did you change your mind?"

She looked out over the living room, her eyes seeming to search each crack and crevice of the room. Konstantine saw a couple of her paintings leaning against one wall, ready to be hung.

He delighted at the idea he would get to do that for her, if she allowed it. They would make this place a home together.

Together.

"For a long time I didn't have an apartment," she said finally. "Mostly I crashed in empty vacation rentals or unsold houses or unused hotel rooms. Sometimes I'd stay in warehouses, in the upper lofts where no one would come across me. It was like that for a long time, while I hunted Angelo."

Konstantine pushed a stray hair off her cheek but didn't interrupt.

"It was Lucy who talked me into getting a place. We'd looked at a lot of them, but I'd refused until she'd found that one. I liked how high it was and I liked the view of the river.

It felt safe up there. So I bought it. And when you asked me to move in with you, it felt like—it felt like it had when Lucy pushed me to—it felt like you were asking me to—"

She broke off.

And Konstantine wasn't sure she'd ever spoken to him like this before. Of her thoughts and her feelings. It was very clear she was struggling to share them.

But she seemed to find her footing again. "I had agreed to get an apartment, but it wasn't a home. Even with Lucy, it had been *her* home and I haven't had a—not since my parents died. I haven't because I thought that if I made a *home* with anyone, if I tried and then—"

Her words fell away.

Finally, she met his eyes. "Do you think Octavia will like it here?"

He knew she was directing his attention away from her words and what she'd just confessed, but it was all right. He would not push her now.

He thought he understood what she was trying to say anyway.

"*Sì*," he said, his heart full of tenderness. "She will be a queen at the window surveying her domain."

"We can put out a bird feeder on the balcony for her and get her a cat tree," Lou added.

Konstantine had no idea what a cat tree was, but it didn't matter. He wanted to tell her something before they got too far away from what she'd said.

"We will keep this place safe. Together. We will keep each other safe," he promised her. "And you aren't a child anymore. Any fool who dares to come into your house *now* to harm us —I pity them."

This, at least, earned him a smile.

"Do you want to know the real reason I picked this one?" she asked. Her mischievous smile was back.

"Of course."

She untangled herself from his embrace and went to the coffee table. She lifted a small remote and pressed a series of buttons. One by one, the panels in the walls began to slide away.

Inside them were secret rooms, backlit with gleaming glass shelves. In one, he recognized her father's battered bulletproof vest encased, and beside it, many of the guns and knives he'd seen her use before. The other two enclaves were empty, waiting to be filled.

"I have more *room*," she said, her smile triumphant.

He stood beside her, admiring each weapon closet in turn.

"This is wonderful, but it isn't the best part," he told her.

He wrapped his arms around her, burying his face in her neck.

"I don't see what could be better than this," she said.

He laughed into the hollow of her throat. "I assure you, the *best* part will be christening every *room*, every *surface* of this apartment together."

"Will it?" she said, her brow arched. "When will we be doing that?"

"Now. Let's begin *now*."

It was her turn to hook her arms around his neck and hold him close. "We still need to get the bed."

"No, *amore mio*." He found her lips again. "The bed can wait."

Did you enjoy Silver Bullet? Louie's story continues in *Hell House (Shadows in the Water #9)*

GET YOUR THREE FREE STORIES TODAY

Thank you so much for reading *Silver Bullet*. I hope you're enjoying Louie's story. If you'd like more, I have a free, exclusive Lou Thorne story for you. Meet Louie early in her hunting days, when she pursues Benito Martinelli, the son of her enemy. This was the man her father arrested—and the reason her parents were killed months later.

You can only read this story by signing up for my free newsletter. If you would like this story, you can get your copy by visiting ➜ www.korymshrum.com/lounewsletteroffer

I will also send you free stories from the other series that I write. If you've signed up for my newsletter already, no need to sign up again. You should have already received this story from me. Check your email and make sure it wasn't marked as spam! Can't find it? Email me at ➜ kory@korymshrum.com and I'll take care of it.

As to the newsletter itself, I send out 2-3 a month and host a monthly giveaway exclusive to my subscribers. The prizes are usually signed books or other freebies that I think you'll enjoy. I also share information about my current projects, and personal anecdotes (like pictures of my dog). If you want these free stories and access to the exclusive give-aways, you can sign up for the newsletter at ➜ www.korymshrum.com/lounewsletteroffer

If this is not your cup of tea (I love tea), you can follow me on Facebook at ➜ www.facebook.com/korymshrum in order to be notified of my new releases.

ACKNOWLEDGMENTS

Ah yes, the curtain has fallen and it's time for the bows. Thank you to everyone who has read the book and thanks also to those who help to make each story what it is.

Nods to Kimberly Benedicto, Kathrine Pendleton, Angela Roquet, and Monica La Porta for being my first readers. Extra applause to Monica, who makes sure that the Italian I use makes any sense at all.

The award for best editor goes to Toby Selwyn for his keen eye and charming wit. The best cover designer is the ever-humble Christian Bentulan, who continues to make each cover even prettier than the last. And finally, all hail the best assistant Alexandra Amor, Lady of the North, for all the magical things she does—which is much too much to list here.

And as always, many thanks to my lovely street team. Thank you for reading the books in advance, reporting those lingering typos and posting your honest reviews.

Without all of you, none of this would be half as fun.

ALSO BY KORY M. SHRUM

Dying for a Living series

Dying for a Living

Dying by the Hour

Dying for Her: A Companion Novel

Dying Light

Worth Dying For

Dying Breath

Dying Day

Shadows in the Water: Lou Thorne Thrillers

Shadows in the Water

Under the Bones

Danse Macabre

Carnival

Devil's Luck

What Comes Around

Overkill

Silver Bullet

Hell House

Castle Cove series

Welcome to Castle Cove

Night Tide

2603 novels

The City Below

The City Within

The City Outside

Jack and the Fire Eater

Learn more about Kory's work at: www.korymshrum.com

ABOUT THE AUTHOR

Kory M. Shrum is author of more than twenty novels, including the bestselling *Shadows in the Water* and *Dying for a Living* series. She has loved books and words all her life. She reads almost every genre you can think of, but when she writes, she writes science fiction, fantasy, and thrillers, or often something that's all of the above.

In 2020, she launched a true crime podcast "Who Killed My Mother?", sharing the true story of her mother's tragic death. You can listen for free on YouTube or your favorite podcast app.

When she's not eating, reading, writing, or indulging in her true calling as a stay-at-home dog mom, she loves to plan her next adventure. She can usually be found under thick blankets with snacks. The kettle is almost always on.

She lives in Michigan with her equally bookish wife, Kim, and their rescue pug, Charley.

Learn more about Kory and her work at
www.korymshrum.com

Made in the USA
Monee, IL
15 April 2024